WHEN
KILLERS
CRY

K.A.Edwards

GLUE fiction

www.glue-publishing.co.uk

First published in Great Britain in 2015
by GLUE fiction, an imprint of GLUE Publishing.

The moral right of the author has been asserted.

Visit www.glue-publishing.co.uk for more information.
Connect with the author at www.glue-publishing.co.uk

ISBN: 978-0-9932915-4-8

In loving memory of my parents Belinda and Denzil

Evil is unspectacular and always human, and shares our bed and eats at our own table. — W. H. Auden

PROLOGUE

Every killer knows that the victim, for the main part, is unsuspecting. They seldom expect to die and this particular victim was no different, going about his business with no inkling of the finality of each event. He said a distracted goodbye to his wife and children, kissed their cheeks, and vanished from their lives forever. He took his final journey down the tree-lined road he travelled on every day with no sense of his own mortality. The greasy hamburger he swallowed at lunchtime was the last meal he ever ate and as he withdrew his hard-earned money from the bank, he never suspected that he'd not live to spend it. He continued with his daily life as if it would go on forever.

Most people aren't born natural killers. It takes years of training and hours of practice to perfect the art of murder. It's a skill, a vocation and it doesn't suit everyone, but some unique individuals find assassination a perfect fit for them and the South Africa of 1981 was an idyllic stamping ground.

It wasn't too difficult to find a slot in the great machinations of the apartheid engine and to become an irreplaceable cog that ground on ceaselessly no matter what, grinding up and spitting out enemies of the regime. The masters were only too happy to have conscienceless soldiers to do their bidding and even though the relationship could be complicated, for some it was ideal. Sacrifices had to be made, but it was essential to remember the bigger picture, to see that the time denied to family and friends wasn't lost, but had been spent valuably to guarantee the greater good.

Most soldiers knew what their mission was. They obeyed without question and weren't involved in politics, didn't have their own opinions or beliefs. They formed the backbone of every strong country, gave it stability within by dealing with those who wished to destabilise the precarious balance of power, and kept its borders safe from insurgents that planned to destroy and undermine the way of life that was beloved by all. Some worked in full view of the public and the media, doing their jobs with pride, unashamed when their deeds were exposed to a watching world. They strutted and preened giving displays of strength and might, hoping to instil pride in the hearts of the nation and fear in the hearts of the enemy. Their leaders spoke with vigour, appearing on the radio and television espousing their beliefs and their hopes for the country. And millions applauded.

But others, no less important to the stability of the nation, did their work under a cloak of invisibility. Few knew who they were or even that they existed. They were an immense unseen army that floated in and out of communities at will, undetectable, watching, recording and informing on those whose hearts were not set upon the right path, enemies of the state deviating from the dream of creating a nation that was free from perversion of every kind.

They all knew that deceit was the key to fooling a target into making false conclusions. A skilful disguise, a careful word and the ability to morph into the shape and persona of a stranger would get the killer so close it would be over before even the smallest inkling of suspicion surfaced. This time was no different.

The victim walked past an abandoned vehicle and peered in curiously, shrugged and continued towards his own car parked on the third floor of the multi-storey car park. In an instant his killer was next to him, darting forward in deadly silence. The victim turned, a smile tugged at the corners of his mouth and stayed there forever. He didn't even know what hit him as the bullet shattered his brain and he fell to the ground still smiling.

CHAPTER

One

Pretoria, the administrative capital of South Africa, is a large city where lush vegetation mingles with attractive historical buildings and modern architecture. The Magaliesberg mountain range looks down, eternally protective of the city as it sprawls up hills and through valleys continually conquering the land between the Highveld and the Bushveld, in the northeast of the country.

During spring the streets are awash with flowering Jacaranda trees, their mauve, bell-shaped blossoms carpeting the ground. From lofty vantage points a vast impressionist canvas stippled in daubs of purple and green stretches towards the horizon as the trees bloom, creating floral tunnels for the city's inhabitants to drive through.

Hannah Smith drove towards her office in the city centre, wishing it were the end of the day and that she didn't have to endure interminable hours at work. She was tired, her energy sapped by the heat and a string of sleepless nights. The past week had been frustrating, with endless phone calls to her many sources proving futile, and she was beginning to think her boss was right and she was chasing conspiracies where there were none.

Yet she was unable to let it go, for through every moment, at work, at home, in the darkest nights, the memory of a bloated, brown body that had tumbled out of the surf in front of her, persisted. It scythed into her life, propelling it in a direction she'd never anticipated.

He was naked, missing fingers and toes, extremities nibbled by fish and crabs. Lying in front of her, skin marbled and flaky, eyes milky, the wounds on his body were unmistakable. White bone poking though brown flesh and circular burn marks, disinfected by the salt, were evidence of a severe beating, but it was the ragged-edged bullet hole in his head that confirmed he had been murdered.

Hannah found herself consumed by a profound sense of destiny, as if he'd washed up at her feet for a reason, settled on that wet holiday beach because she was the only one that could help him, even in death.

Despite her efforts the local police remained disinterested, telling her he was a vagrant that no one would miss, and if she hadn't persisted, the man would have been cremated or buried in an unmarked grave, with no one any the wiser as to who he was or why he'd been tortured and killed. Despite the obvious dangers associated with such an investigation, she was compelled to find out more about the man, no easy task in the present climate. For an ambitious reporter like her, it was the perfect opportunity.

Hannah rounded a bend and to her surprise saw Detective Tom Maartens, a man she knew as a result of her investigations, on a corner nearby in deep conversation with a white man in a smart navy blue suit. Wary as she was of the hefty policeman, she was intrigued to see him here, away from his own little patch of dominion.

She stopped at the red lights adjacent to the two men and realised they were in the midst of an intense argument. Maartens was gesticulating angrily and the other man seemed nervous, stepping back as the policeman's finger waved under his nose. Maartens' hand hovered near his gun and as he reached for it the suited man held his hands up, as if in surrender. Maartens backed away still obviously angry. The lights changed and the car behind her hooted. Hannah reluctantly drove off and spent the rest of the day wondering what Maartens had been doing so far off his beat, and who the man was he'd been berating.

She soon forgot about him as her day filled up with meetings and bad tempered confrontations with cantankerous editors. It was another wearisome time for her and she was relieved when it eventually ended and she was free to go home for the weekend. She drove out of the city, irritated by the usual Friday afternoon rush hour and hoped she'd make it home before the weather broke.

As was usual in the Highveld, the afternoon storm built up suddenly, billows gathering with unexpected speed in a cobalt sky, the skyline sharpening in sombre contrast to the oily brushstrokes of charcoal-grey streaked across the heavens. Then, as gusts of wind blew litter and lifted dresses, the clouds burst like ripe fruit and the heat of the day was extinguished.

Despite the storm the city was sultry, the weather oppressive and the streets were patchy with evaporating wetness, streams of water flowing uninhibited down the verges, spilling out of gutters and pooling in low, badly drained areas. The smell of rainwater and hot tar blended with the fragrance of sodden grass and the clogging fumes of the traffic.

Driving along the steaming road, the imposing Union Buildings louring against the horizon drew Hannah's eye. An orange, white, and blue flag fluttered above the sand-coloured structure and the expansive green gardens below. Immaculate lawns and well-tended flowerbeds seemed intent on distracting from the reality that this was the seat of government, the place where apartheid was written into law.

An occasional flash of lightning lacerated the sky and as thunder rumbled, Hannah could not shake the feeling that it was a portent of things to come. Despite the beauty of the tree-lined streets that were woven into every strand of her life, she was becoming sensitive to an undercurrent of discontent. A cloud hung unseen over the country, threatening to disgorge violence and bloodshed. Few could see it and those that did chose to ignore its presence in the hope that it would dissipate of its own accord.

She turned towards Sunnyside, a busy commercial part of the city. Sunnypark, a vibrant shopping centre, was teeming with shoppers, the forecourt filled with schoolchildren relieved to be free from lessons for the weekend and Esselen Street, a main access route to the centre of town, heaved with traffic belching smoke and bad temper into the atmosphere.

While most pedestrians crossed the road in an orderly fashion at the lights, others jaywalked thinking themselves impervious to the danger of oncoming taxis and cars. A pack of giggling teenage girls and nonchalant boys stood in a chaotic line outside the Oscar cinema, queuing for tickets to the latest must-see movie. A couple of *troepies* stood on the roadside trying to hitch a lift with an outstretched thumb and a hopeful expression. They were dressed in army brown, carrying bulky rucksacks and would probably spend most of their weekend trying to get home. After two days of freedom doubtless involving much beer drinking, they would head back to a military base to continue their National Service and complete their conversion from schoolboy to soldier. It was another normal day in the capital city.

Hannah rounded the corner of the shopping centre, and a gathering crowd at the entrance to the car park attracted her attention. A yellow police van, followed by an official car drove in at speed, startling the elderly black man operating the electronic ticket machine. When a coroner's van arrived and manoeuvred up the narrow winding ramp, Hannah was unable to resist, and showing her press pass, followed the other vehicles into the gloomy building.

With the flashing of blue lights and the persistent rain, the concrete crime scene had the atmosphere of a badly lit horror film. The sense of unreality and the gentle pat, pat, pat of raindrops accompanying the soft swishing of car tyres on the wet roads outside made Hannah feel as though everything was happening in slow motion, the quiet and dull atmosphere incongruous in this busy area of town.

A few mud-spattered cars were parked nearby but the second floor of the mausoleum-like car park had been cordoned off and was mainly deserted, except for the solemn-faced policemen and the distressing pile lying in a heap under an orange blanket. One foot, wearing a well-polished black shoe, peered out from beneath the shroud.

Hannah parked and made her way towards the enclosed area. She jumped over a puddle and moved forward, eyes keenly studying the scene, eager to spot anything that would give her a clue to what had happened. She could see Detective Tom Maartens talking to one of his colleagues and even from a distance saw that he was not amused. He turned and frowned when he saw her, shook his head and walked over. The look on his face made her involuntarily take a step backwards, for a moment experiencing the spark of fear that was not uncommon in the general populace. This was South African officialdom at its most intimidating and she was putting herself at risk confronting it openly.

Maartens approached, his sturdy frame exuding the power of his position. There was an odd gleam in his eyes and a crinkle between his brows as he stopped and put his hands in his pockets, the casual stance emphasising his menace.

'Smith. I might have known you would show up here. Always know where to find the dead bodies. You're beginning to get on my nerves.'

Hannah didn't disillusion him. Let him think she was better at her job than she was. It was obvious this was another murder so she did her best to goad the dour detective into revealing what he knew.

'What is it this time? Another bullet to the back of the head?'

'Yes, it is, but there's no reason to suspect there's any connection with the other murders you've fixated on, so don't go getting ideas into that feather-brained head of yours. Probably a robbery.'

'Ja and I'm the Pope. Pull the other one, Detective.'

Tom looked at his watch, clicking his tongue in annoyance. 'Dammit! I missed the end of Jack's game. And they were winning. Just once I'd like to be there at the end of a match without some oke getting his brains splattered all over the street.' The vein in his temple began to throb.

'I doubt if he planned it like this, Detective,' said Hannah and pointed at the body. 'His plans were also interrupted, you know. Very inconsiderate of him to prevent you from worshipping at the shrine of the national religion.'

Maartens grinned. 'One minute I'm watching my son being run over by a pack of fifteen-year-olds and the next some kid is handing me a note demanding that I get myself here as soon as possible. Why is it someone always gets murdered in the middle of a rugby match or while I'm away on holiday? My son Jack's playing his first game for the under-sixteen second team today. He was so proud and I'm missing the end of it.'

'But then, murder rather leaves rugby for dead, don't you think?' said Hannah, irritated that he seemed more interested in his family than the fact that there'd been a killing in an affluent part of town.

Tom raised an eyebrow. 'Seriously, Miss Smith, this murder isn't related to the others. It's a robbery gone wrong.'

'Could be. Could also be another activist or person that's landed himself on the wrong side of the authorities,' she remarked, watching his face.

It was obvious to her from the outset that this killing was nothing like those she was already investigating, the circumstances differed greatly, and this victim was white, but there was the chance of a story here and perhaps provoking Maartens would reveal what it was.

He neatly swung the conversation back in her direction. 'I don't understand why you're still so obsessed with that body you and your friend stumbled across. It's been months and I'm sure the police in Natal are doing their best,' he said.

'Perhaps if the cops down there had done their job properly, I wouldn't be so interested. I can see that this body here is already getting a whole lot more attention than the one in Natal did,' she replied. 'I'm sure in your line of work you've seen plenty of beaten and decomposing bodies, but Danielle and I haven't. I know you think my interest is just reaction to a traumatic experience but there's more to it than that.'

'Anyone finding a body rolling round in the surf would be upset and I'm not surprised you're frustrated, but these things take time. There are procedures that have to be followed and surely you understand how difficult it is to identify a naked body, especially a black one. Your decision to discover the man's identity yourself is ridiculous, even for an interfering reporter like you. I don't know what I was thinking giving you access to those missing persons files,' said Maartens, jingling the coins in his trouser pocket. It wasn't the first time he had expressed his disdain.

'I know it's not unusual for black bodies to remain unidentified, but what kind of reporter would I be if I didn't look into it? My research has turned up some anomalies and you personally have gone out of your way to convince me to drop my investigations. It makes me wonder what you're covering up.'

The words tumbled out before she could stop them and she felt a tremor of alarm as he put his hands on his hips and glared at her. Challenging a man in a position of power wasn't the wisest thing she'd ever done. She rubbed her arms.

'And what is it exactly, that has made you so certain that murder has anything to do with this one or any of the others that you have so conveniently uncovered?' he asked.

CHAPTER

Two

Articulating the thoughts that had been circling her mind for the past months and attempting to convey her gut instinct in a credible way wasn't easy. For someone who was naturally eloquent Hannah felt surprisingly tongue-tied in front of this man.

'Not long after Dani and I found that body washed up on the beach, some hikers uncovered a charred body in a shallow grave in a remote part of the Drakensberg Mountains. It didn't even make the news but I spotted a report that came into our office so I took a closer look and noticed similarities,' she said. 'Just to make things clear, I'm not like most journalists, who write what the government wants to hear – for me, it's the story that matters, no matter how uncomfortable or dangerous that might be.'

'And?'

'The autopsy results showed bullet holes in virtually identical places and ballistics revealed that the same gun had been used in both killings, and not only that, the men had been drugged. I had a good look at the crime scene photographs as well as the post mortem and forensics reports and I'm convinced both men were killed by the same person.'

He fixed honey-coloured eyes on her. 'I'd be very interested to know how you got hold of autopsy results and crime scene photographs.'

'You don't seriously expect me to reveal my sources, do you?'

A contact in the police laboratory had leaked them to her and Hannah was in no doubt as to what would happen to him if she revealed his name. She hoped Maartens wouldn't quote the law or worse, try to enforce it. She'd sworn to protect her sources no matter how illegal that action was and she'd already said too much to this man.

'Consider this a caution, Miss Smith. Just because I've helped you out in the past doesn't mean I'll allow you to take advantage of the law. Don't look so panic-stricken, you aren't in serious trouble, not yet anyway,' he said.

She unclenched her fists and took a steadying breath. 'After the second body was found, I wondered what linked the men and discovered that they matched the descriptions of two political activists who had disappeared without a trace, so I started looking into cases of missing activists and dissidents,' she said.

'I think you're looking in the wrong direction,' he said.

'Maybe, but I found a number of cases going back four years and information about three more bodies that were found in similar circumstances. They still haven't been identified, which isn't unusual because they were all black, except that they'd been drugged and shot in a similar fashion.' She had revealed none of these findings to the police, assuming that if she'd seen the similarities, so had they. She watched Maartens apprehensively, realising she had revealed far more than she ever intended.

'You don't honestly think that this poor guy here is connected in any way to those cases, do you?' he said.

Hannah absently weaved a strand of hair round her fingers as she wondered why the detective was trying so hard to make her think this murder was random. It was possible he was simply humouring her and that his agenda wasn't as transparent as it seemed. It wasn't inconceivable that he would feed her the party line in order to divert her. She wasn't sure who she could trust these days, and Maartens was naturally reticent, all policemen being well conditioned in the art of diversion and denial, but had hoped she wouldn't have to try her not inconsiderable feminine wiles to get information out of him.

'I can assure you that this murder has nothing to do with the others. It's a mugging that got out of control, that's all,' he said again, turning away. Hannah stepped in front of him and held up a hand.

'How stupid do you think I am? It's blatantly not a robbery. For one thing I can see a wallet sticking out of his pocket, and that looks like a very expensive wristwatch to me. Also, how many robbers shoot their victim so precisely in the head?'

She gestured back to the body. She'd been watching the coroner closely and even from a distance could see a congealed mess of tissue and brain matter. She couldn't realistically tell the origin of the injury, but hoped Tom would let some other snippet of information slip. He didn't.

'You must have extremely well-developed powers of observation. I'm not denying that it's suspicious, but the body's not even cold yet so it's a bit much for you to expect me to have solved it already.'

'And there I was thinking you were Superman,' said Hannah.

'These things can't be rushed, as you know, Miss Smith.' He turned away again.

Hannah watched him closely, irrationally convinced that she had in fact stumbled upon something important and that he had information about the victim that he wasn't telling her. She didn't know him well enough to know what tactic was best to get him to talk and obviously she wasn't asking the right questions so she decided to try another tack. Feeling slightly foolish, she leaned forward, stuck out her chest, and licked her lips.

'Come on, Detective. Give a girl a break. How am I going to get anywhere if you keep brushing me off like this? I have a story to write and no matter what you say a white man shot in a car park in the middle of Pretoria is bound to raise a few questions.' She was unable to resist the temptation to flutter her eyelashes.

Tom twisted the wedding ring on his left hand and regarded her with a bit more interest.

'Unless there's a serial killer on the loose, you must concede there could be a political motive to at least some of the murders. Can't you at least admit that they might be politically motivated?'

'You can't possibly know anything about the victim at this stage, so even for someone with a vivid imagination like you, it's a bit of a jump to assume it's a political assassination, isn't it?' he replied.

'I thought you knew all journalists are paranoid conspiracy theorists. And 'assassination' is a strange word for you to use, isn't it? Particularly as you say you don't know anything about who that man over there is.' She pointed back to the body. 'More importantly, are you suggesting that the other killings were assassinations?'

Tom swallowed and stared hard. She folded her arms so he wouldn't see them shaking and forced herself to stay focussed on his face. He glanced over his shoulder. Hannah followed his gaze and noticed one of his colleagues watching them.

He shifted his weight and muttered, 'Look, I've said far too much. If you insist on investigating this any further, do me a favour and be careful. There are things happening in this country that could land a girl like you in a lot of trouble. But keep me informed about how you get on, okay?'

'Okay.'

He then adopted an official posture and said, 'Now, if you don't mind, Miss Smith, I need to supervise the removal of the body and I can't be wasting any more police time on you. My poor wife is cooped-up in the tuck-shop selling hotdogs and she's not going to be amused if she has to get a lift home in a car full of smelly teenagers. So if it's quite all right with you, I'd like to finish off here.'

'Go ahead, Detective. Don't let me get in the way. I'm sure you have someone to boss about, not to mention that enthralling rugby match you need to get back to.'

Maartens stalked off with an angry click of the tongue. Hannah surveyed the scene with interest, looking for anything that the killer might have left behind. A crowd of mainly black onlookers milled about, craning their necks for a better view, moving out of her way as she walked back towards her car. She shot a quick glance at the interested faces, wondering if the killer was amongst them, watching.

The new murder was certainly different from the others, where the bodies had been found by chance in remote areas. This was a busy part of town in a public parking area, but was possibly merely another indiscriminate act of violence in an increasingly volatile society.

She tried to get as close to the body as she could without causing too much comment and as it was lifted onto a stretcher, the blanket fell away and she caught a glimpse of the man's face. She inhaled sharply as she realised that the last time she'd seen this corpse, he'd been alive and well and arguing with Tom Maartens on the corner of the street.

Hannah headed home, trying to make sense of what had just transpired. She was developing an instinct and the way the police had been handling the scene, and the set of Tom's face, not to mention his lying to her about knowing the man, told her there was more to this killing. His sudden about-turn and barely veiled warning had piqued her interest too. She wondered what he was hiding, and if he was to be trusted.

The reporter was brooding, reflecting on the tension in the country. With the dawn of the '80s, she had hoped things would change but it seemed as if the situation was spiralling to a head as sanctions and the oil embargo squeezed tighter and pressure from the outside world for the Nationalist Government to relinquish the grip of apartheid mounted. During the past few months she had found herself being pulled deeper into political intrigue and what she was uncovering unsettled her, causing her to constantly look over her shoulder, never sure if that day would be her last.

CHAPTER

Three

Something about crime turned Hannah into a piranha. She loved a challenge and the seedier side of life had always fascinated her. Having grown up a privileged and spoilt child whose love of second-rate crime novels was the despair of her mother, it somehow seemed that the people who lived in the areas her mother delicately referred to as 'unfortunate' had a much more interesting life than she did. Nothing intrigued her more than lines of dirty washing strung across rank-smelling, junk-infested, barren gardens, and snotty-nosed children running to hide from beer-reeking, cigarette-dangling, overweight mothers in too tight crimpolene dresses.

These glimpses into an alternative life had been seen through dirty windows on the tedious train journeys home from university in Johannesburg and they kindled a flame in her that refused to be quenched. To her, struggle was imbued with romance, a romance that had been lacking from her sterile upbringing. Hannah supposed she could have become a social worker, but she didn't want to help the people she saw through the train window, she wanted to write about them and their desperation in exquisite detail, covering the minutiae of their pitiful lives. She wanted to find out what went on in their dismal existence and to understand the forces that drove them on day by day.

The decision to become a journalist had horrified her mother and caused her father to 'harrumph'. Her brother, a constant disapproving figure that lurked in the background of her life, had dismissed her ambitions out of hand, but she'd always been very good at getting her own way and she did again.

The youthfully exuberant Hannah had been naïve enough to believe that it was only in these rat-infested slum areas that crime occurred but had subsequently wised up. Crime had many faces, and in apartheid South Africa there was plenty of it in all areas. Death suffered no identity crisis and attacked senselessly wherever it desired. She embarked on her great adventure to inform and enlighten the world through her pen and only discovered much later to her chagrin, that her father, usually uninvolved in her life, had done some serious string pulling to get her appointed to a well-respected newspaper. When she discovered that she had not received the job on merit, she set about zealously trying to prove herself.

It had been a small jump from writing the obituaries, fascinating in their own ghoulish way; to writing about women's issues before finally being given the opportunity to try her hand at crime and it was in the investigation and resolution of murder that she found a strange fulfilment. She was also discovering that while apartheid was aimed at subduing only one sector of the population, it affected everyone in some way and as the armed struggle intensified, not one South African, no matter their colour or creed, escaped its consequences.

Despite the manner in which she had acquired it, Hannah loved her work and those that didn't approve, like her mother, and who thought she should be raising a brood of screaming brats in some leafy suburb, could take a leap into the nearest ditch. Her male colleagues had grudging respect for her tenacity and were starting to realise that, despite being one of the weaker sex, she was surprisingly good at her job. She was beginning to build a reputation as someone who could dissect misinformation, target what she perceived to be the truth and prove her case. Recently, she'd become aware that Frik van Niekerk, a colleague with flexible morality, was starting to take notice of her and her instinct told her that it wasn't simply because she was an attractive woman.

Hannah drove away from the crime scene convinced that Tom Maartens knew more than he was telling and his opinion of her work did nothing to dissuade her from investigating what she knew was more than simply another unidentified body. Not even the smoggy stop and start of the noisy homeward-bound traffic could quell the effervescence in her soul that she always felt when she knew she was on to something big.

She was exposed to more than the average man in the street through her contacts within the media and was very aware of a swirling maelstrom beneath the seeming calm. She suspected she was on the brink of making a monumental discovery, as she had been frightened a few times during her investigations. No death threats but a few pointed remarks and hints from other reporters that she was putting her nose where it wasn't welcome. Even if the other deaths proved to be nothing more sinister than a pathetic reflection of life in South Africa, Hannah knew intuitively that this killing in Pretoria was a political hit and was determined to prove it. The first thing she needed to do was to find out more about the victim.

It was Monday morning following a frustrating weekend for Hannah, who had spent the last two days impatiently marking time and working out a strategy for tackling her investigation. She went in to work early, navigating her way through streets that were already beginning to clog up with traffic as school busses and commuters began their journeys.

The newspaper offices were alive with the clacking of keyboards, ringing phones and eager copywriters, artists and other staff going about their business. Hannah sat at her desk tapping a pencil against her teeth. She peeked over her shoulder, but everyone else appeared to be too engrossed in producing the next issue to take notice of her. Frik van Niekerk's office door was closed and through the frosted glass she could see that he was deep in conversation with someone on the other end of the line.

She picked up her phone and dialled a number she'd been forced to commit to memory as it was too dangerous to leave lying around. After a couple of rings a quiet voice answered.

'Yes?'

'Hello. It's Hannah. Can you talk?'

'No. Now is not a good time. Can you meet me at four thirty? The usual place?'

'That's great. See you then.' Hannah put the receiver down and sat back, her skin crawling when she realised Frik van Niekerk was standing in front of her desk, watching her in silence, his lizard eyes narrowed. He smoothed a lock of greasy hair across his forehead, trying in vain to cover the balding pate.

'Problem, Hannah?' His voice was surprisingly high for a large man and he had a very strong Afrikaans accent, rolling his r's in a guttural manner.

'No,' she answered. 'Just making plans with a friend.'

'Boyfriend? I'm sure a pretty little thing like you has plenty of guys wanting to…take you out.' He leered in what he obviously thought was a seductive manner. Hannah resisted the urge to shudder.

'Was there something you wanted, Mr Van Niekerk? I'm very busy at the moment.'

He licked his lips and flared red-veined nostrils, plucking at his collar with polony fingers. 'No, just checking everything was okay. You seem a little tense.'

'I'm fine, thanks. But I have a lot of work so if you don't mind -?'

He hitched up his trousers, smoothed his hair, and walked away. Hannah opened the file on her desk, but could feel his eyes on her. For the rest of the day she was careful not to do anything out of character that might alert him to what she was working on.

Frik van Niekerk was a battle-hardened, craggy-faced reporter with an acid-filled pen and a weary expression. Hannah suspected he was a spy for the state, and was wary about revealing too much to him, fearful of where her opinions would be repeated. The press was basically a voice of the government, the English press less so than the Afrikaans, but they were still essentially expected to support the policies of the government and its various departments, the SAP being one of these. To attack the police and bring its reputation into 'disrepute' was not considered acceptable. The Police Act made it an offence to publish 'any untrue matter' and so the burden of proof fell to the journalists that relied on witnesses who feared for their safety and did not want to be identified.

Almost a hundred laws affected the way the press operated, ranging from blatant prohibition of certain publications to the threat of being prosecuted for printing what was deemed to be subversive material. Although they were allowed to print and publish opposition statements, these were severely curbed, so while Hannah and her liberal colleagues did not defy the laws, they tried to exploit loopholes and find ways of beating the system. The combination of legislation, self-censorship, and agreements negotiated between the state and the Newspaper Press Union succeeded in greatly eroding the fundamental freedoms of the press, and The Criminal Procedure Act inhibited and affected the national flow of information, ruling out the right of journalists to protect their sources. Hannah hoped she would never be called upon to protect Tom Maartens, who despite appearing co-operative was nonetheless part of an incompetent police force that frequently behaved like the security arm of the National Party. And there was still the mystery of his connection to the dead man. But Maartens wasn't the primary source that Hannah needed to safeguard.

At four o'clock Hannah left the office, ignoring the querying look from Van Niekerk, and drove into a quiet cul-de-sac in a hilly suburb to the east of Pretoria. She parked her car and after checking the street to ensure she had not been followed, walked through a partially hidden gate that led into a derelict and overgrown park. A few rusty swings and a lopsided slide were all that remained of the children's playground.

The grass was knee high, partially obscuring a corroded drinking fountain marked '*slegs blankes* - whites only', just in case any literate non-white considered quenching their thirst there. She sat down on a wooden bench, leaning her back against the painted notice on the backrest informing her that this was the bench she, a European person, should sit on. Nearby was another bench solely for the use of any non-Europeans that decided to grace the park with their presence. A line of industrious ants marched in formation across the mahogany earth, oblivious to what part of the park was for their exclusive use.

She could hear the droning of traffic in the distance accompanying the melancholic call of a bird in a tree and the guttural croaking of a frog bemoaning its fate in a stagnant pond. She closed her eyes and imagined the undulating sound was the sea breaking on the shore, but the scent of wet earthy grass and the fetid smell of slimy water were almost overwhelming, rudely distracting her from the pleasant images in her head.

A footfall disturbed her reverie and she opened her eyes to find a very tall man with ebony skin and intense chocolate eyes standing in front of her. He was dressed in grubby grey overalls covered in oily stains and she noticed a smear of red paint on the sleeve. Hannah smiled and his solemn features transformed.

'Themba, *dumêla*. It's so good to see you.' She grasped his hand, greeting him in Sotho. Themba grinned and patted her arm.

'*O kae*, Hannah?' he asked in a rich baritone. 'How are you?'

'Well, thanks. And you?' She studied his face and saw a deep laceration on his head, just below the hairline. His right eye was puffy, drooping at the corner, a yellowing bruise covered his left cheek, and a ragged scarlet line untidily dissected his perfectly formed bottom lip.

'What happened?'

'It is nothing. I had a run in with a couple of policemen a few days ago. They were just checking I had my passbook and when they found everything was exactly the way it is supposed to be they were so disappointed they gave me a good hiding to encourage me never to forget it. Preventative measures, I am sure you understand.' He laughed. 'If they only knew, hey, Hannah?'

'Bastards,' said Hannah. They sat down on the whites-only bench.

'I have something for you about a raid on a squatter camp last night. Thought maybe you could persuade someone to publish it, though I do not hold out much hope. We both know your newspaper has been infiltrated and is being manipulated by the police. All the stories have the same pattern. They quote the police, the intelligence services, the official lies of government ministers and they do not bother to quote anyone else. And these are printed. Heaven forbid someone should actually print the truth for once.'

Hannah nodded, 'You don't need to remind me about police infiltration.'

Themba handed her a large buff envelope, which she put in her handbag. She gave him one in return. He swiftly concealed it on his body, without checking the contents.

'Any new information about your family?' asked Hannah.

'No, nothing as yet. So, what can I do for you?' he asked, watching the entrance to the park.

'I don't know if you heard about the guy that was killed in a car park in town on Friday afternoon. He was shot in the back of the head, just like the others and I was wondering if you knew who he was and why someone would want him dead. Also, what's his connection to Maartens? I saw them arguing earlier that day.'

'We heard about him and I have already done a bit of checking, as I suspected you would want to know more. He was a lawyer who represented a number of ANC members and he was a bit of a risk taker, openly acknowledging that his clients are members of a banned organisation. The Security Police have had him under surveillance for some time and he had just returned from a trip overseas, probably Cuba, so you can imagine how popular that made him. Although, considering his big mouth I do not think we can rule out the possibility that he was killed by one of his clients just to keep him quiet. If I had to hazard a guess though, I would say it was the cops, but somehow that does not seem quite right. I will see what else I can find out. What about your policeman friend?'

'I'd hardly call him my friend, but he did warn me to be careful so I'm certain he knows something he's not telling me. I'll have another crack at him and see what else I can find out.'

'Are you sure you can trust him?' asked Themba. 'I am not too keen on involving someone that I have not checked out thoroughly and the policemen I have met so far have all been on the other end of a gun.'

'Initially he was very loath to help me, but lately he's been a bit more co-operative. He resists just enough to make me think he won't help, but then he relents and I've received some useful information from him. I thought it was because he's starting to have faith in me and knows I won't publish his name or get him into any trouble, but now I'm not so sure. It might be that he's been told to keep an eye on me. Could you see what you can find out about him? If he's involved in one of the dirty tricks departments, I've made a big mistake. Better to be safe.'

'I will see if I can get hold of his service file,' said Themba. 'I have a guy in the police records department. It is amazing how far ten rand goes these days. I will also ask around, because if he is dirty someone will know.'

The gate squeaked as three brawny white teenagers tossing a rugby ball thrust it open and burst into the park. When they saw Hannah and Themba they froze and the ball dropped to the ground. Hannah suppressed a laugh at the expressions on their faces. The largest, a powerful-looking boy with almost no neck, extremely short dark hair and tight shorts, stuck his jaw out belligerently and came towards them. He was wearing a school uniform a good two sizes too small, the grey fabric straining over his bulging biceps and hairy muscled thighs.

'Is jy okay, *tannie*?' he asked. 'Is you all right, auntie? Are this kaffir troubling you?' he said, in an appalling accent.

Themba had risen swiftly and was standing with his head bowed. Why was it, wondered Hannah, that most English children could speak quite presentable Afrikaans, yet Afrikaner children could barely string a sentence together in English?

'*Alles is reg.* Everything's fine, thanks. He was just asking if I had a cigarette for him.'

'Ja, but he were sitting on the wrong place. Next to you.' The boy looked pointedly at the painted sign on the bench.

'I know, but he probably can't read and he was just leaving. You can go now, boy.' She dismissed Themba and picked up her handbag, irritated that their meeting had been so precipitously interrupted.

Themba arranged his features into a suitably contrite expression and putting on an appropriate accent, said, 'Thank you, madam. I go now. No trouble. I want no trouble. Please, master.'

The teenager glared at him, somewhat pacified at being addressed with such respect, but still took a threatening step towards him, raising his arm as if to strike. Themba cowered, turned, and ran. The teenagers laughed and yelled insults at his retreating back. Hannah bit her tongue, her face growing warm. If they only knew whom they had just chased off.

CHAPTER

Four

Hannah first met Themba Ntini in 1978 whilst covering the terrorist bombing of a power station. She'd arrived at the H.F. Verwoerd Hospital in Pretoria to question the night watchman injured in the blast and was surprised to find a black reporter from an opposition newspaper already there. After the momentary obligatory frisson of fear at the sight of him, she'd taken to Themba instantly, amazed at the ease with which he extracted information from the scared man, and was greatly impressed with the manner in which he conducted himself and the interview. She discovered that his excellent English was the result of a mission school in the Eastern Cape and a high school education at an expensive private school in East London, courtesy of a church scholarship.

Over the years they ran into each other repeatedly and despite their personal situations making such a relationship difficult, not to mention dangerous, had become firm friends.

Themba was now one of Hannah's most valuable informants and a freelance journalist working clandestinely in the townships. The government was anxious to prevent objective reporting by the international media and so the freedom movement developed secret channels for sending information overseas. Themba was becoming an increasingly important conduit.

In the 1970's he'd been employed as a journalist by a white controlled newspaper, but his refusal to stop speaking out on controversial subjects and his ferocious attacks on the government and the policies of apartheid, had subjected him to frequent intimidation, interrogation and on one occasion detention for forty-six hours during which time he was beaten but never charged.

While he was on staff at the paper, it was rarely free from threats that characterized the regime's vindictiveness toward those who opposed apartheid. The Security Police began tapping the newspaper's telephones and inevitably the activities of the entire staff were monitored. When intimidation from the authorities became too much, the white owners of the newspaper fired him.

That same day Themba was picked up by the police and questioned about his future plans and his supposed connections to any banned organisations such as the African National Congress or the Pan Africanist Congress, the PAC.

As it turned out, being in detention saved his life. On returning to his home in Mamelodi, a sprawling township on the outskirts of Pretoria, he found his family gone and the house wrecked. His wife and three small children were still missing, presumed dead.

Hannah's numerous queries to the police were met with disdain and the arrogant assumption that whatever had happened to Themba's family was of his own making. The neighbours were too afraid to speak out and so Themba had gone back to work, hoping that someone would one day summon enough courage to tell him the truth about what happened that day.

Finding himself out of work and blacklisted in the world of journalism Themba contacted Hannah offering himself as an informant and told her of his decision to go freelance. Despite her misgivings about his safety, Hannah agreed enthusiastically and their friendship was sealed. She supported him financially in a small way and also steered other liberal reporters to him.

Themba then went underground, building himself a network of supporters and informants who helped him disseminate information about the sentiments and aspirations of black people in the townships. He seemed to have a never-ending list of contacts and people in places of importance who were willing to help. He covered newsworthy events at great personal risk and as white reporters could not enter segregated townships, proved an invaluable source to Hannah and others from the international press trying to report the truth.

While most English newspapers reported from the perspective of how events affected whites, Themba was able to relate the bitter reality of life as he endured it to the international press that was not bound by South African law. Many local papers adopted the opinion that if the police did not confirm an event, it hadn't happened, but Western media was able to recount eyewitness accounts fairly and without fear of retaliation.

Themba worked tirelessly and boldly and Hannah lived in a state of high anxiety, fearing daily that she would hear he'd been detained or disappeared. Police powers enabled them to detain and question a suspect without trial and it was not uncommon for black informants, activists, and reporters to suddenly and inexplicably disappear without a trace never to be heard of again. Each time she met with Themba, Hannah wondered if it would be the last.

Expressing her fears to him he'd laughed and replied, 'I should get paid every time I'm detained. After all, whites get a salary when they go to the army and going to jail is like National Service for us blacks, so why shouldn't we get paid?'

For all his flippancy, Hannah knew that Themba was aware of the constant danger and took great care to stay out of trouble. They never spoke about what would happen to Hannah if their relationship were made public.

The next day, Hannah went to her office as usual and reread the report Themba had given her about the raid on the squatter camp by the police.

Last night, as squatter camp inhabitants were preparing for bed, the silence was broken by the shrill sounds of screaming. Large khaki-clad men with batons and sjamboks, the traditional leather whip popular among Afrikaners, burst through the informal settlement causing mayhem as they went on a rampage destroying everything in their path.

I witnessed a small girl of no more than six years old being forcibly ripped from the arms of her sobbing mother, who was arrested and violently thrown into the back of a van, with no obvious regard to either her or her child's welfare. The painfully thin

*girl sank to the ground and but for the kindness of strangers would
no doubt still be there alone among the ruins of her makeshift home.*

*People fled in terror as their homes were bulldozed and then set
alight by men whose primary objective seemed to be annihilation of
the camp and the people that lived there. As usual, the police, who
are supposed to bring about law and order, seemed hell bent on
destroying as many people's lives as possible.*

*When will this plunder and lack of basic human decency be
called to account? For how much longer must the people suffer under
a brutal regime that is intent upon throwing its citizens into the
streets and leaving the homeless without food and shelter? When will
this government be called to account?*

She took the article to her editor, Johannes Jordaan,
knowing he would find it seditious and never dare
publish it, although she found some satisfaction in
knowing that the same article would appear, uncensored,
in international newspapers. Although Hannah's editor
considered himself devoid of ideology, he harshly
censored information passed to him by Hannah and
other reporters that were known to have black
informants.

Jordaan scanned the copy then asked, 'Anyone die?'

'No, not this time.'

He shrugged and intoned the standard response, 'Not
a big story then, is it? Is this what you've been working
on? We've hardly seen you all week.'

'No, I know, I've been chasing down a few leads on
another story. I'm still looking into those activist murders
and the man that was shot in the car park. Before you say
anything, I know you don't consider dead activists very
important, but I think there's something a lot more

sinister behind these killings, and I'd like to carry on if that's okay with you?'

Jordaan pursed his lips and thought for a moment. 'Mm, okay, for now, but I don't want you wasting your time on something that's not going anywhere. Frik reckons you're on a wild goose chase.'

'He would,' said Hannah.

'You can't go getting all wound up about a couple of dead black men, Hannah. The blacks are always killing each other; it's the way of Africa. It will turn out to be some tribal vendetta, you'll see. It would be better if you concentrated your energies on the Pretoria killing,' he said and after subjecting her to a stern gaze, left her alone.

Thankfully Frik van Niekerk was out and for a while Hannah was free from the constant fear that she was being watched and took the opportunity to ring Arnold Coetser, a friend from university.

Coetser was a lawyer at a struggling law firm in Johannesburg who had been in love with Hannah since they met and she cruelly took advantage of his feelings to pump him for information. One of the first conscientious objectors, he'd spent time in prison instead of the obligatory two years in the National Defence Force. Officially, his incarceration had broken his spirit and he now worked as an immigration lawyer; unofficially, his zeal had increased and he worked for the underground movement, smuggling dissenters and militants in and out of South Africa and providing false documentation for those fleeing the country to escape the security forces or the draft.

'Hi, Arnold, it's Hannah,' she said.

'What do you want?' he said.

'A lawyer was shot in Pretoria last week.'

'David Bosman. I knew him quite well. He was brilliant but arrogant. A lot like you, actually. He thought he could get away with speaking his mind and after a couple of beers he shot his mouth off about the guys he'd helped escape. He even spoke out about a recent trip to Cuba, as if that would win him any friends. I'm not surprised that bunch of thugs from the security forces got him. He made them look bad.'

'You think it was the authorities that killed him?' asked Hannah.

'Who else?' he asked. 'Look, I know you're always looking for conspiracies where there aren't any, but this guy was spectacularly stupid when it came to his own safety. He's been under surveillance for years and they probably decided to get rid of him permanently instead of just banning him. Other than that I don't know anything that could help you.'

'Thanks, Arnold. I owe you,' said Hannah, and rang off, wondering if he was right and she was looking for non-existent assassins.

CHAPTER

Five

Killers weren't born they were created. They developed over the years, through childhood, into adolescence, the result of years of indoctrination and propaganda. True hatred had to be taught and encouraged. It grew darker and blacker with each passing year, then blossomed and flourished and wound its self round every sinew and joint and seeped into the blood until it was flowing strong and pure.

For one, the urge to kill started at a young age, from that first terrifying day at primary school when prissy little girls in pristine uniforms turned up their noses and smirked at the scruffy second-hand uniform and raggedy lice-shaven head. It was there, in the drab classroom with the blue-haired teacher and the neatly covered books that the situation was primed and the seeds planted. Most of the dewy-eyed pupils took what they heard, thought it over for while, and later, when free thought began to emerge, rejected it.

But one of the faceless hordes absorbed it all; every nuance, every racist word, every piece of Christian

National Education was swallowed whole, nestling in the killer heart and deep within each fibre, growing, expanding, full of potential.

In the black schools, such as they were, they taught their children that the whites were the oppressors, the enemy, and instructed them on ways to rebel and showed them how to riot and revolt and go on marches and participate in mass demonstrations and strikes. Any black thirteen-year-old could make a petrol bomb in less than ten minutes and knew exactly what to do with it. They burned their schools to the ground and the teachers were too afraid to teach so the children ran wild destroying their books and smashing up what was left of the building. Such freedom. But not for everyone. White children had to obey, bide their time and wait until they were grown, powerful and unfettered.

Now the waiting was over. The years spent suppressing what was natural had come to an end. The killer had been patient and delayed the inevitable, yearning for the perfect opportunity, never forgetting those lessons learnt long ago. And when the right opportunity presented its self, all caution was thrown to the dusty wind and life could begin.

***

A week later Hannah opened the door of her flat, planning an early morning swim. She slung her towel over her shoulder but as she closed the door and saw what was stuck there, it fell unnoticed to the ground and her body went numb. In the centre of the door, secured with a drawing pin, was a photograph of a dead cat. A cat the exact size and colouring of her own beloved pet.

She ran down the steps, calling, trying to suppress the rising panic.

'Kitty, here, kitty. Where are you? Puss, puss?'

When the large tortoiseshell came sauntering out of the bushes with an indignant expression on its face, she grabbed it roughly, almost in tears, and buried her face in its fur. The car protested loudly and wriggled away, running up the steps to her door, where it sat mewing, demanding food as it always did.

Hannah ripped the photo down and went inside, gave the cat extra food and a bowl of milk and sank down on her couch. She stared at the photo, turned it over and studied the back, but there was no clue as to where it had been taken or who had stuck it on her door. It was a warning, obviously, but from whom?

In a daze, Hannah drove over to the Maartens' trim home. It was probably a ridiculous thing to do, but she couldn't think of anywhere else to go and was too afraid to stay home alone. Her hands were icy cold and the hair curling into the nape of her neck damp. She tried to slow her breathing, but shock was setting in and she wasn't sure she'd be able to control her emotions on seeing Tom.

She tried to focus on something else and decided this was the perfect opportunity to ask Tom if there was any new information about who might have killed the lawyer in the car park, presupposing he hadn't done it himself. She hoped he would be willing to share any evidence the police had collected, and wanted to tell him about her own investigations. The recent confidence she'd felt after receiving new information from one of her sources had disappeared, but still, she couldn't wait to confront him with it.

After Arnold's assertion that the authorities had killed Bosman, she probed into the lawyer's background but came up against a wall of denials about his activities and a barricade of people intent on wrecking her investigations. She was going to need a lot more fortitude if she proposed exposing the truth and was learning never to take no for an answer.

Despite her relative inexperience in the field, Hannah had realised early on that investigative journalists in South Africa often depended on a whistle blower within the system to get their story. She was hoping Tom was one of them and despite her qualms about his trustworthiness, decided to take the chance, telling herself that for now she would simply have to risk it. She told herself that her ability to read people would tell her whether or not he was involved in anything dodgy, and the minute she found anything implicating him, she would back off. Hannah was very proud of her instincts and they had never let her down before. He might have been talking to that man the day he was murdered for any number of reasons.

After pulling up outside the Maartens' home, Hannah sat for a moment, composing herself before getting out and hesitantly walking up the drive. The house was very orderly, the verdant garden well kept, flowerbeds immaculate, the smell of freshly mown grass lingering in the air. The house had obviously been painted recently, the white walls pristine in the sunshine, with a few irregular splashes of mud along the lower edges and a riotous purple bougainvillea climbing one corner. The paved path leading up to the front door was tidy and slightly damp after a recent shower of rain, the grass between each slab neatly trimmed. A hadada screeched overhead as Hannah lifted the brass knocker, making her jump.

Tom's son Jack opened the door, vivid blue eyes regarding her warily. He was holding a half-eaten apple and still chewing. As tall as she was and almost gangly, still needing to grow into his elbows, he was dressed in the uniform of all fifteen-year-old boys, jeans, pale green T-shirt and a slight sneer. Fair hair with natural highlights from the sun flopped over his forehead. Hannah wondered how many teenage hearts he had broken in his short life. He lifted a long finger and languidly flicked the fringe out of his eyes, staring at her with a touch of insolence.

Luckily Hannah wasn't there to impress him and didn't much care what he thought of her. Her self-image was intact enough not to be concerned with the hostile looks of an adolescent. He raised an eyebrow, just as she'd seen his father do, so very aloof as he lounged against the doorjamb. A brindle dog pressed up against his leg and eyed her with his tongue out. Hannah's parents had a Staffordshire bull terrier and she knew from the look on this one's face that she was in more danger of being licked to death than she was of being mauled.

'Yes?'

'Is your father home? Could you tell him Hannah Smith, from the newspaper, is here, please?'

Jack opened the door, inviting her inside. He took a bite of his apple then padded off leaving her staring at the arrangement of artificial roses on the table in the hallway. She tentatively touched them and the smooth plastic dewdrop, to make sure they were indeed imitations.

Hannah looked round the room with interest, not sure what she expected to find. A wall of crime with a hangman's noose and a bloodied knife perhaps? She was met only with a vast expanse of floral wallpaper in pinks, blues and mauves and a number of Renoir prints tastefully framed.

The air was scented and Hannah wrinkled her nose, recognising the smell of jasmine from her grandmother's garden. She was wondering whether or not she liked this preponderance of flowery decoration that assaulted her senses when a vision in pink floated into the room and held out a slender hand. Hannah had the impression that she was about to be swallowed whole by a giant rose.

'Hello. You must be Miss Smith. I'm Tom's wife, Laurel. Tom will be with us in a moment.' Laurel's voice was soft and husky, almost as if it was an effort to force it out of the pale throat. Hannah shook the ivory hand, surprised at the firm grip of such a fragile creature.

'Hello, thanks so much, I hope I'm not intruding but I need to speak to Detective Maartens.'

The pleasant yet slightly vacant face that smiled at her was perfectly made up, the subtle make-up serving to highlight her luminescent eyes and porcelain skin. Sharp collar and cheekbones emphasised the gauntness of her frame. Hannah could see the outline of the woman's hips protruding through the clinging fabric of her skirt. The distinct fragrance of something sweet and expensive stroked Hannah's senses. Laurel was a naturally alluring woman, yet Hannah had the strange impression that she worked hard to maintain the svelte poise. Her flowing movements appeared calculated, as if she had practised moving in front of a mirror for hours. She ushered her guest into the lounge with a gracious sweep of the hand and indicated that she sit down.

Hannah started at the creak the pink leather couch gave as she sank back awkwardly in the soft cushion, her feet almost lifting off the ground while she struggled to maintain her composure. Laurel watched with a slight smile and blinked a few times.

'Can I get you some tea? Coffee? Something cold?'

'Tea would be wonderful, thanks,' Hannah replied and wondered how this butterfly had ended up married to the wasp of a man she knew as Tom Maartens, detective. The house was immaculate, the furnishings of a high quality and, Hannah knew, very expensive. She wondered how Tom managed it on a policeman's salary.

'Won't be long, I'll get the maid to make a pot,' said Laurel, gliding out of the room.

On the few occasions she had met Tom Maartens, Hannah had been struck by his hardness and irascibility. She'd only ever heard him speak with clipped irritability and had seen his minions flinch in the face of his anger, yet she liked him. Despite the temper a gleam in his eyes made her sure it was all an act adopted to compensate for his stature. She wouldn't have liked to cross him and had taken great care to stay in his good books because she needed him if she was going to make any sense of recent events. She liked to think that he needed her too.

Laurel fluttered into the room in her cloud of cloying perfume, nearly dropping the tray as she put it down on the edge of the oak table. Tom, who stretched out a hand

and steadied the tray before it could topple on to the Persian carpet, followed her. Laurel gave a little giggle and an attractive flush covered her cheeks. She fluttered her lashes coyly at her husband and simpered, making Hannah feel like an intruder.

'I don't normally carry such heavy things, I have delicate wrists, but Priscilla our maid is at a tricky stage in making our dinner. I don't know about you, Hester, but I can't abide lumps in the sauce.'

'It's Hannah,' said Tom.

Laurel blinked. 'Sorry, I have a terrible time remembering names, don't I, sweetie?' She sat on the arm of a chair, evidently about to settle down for a chat. Her husband switched a piercing gaze to Hannah.

'What can I do for you, Miss Smith?'

Hannah opened her handbag and took out an envelope, which she handed to him. 'I found this pinned on my door this morning.'

Laurel, peering over her husband's shoulder, gave a squeal. 'That's horrible. Who could possibly hate you enough to do something so spiteful, you poor thing?'

Tom examined the photograph of the dead cat. 'Have you told anyone else about this?'

'It's all part of the job, isn't it? I presume it's some kind of warning.'

The picture had shaken her but it had also strengthened her resolve. The realisation that she was being watched and that somebody hoped to scare her off only made her more resolute, as it was obvious she was on to something significant. Tom put the photo in his pocket and sat back then he examined her, making her feel like an insect under a microscope. For some peculiar reason Hannah was suddenly stuck by the unusual mustard colour of his eyes, an odd effect of the sunlight shining in through the open window. He had the look of a lion about him, a predatory one, and as he sat down opposite her, she realised that his movements had a feline quality about them. He wasn't very tall by South African standards but his muscular body exuded power and he possessed a natural magnetism.

'I'll look into this. Although, I must warn you that it's highly improbable we'll find out who sent it,' he said.

'That's what I thought you'd say. More importantly, I have some new information about the murder in the car park,' said Hannah.

'Oh?' He continued staring at her.

Hannah was not intimidated and met the challenge in his yellow eyes head-on. She glanced across at Laurel, who flicked an imaginary speck of lint off her lap.

'Thanks for the tea, Laurel love,' said Tom.

Hannah hoped the woman would get the message that she wanted to be alone with Tom so they could talk, and wondered if she was the type of wife that considered any woman with a pulse a hazard to her marital bliss.

Laurel moved a rebellious highlighted lock that had escaped the layer of spray. 'You know, I can't bear all this violence and murder that you're involved in. Such a horrid job my husband has, and I do so wish he would give it up because I've enough money for both of us. I do love having lots of money, don't I, my love?'

Hannah watched the large blue vein throbbing on Tom's temple with interest. She'd seen it beating before when he was angry with a subordinate for disobeying instructions.

Laurel instantly seemed uncertain, knowing she had revealed too much and stood up. Her eyes flickered and a line creased her smooth forehead. Hannah sipped her tea feeling like a trespasser and waited for the explosion of ill temper but Tom only smiled.

'Hannah and I would prefer to be alone to discuss some business if you don't mind but you don't need to stay, love, it'll only upset you and we won't be long.'

Laurel put another spoon of sugar in his tea, seemingly reassured at his kind words. She stirred it, patted him on the hand, and drifted off, once again a poised and serene figure. Hannah was surprised by a soft look in Tom's eyes as he watched his wife's retreating figure.

She was about to tell Tom her latest news, when Jack sauntered through the lounge and walked out onto the adjacent veranda, settling down almost, but not quite out of sight, eating a packet of Marie biscuits. He left the glass door open and pretended to read a Mad magazine as his father and Hannah talked. It was obvious to Hannah that he was listening to their conversation and she wondered if she should ask Tom to make him leave.

'What a treasure. Don't know how she puts up with me. Okay, Miss Smith, what new information do you have?'

'I was wondering, now that you've had time to conduct some investigations, what the connection between David Bosman, the murdered lawyer in the car park, and the body that was found near Harrismith last month is?'

Tom took a sip of tea and placed the cup back in the saucer. Hannah could tell he was surprised that she'd already identified Bosman and hoped he was impressed at how good she was at her job. And this was only the beginning of what she knew. She waited for him to confess that he'd known the man, but he didn't.

'What specifically has led you to reach the conclusion that they're connected?' he said.

'I'm not a total idiot and they both died by a bullet to the back of the head. Before you argue, I know quite a lot about ballistics and I have a contact in the lab that isn't as tight-lipped as the rest of you. I asked him to do some tests for me and he told me the bullets from Bosman positively matched those from the Harrismith body. I've also asked him to do an analysis of bullets taken from other unidentified victims. Are you still going to tell me it's not the same killer?'

Tom shrugged and she saw the shutters come down in his eyes. It was a long shot asking for a comparison to be made, but her hunch paid off and she was feeling arrogantly self-assured and not a little smug to have proved conclusively that two of the deaths were linked.

'Come on, Detective. I know the South African police don't like sharing their toys with other children but I have a story to write so a bit of co-operation would be appreciated. We *are* on the same side, aren't we?'

Tom shook his head and spoke softly, but his voice had an unusual undertone that puzzled her. 'It could be a coincidence; you know how easy it is to buy a gun.' Hannah snorted.

'That's the trouble with you reporters; always sniffing out stories that don't exist and you're the worst of all of them. I never met anyone with such a vivid imagination but as I've said before, I'll let you know if we find out anything new. In the meantime why don't you find some mouldy ex-rugby star and his beer belly to write about or something else that will amuse your readers?' It wasn't the first time Tom had commented on, and disapproved of, her chosen profession.

'You and my mother should form a club,' she retorted, glaring at him.

'I'm sure a girl with your talent can find plenty more interesting things to write about than dead bodies. Like Laurel says, it's such a horrid job, particularly for a girl like you. Leave the crime investigating to the men.'

Hannah had to get through to him and persuade him to open up about what he knew. 'Playing games isn't doing either of us any good so I'm going to be honest; I was surprised to discover that the same gun was used on that man in Harrismith and on the lawyer. Despite what I said when I saw you in the car park, I didn't think they were connected, but now I know they are and that puts a totally different perspective on every case I'm looking at.'

She hesitated for a moment then decided to tell him what else she had discovered. 'Did you know that over the last two years, twelve bodies have been found, all shot the same way, all with the same type of weapon? Seven of them had been drugged. And did you know that it's been proven these last two victims were quite involved politically?'

'I did. We aren't complete monkeys, despite what you think. The body they found near Harrismith was a particularly nasty agitator who disappeared from his home in Soweto about three months ago.'

At least he was still willing to give her some new information. 'I knew that already. I too am very good at my job. Did you know David Bosman was working on getting him out of the country? Why did it take so long for you to identify him?' Hannah hoped Tom would finally confess to knowing the man, but once again he didn't, and her chest tightened. She bit her lip, eager to confront him and ask why he and Bosman had been arguing the day he was killed, but she restrained herself. Exposing everything she knew wouldn't be wise.

'You know what it's like, so many of these guys disappear all the time it's impossible to keep track of them. For all we knew he'd gone into exile in Botswana or something.'

'And we all know the South African police couldn't care less about a black activist that goes missing, don't we?' she said.

'So young to be so cynical, Miss Smith.'

'Maybe, but only about authority and the government in particular. I'm a bit sceptical about those who wish to control the people they govern like the Nats do. In a democracy, or even a sham of a democracy like ours, journalism's meant to call those in power to account,' she said.

'In that case I've no doubt you already know that Bosman had decidedly cosy connections to the ANC, which despite what you might think from a moral standpoint, is still a banned terrorist organisation,' he said.

'Yes, he did and we can see why he needed to die, can't we? An attorney who was doing no more than his duty in providing representation for people facing criminal charges is committing a terrible crime, isn't he? What about the dismembered body they found two weeks ago in Hartebeespoort Dam? He was only a gardener. Granted, a gardener who had been detained a number of times and was one of the young lions of the ANC Youth, but you can't seriously expect me to believe that there's no link between him and the others?'

Tom inclined his head slightly to the side. Hannah could tell he was disconcerted and wondered if she should have shared her knowledge with him earlier. He narrowed his saffron eyes and considered her until she squirmed.

'Hannah, I'm going to tell you something but you need to promise me you won't let on to anyone else what I think. I'm only informing you because it's apparent you have already started putting the pieces together.'

'Whatever you say here is off the record.'

'Since you started digging around I've been doing a little undercover investigating of my own and have reached the same conclusions you have. It's time we honestly compared what we know and in the spirit of co-operation…I've been having a thought that perhaps what we have here is a professional killer.'

'An assassin, you mean?'

CHAPTER

Six

Jack lowered his magazine and leaned through the open door, peering at his father and Hannah over the top of it, a biscuit poised half way to his lips, a furrow between his eyebrows. Hannah glanced at him. Assassination was an intriguing topic for anyone, never mind a testosterone-driven teenage boy.

'Go to your room, Jack,' said Tom. 'The last time I looked in there the floor was covered in dirty clothes and muddy rugby boots and I won't even mention the smell.'

'Priscilla can clean it later,' said Jack. 'That's why you pay her.'

'Jack,' said his father, beginning to look annoyed, 'I don't think I like your attitude. Do we need to discuss this later?' Jack stood swiftly, obviously recognising the threat in his father's voice. He came inside and walked past them, clicking his tongue in a last act of defiance before leaving the lounge.

Hannah watched the doorway for a moment before asking, 'Do you think it's your boys from Vlakplaas?'

Tom caught his breath. 'What?'

'You know, Vlakplaas, renegade policemen roaming the countryside like a posse of bounty hunters eliminating enemies of the state.' She waited.

'Of course I do. When investigations are stonewalled at every turn, not only by your colleagues, but also by your usually reliable sources outside the SAP, it makes you think. I know about Vlakplaas, and it pains me to admit this, but I have to consider the very real possibility that some of my friends are in it up to their necks.'

'And you've never been tempted to join them? From what I can gather it's quite an honour to be one of the pack, if you can stomach it.'

She studied him closely, hoping to see some flicker in his eyes that would confirm his innocence or guilt, but his face was blank, barely a muscle moving.

'I can't. I mean no one has ever tried to recruit me. They know better than to try.'

'Tell me Tom, what do you know about the South African police's death squads?' said Hannah. 'I don't know much detail, but be honest, Detective, it's impossible to work in the same environment as the Vlakplaas boys without knowing something about them.'

Tom stood up and walked to the door leading out onto the veranda. He went very still. The room was silent except for the distant sound of a hadeda screeching as it flew overhead. The air was hot and sweetly scented, a remnant of Laurel's perfume. Tom turned and started pacing.

'I'm not deaf or stupid and you can't help overhearing the boasting of men that take such pride in abduction, torture and murder.'

'From what I've gathered,' said Hannah, 'they live a protected life on that farm outside Pretoria, a band of brothers that operates outside the laws of the country as well as the rules and regulations of the police. Being part of the Vlakplaas unit is like belonging to a close-knit family that's not only paranoid and secretive, but above the law too. They seem to be bound together by obligation and faithfulness and according to my source, the relationships that exist between the superior officers and their minions are extraordinary. Isn't that right, Tom?'

'Couldn't have said it better myself – and you'd better make damn sure you never write anything like that for your newspaper. You're right though. I know how sick it is, but these guys are respected and protected by the rest of the police force and by the community beyond it. It's virtually impossible to prove anything because there's so much intimidation. Not only that, they're experts at incriminating and discrediting anyone that tries to expose them.'

He frowned and plumped up the cushions on the large overstuffed armchair that was slumped in a corner of the room. He sank down into the chair and closed his eyes.

'You mean you're only one of many who know about Vlakplaas and the wholesale slaughter that goes on in the name of freedom and says nothing.'

Tom jerked upright and glared at her.

'I value my life and that of my family too much. If you know anything at all about Vlakplaas surely you understand how impossible it is to speak out against them. It's easy for you to be self-righteous when you don't have to deal with it every day. I'm not going to justify myself to you, Hannah.'

'Then you do think it's the Vlakplaas guys?' she said.

'No, not this time.' Hannah opened her mouth to protest but he shook his head.

'There's a strange feeling to the killings you're talking about that doesn't fit the police profile at all. For one thing, many of them were killed by one clean shot to the head, and then there's the fact that they were drugged. I've been watching the men I know are involved at Vlakplaas and I can see it's nothing to do with them. There's one guy that I know for sure is stationed at the farm and he had a very odd reaction when he saw the photos of one of the bodies we found. No, the modus operandi is wrong. This is something else.'

'Well, ja. There's certainly something about the way these murders happened. They were so smoothly planned and executed.' She grinned.

'Has anyone ever told you that you have a rather weird sense of humour, Miss Smith?'

'Frequently,' she replied.

'What I mean is, a lot of preparation went into these killings. It was only by chance that the body near Harrismith was found at all. It was badly burnt, that's why it's taken so long to get any identification and it's only because a police van was passing by the car park at the right time the other day that the lawyer was found there at all. They must have interrupted the killer before he could dispose of the body.'

Hannah leaned forward, clasping a pink cushion to her chest.

'They may not have known each other personally, but think about who they were – an activist, a member of the ANC Youth League and an anti-apartheid attorney. What we need to find out now is who would want them dead and why. I mean, we need to assess their respective roles in a political context and then find out if they were a specific threat to anyone, stuff like that.'

'Ja, I think I need to do some more digging around. See what you can find out too, will you?'

'Why, Detective Maartens,' said Hannah, feigning surprise. 'Are you asking for my help?'

'You damn well know I am, Miss Smith. At least I can be sure you won't tell me to mind my own business.'

'Did someone warn you off?'

The shutters came down again. 'No, I'm joking. Now, how about another cup of tea?' asked Tom. Hannah agreed, hoping that his mouth would open up again when his stomach was full, but it didn't.

CHAPTER

Seven

Laurel rejoined them, followed by Jack, and it was evident from the start that Tom's wife found Hannah's presence unwelcome.

'I can see from your lovely curves that you like sweet things, Hester, so I'm sure you'll love these biscuits the maid baked,' said Laurel, passing over a plate of peanut butter cookies. Hannah took one reluctantly.

'Hannah, Mum,' said Jack.

The next hour was filled with barbed comments about Hannah's weight and unmarried status. Yet Laurel seemed preoccupied and vague, constantly referring to Hannah as Hester, although Hannah suspected this was more to put her in her place as someone of little significance than an inability to remember names.

She wondered again about Laurel's relationship with Tom who always appeared so driven and focused, yet his wife gave the impression of being barely capable of maintaining a thought to its conclusion before getting another and acting upon it. Perhaps she found all the violence that her husband dealt with too difficult to manage and escaped into her own reality. It would be interesting to sit down with Laurel and find out what actually made her tick, thought Hannah, wiping a crumb off her lips.

What interested her even more was the leeway Tom gave her. Despite the occasional blatantly rude remark about Hannah and her job, Tom never once defended her or reprimanded his wife. Hannah wondered if he would do so in private. Then she chided herself for feeling disappointed at his lack of backbone. The man's character or lack of it, was nothing to do with her.

Jack watched his mother all the time, trying to anticipate her every need and constantly covering for her when she lost a train of thought or said something out of kilter. While his father appeared incapable of commenting on his wife's ill manners, Jack was unable to hide his embarrassment and cast pleading looks at his father to intervene, but Tom was apparently blindly loyal and not about to cause a scene for fear of Hannah writing something about his peculiar mate in her newspaper.

'Is it hard writing stuff for the newspaper?' asked Jack. 'Did you go to university? I never knew women could be reporters. Do you get scared?'

'Jack,' said Tom with a smile, 'Let Hannah enjoy her tea with the interrogation.'

'It's okay. No, it's not hard, I love writing, yes, I did go to university - Wits, and yes, I often get scared.' said Hannah and took another biscuit, mainly to see the expression on Laurel's face.

'Did you vomit the first time you saw a dead body? I would.'

Hannah laughed, 'Actually, Jack, I did throw up, It was horrible. His skin was all greeny-white with parts of it flaking off in huge chunks and his eyeballs had been eaten by fish and the smell...' Out of nowhere the bloated body on the beach sprang to her mind. She frowned. 'But it's not funny, it's terrifying to see someone snuffed out like that. I always wonder what they were like alive, who misses them and what their last thoughts were.'

'Ag, no man, Hester, Jack's far too young to be hearing stuff like this. Tom, please, make her stop.'

'Sorry, Laurel, I really shouldn't have said anything.'

'No. You shouldn't.' Laurel smoothed her hair and checked her manicured nails. Tom drank his tea as if nothing had happened.

Jack wasn't put off at all and continued asking pointed and surprisingly astute questions about Hannah's job. He had a ghoulish appreciation of the darker side of what she did, relishing the more unusual and morbid descriptions. When he wasn't sullenly slumped in his seat, he had a quick mind and an equally speedy tongue.

Hannah caught the sour glance thrown at her by Laurel and realised that Jack's mother did not appreciate her encouraging him or the instant rapport that had developed between them. She would have to be cautious if she hoped to cultivate his father as a reliable ally and firmly quashed the thought that spending time with Tom was an attractive option.

It was fascinating watching the way the family interacted. They seemed close, yet every now and then Hannah saw Jack and his father exchange a look that neatly shut out the rest of the world. Some of the moments when Jack and Tom were together made her feel like an interloper and she was interested to know if Laurel ever felt like that too. She was amused by the look on Jack's face when Laurel tugged at his shirt, patted his hair flat or indicated that he wipe his face.

Laurel was clearly a product of the sixties, and Hannah wondered if her vagueness and air of being from another planet had something to do with her taking drugs when she was younger. She found it increasingly difficult to understand how Laurel and Tom, so different, had ended up together. There was no explaining taste.

It required effort to concentrate on Laurel's chattering, but Hannah smiled and tried to look enthralled as Laurel told her all about her work for various charities and how much she enjoyed serving in the tuck-shop at Jack's school.

'It's a mother's duty, don't you think, Hannah? You couldn't possibly understand how a mother feels about her son, not having your own children, and I suppose you'll not get to experience the joy of motherhood, will you? I mean, you're no spring chicken, are you?'

Hannah cleared her throat. Tom showed no reaction. Jack covered his face with a serviette, pretending to sneeze. Laurel continued, oblivious.

'Mum!' said Jack.

Hannah took another biscuit, wondering if the woman was truly as gormless as she made out. Jack tried to catch his father's eye, but Tom merely continued drinking his tea. The teenager sank down a bit lower and hid behind his fringe. Hannah was appalled. The woman clearly wasn't normal, obviously suffering some kind of neuroses, and she couldn't understand why Tom, who she knew to be uncompromisingly vocal and outspoken, was so unperturbed at his wife's rudeness. All she could think was that Tom was coping with her condition by pretending it didn't exist.

'I love being involved in my Jackie's life,' continued Laurel, seemingly unaware of the tension she had created. Jack winced and rolled his eyes heavenward.

'I know I'm a bit forgetful at times, aren't I, my love, but I do try my best. There is so much to do you can't blame me for being absentminded, can you? But I don't want to miss out on anything, childhood is such a fascinating time to watch. I suppose my brain is so full that some things fall out every now and then. But at least now that he's bigger he can feed himself when I forget, can't you, my darling?'

Laurel giggled like a schoolgirl and plucked a loose thread off her skirt. Jack remained silent and his father continued eating as if nothing was amiss, but as Tom was seeing Hannah out, he put a hand in the small of her back.

'I'm sorry about Laurel, Hannah. She hasn't been very well and has a condition that makes her a bit ...it's nothing to do with you though, please don't take anything she says personally.'

Hannah tried to ignore the electric shock that was running up her back and nodded, overcome with sympathy for Tom and his son.

In spite of Laurel's constant sniping and Tom's attempt at an apology, Hannah went home tired and happy; almost wishing she had a Jack of her own to treat her with scorn and to roll his eyes at her feeble attempts at humour. She firmly suppressed the longing before she arrived home. It didn't do to get involved emotionally.

***

A murder was being planned and correct timing was imperative. The day was still after a recent shower and freshness was always inspiring, giving the spirits a lift. There was no space for error but experience and groundwork paid off every time. Fatigue and undue haste could override every precaution, so rest and preparation for the mission were vital. Knowing exactly what to do, when to do it and how to carry out the execution, ensured there would be no mistake and the man would die at the appointed time.

The area for the attack had been chosen. It had been surveyed and scouted. Every contingency anticipated. The operation depended on knowledge, understanding and the skilful application of techniques that would allow the killer to move, hide, detect and observe the target without being seen.

An array of weaponry was spread out on a table, the precision instruments cared for lovingly. Each day and after every skirmish with the enemy they were stripped down, cleaned and oiled, the barrels run through until they were sparkling and a fresh coating of low infra-red signature paint applied. There could be no sloppiness, a glint might be seen, an unclean gun could jam and the mission would fail.

These beautiful instruments were well utilised in perfecting the job they were created for. They were poetry in motion. The power to end life exploded out of the barrel with the press of a finger, a sparking synapse, a momentary reaction and the prey died. Gone for time without end just like that. It was destiny fulfilled.

CHAPTER

Eight

Hannah woke with a start. She could hear an engine revving and buried her head under the blanket. Then she heard shouts and barking dogs and leapt out of bed. She ran to the window and in the road outside saw a yellow police van with mesh on the back and Alsatian dogs in a little cage. A burly policeman with a snarling beast straining at the leash was pushing Philemon, the gardener, into the back of the van to join the other fearful faces crowded in the tiny space. She shivered, realising it was a sweep to pick up anyone without a passbook.

Hannah lived in a complex of ground floor flats. Philemon maintained the beautiful communal gardens and attended to the swimming pool that he was not allowed to swim in. Despite having no education, he was a diligent and competent worker. He lived in a poky room on the premises and acted as general factotum and handyman as well as gardener.

Hannah spoke to Philemon often on her way in and out and had helped him furnish his room, giving him a television set and some reject furniture from her parents.

She provided paint and helped him with a constant supply of paraffin for his stove. This wasn't the first time he'd been picked up. If he hadn't returned by the end of the day, she would go down to the police station to bail him out.

Hannah went back to bed and pulled the duvet over her head, grateful for the weekend and a chance for a lie-in. She was just nodding off when Grace, the maid, came into the room with a cup of tea, which she put on the bedside table.

The large black woman, dressed in a mauve cotton dress with amthcing apron and headscarf, picked up the dirty clothes tossed carelessly on the floor along with assorted underwear and garments from the day before and deftly tidied away the mess of assorted objects strewn around the room. Hannah sat up in bed and sipped her tea.

'Philemon was arrested again.'

'Yes,' answered Grace, subdued.

'I heard there's been trouble in the townships again,' said Hannah.

'People, they just want a better life. They do not do it to cause trouble,' said Grace.

'I was just wondering if you had a problem getting here this morning. I don't know if the buses are running.' She climbed out of bed and put on her dressing gown. 'What do you think, Grace? Are things going to change anytime soon?'

Hannah hadn't expected any response and was surprised when Grace answered.

'Perhaps it would be a good thing not to ask too many questions. There are some things that are too hard to explain and you can never understand the way things are for us. It would be best if you were not so curious, especially with friends like yours.'

Hannah was speechless. If she didn't know better, she'd think the maid's tone was slightly threatening. Grace took a tissue out of the pocket of her uniform and dabbed her eyes.

'Gracie? What's the matter?'

Hannah was concerned. She wasn't used to seeing emotion from her maid and had certainly never considered that Grace, who came from a rural area, had three years of education and could barely write her own name, might have a valid opinion about anything significant. Hannah thought of her as a simple country girl, despite her age, and she certainly had a quiet naiveté, going about her menial tasks without complaint. For over thirty years Grace had cooked and cleaned and babysat for Hannah's family and when Hannah moved into her own flat, she insisted on coming in once a week to help out. Black or not, she was like a mother to Hannah who'd always thought they had a good relationship.

'Gracie, please don't cry. You don't have such a bad life, do you? It would be much worse if you were still on the farm or in a township. You have a good job here and with my folks. You have your own furnished room and food so you don't have to pay for anything yourself. My mother even buys uniforms for you to wear. And they're so pretty, a different colour for every day of the week. You like clothes, don't you?'

Grace shook her head and started making the bed. Hannah guiltily put her shoes in the cupboard and closed an overflowing drawer.

'You do not understand how it is for my family and me,' said Grace. 'You live here in this flat but I live in a small room at the bottom of your mother's garden on my own and my family live far away from me. You think I like eating pap and cheap meat off a tin plate and drinking strong sweet tea and you give me thick sandwiches with jam but no butter, and you think this is the way it should be and that you are being kind, but you do not know the truth about these matters. You are a white person and the government gives you everything for free. You get all this for nothing and you don't even have to pay. You cannot understand.'

It wasn't the first time Hannah's maid had expressed the sentiment that white people were given everything for nothing, but her lack of education made it very difficult for Hannah to explain how the system actually worked. Tremendous propaganda was spread in the townships about how the white government supplied such things as jobs, housing, electricity, water and even vast sums of money, for free to all whites. And, she was the first to admit, that for any black working in a white area and observing the seeming affluence of the people that lived there, it must appear as if the lies were fact.

'We don't have it that easy either, you know. I don't get everything for free, despite what you've been told. I work hard for what I have and yes, I do have more advantages than you, but I have to work, just like you do, and I use my salary to pay for what I have, just like you do. I don't agree with the way the blacks are treated by the government, Grace, and it's difficult for all of us that want a better life for all South Africans. There are many people working against the system, trying to get it to change, but it's not going to happen overnight.'

The disbelieving look on Grace's face said it all. No way she was going to fall for this particular piece of racist propaganda either.

'We've already had three bomb scares at the office this year,' said Hannah, trying to impress the fact that life was hard for everyone. 'And the petrol price has gone up again and that means food prices will go up too.'

As she said it, she realised how inane it sounded. She simply could not make Grace understand that few escaped apartheid unscathed, despite the obvious degrees of suffering. It was virtually impossible to explain the mechanics of the economy, and how could she ever describe her job or how she was doing her utmost to make things better for people exactly like her maid?

She wondered what Grace would think if she knew of her friendship with Themba. Illegal cross-racial relationships were as hard to explain as fraternization with the police and she mulled over the suspicion that it was her connection with Tom that had caused Grace to give voice to her opinions. She had the unsettling thought that if the situation in the country ever escalated to a state of all-out war, she wasn't entirely convinced Grace wouldn't murder her in her bed.

**

The killer did not always operate alone. Many men felt the same, appreciated the thrill of the chase and the climax of the kill, and in a country built on nationalist pride and entrenched racism, it was easy to find a team whose ideals melded perfectly. They might not all be driven by the same desires, but as far as murder was concerned, they were united. It was easy, most were already trained to kill, as were all white boys, and crafting them into a skilled team was easy.

Until now they'd been safe, unseen and invisible, going about their business, but recently there were unsettling reports about someone prying into their business. It was unfortunate and inconvenient, but a woman had stumbled across their work and she was now intent on exposing them.

They tried scaring her but it seemed she was made of sterner stuff than they'd imagined and she had not heeded their warning. She continued to investigate their work, looking into their affairs with no regard for her own safety, asking questions everywhere and they knew it was only a matter of time before someone answered her questions honestly and pointed her towards their exclusive unit.

Thus far they'd remained concealed and hidden from the world, content to go about their business under cover of darkness protected by the knowledge that they were invisible and that only a few knew of their existence. It was a pity, but they would have to intensify their efforts to scare her off or she would expose them and cause untold damage to their mission. At first the unit's leader had been unconcerned, convinced the journalist would back down in fear, but in the last few days something had changed and the order had come down for harsher tactics to be employed. But first they had someone else to take care of.

CHAPTER

Nine

Hannah wandered around her quiet flat oddly on edge. The off-white walls had a hint of cool green and all the furnishings were co-ordinated. She'd recently redecorated and the floor was now covered in a luxurious deep pile carpet with a few strategically thrown hand-woven African rugs. The curtains draped at the ceiling-height windows were soft and cream, nothing frilly or fussy. She didn't like finicky decoration and there was a minimum of ornamentation but plenty of clutter, as her life spilled from one room to the next. The lemony atmosphere was tranquil and homely, but for once her usual haven did nothing to still the turmoil inside her.

Discarded magazines lay strewn across the coffee table and a pile of books sat drunkenly on the top of a rickety bookcase. Notebooks filled with untidy scrawl and indecipherable memos lay scattered on the floor in front of the sofa and on a nearby small table. A chewed pencil was carelessly tossed into the empty fruit bowl joining a broken cassette box and a Nina Simone tape.

The only programme on TV was a dreary documentary about the Voortrekker Monument, so she turned off the sound, sat down on the couch and phoned Dani.

'It's me.'

'Long time, no hear. I thought you'd given up journalism and run off to join the circus. I've been fending off queries about you all week. You can't just keep popping in and out of the office without telling anyone where you're going.'

'I'm a spy for the state, you know,' said Hannah. 'You'd better treat me with due respect.'

'I'll call you Mata Hari, shall I? I managed to convince Frik that you were working on a story and that you'd be back with a full report next week. I think he has the hots for you.'

'Perish the thought. But thanks for running intervention. Actually I have been working non-stop for the last week and I didn't have time to check in with you, but I've kind of run into a brick wall. I need a break.'

'Frankly, my dear, I'm shocked and surprised that you aren't engrossed in the latest thrilling epic about our brave Voortrekker forefathers.' Hannah glanced over at her television set and grimaced.

An image of the austere Voortrekker Monument perched on a hill outside Pretoria appeared on the screen. Afrikaner men and women dressed in traditional costume were doing volkspele, the specific type of folk dancing so beloved by them. A robust red-faced woman in grey bonnet, skirt and apron, twirled enthusiastically, nationalist fervour burning in her eyes.

'You know what I think about this, Dani,' said Hannah. 'It's supposedly a reminder of the courage, determination and persistence of the Voortrekkers that embarked on The Great Trek in an effort to escape the oppressions of British rule and forge a new life in the hinterland of South Africa, and we both know how the building is revered as a symbol of the sacrifices made by these pioneers, who conquered the indigenous inhabitants and saw themselves as God's appointed and anointed peoples.

'It's meant to encapsulate Afrikaner strength, and since it's on one of the highest hills above the capital city, it's impossible to miss, a constant reminder of the apartheid regime and its policies. But it's nothing more than a shrine of indoctrination that falsifies the history of South Africa and its people.

'What is it with the powers above that they think they need to shove a bit of propaganda down our throats at every possible opportunity? Perhaps they think it will encourage an upsurge of patriotic feeling for our forefathers and all they suffered to make South Africa the wonderful place it is today.'

Dani laughed. 'Well done, beautifully put. Pity you can't write that in your next article.'

'You're right, it is a pity I can't write what I think, but I value my freedom too much for that. I'll have to content myself with spouting off into the ear of my best friend and, might I add, very loyal secretary.'

'I prefer the title Personal Assistant if that's okay with you,' said Dani.

Hannah picked up a bottle of nail polish from the nearby coffee table and cradling the phone in the hollow between shoulder and ear, began to paint her toenails.

'What are you up to?' She wiped a fleck of polish off her skin, while Dani told her about her day's shopping at a recently revamped shopping centre.

'Sorry to bore you,' said Dani, and Hannah realised that she wasn't paying attention.

'It's not you, fascinating though your retail therapy tales are, I can't stop thinking about the story I'm working on.'

'You mean the guy that was murdered in the parking lot? I don't know any more, Hannah. What's this country coming to when self-respecting white people can be murdered in cold blood in supposedly safe suburbia?'

'It wasn't cold blooded murder.'

'No? What other kind of murder is there?'

'Killing for money.' It sounded even more ridiculous said aloud for the first time. Dani took a deep breath.

'Like contract killing? You must be joking. This isn't America. This is sunny South Africa.'

'Dani, I'd think that you of all people would have realised by now that it's only sunny on the surface. There's stuff going on that you don't want to know about.'

'Look, you're the investigative reporter here. I'm only the supportive secretary slash best friend. I'd prefer not to be apprised of everything you know, if you don't mind. I have enough things to cope with without worrying about the state of the nation.'

'I know. You're a typical South African hiding your head in the sand. Well, I don't think you're going to be able to do that for much longer. Damn!' She dropped the small brush, leaving a smudge of pink on the top of her toe and on the fluffy beige rug.

Dani gave a wry chuckle. 'For now, that's the way I prefer it. No good worrying over things I can't do anything about, is there?'

'This will interest you. I had tea with Detective Maartens and his family on Saturday,' said Hannah, changing the subject swiftly as her blood pressure started to rise at Dani's blithe attempt to remain ignorant.

'Did you? And what was that like considering he might be a government spy?'

'It was quite an eye-opener. His wife is something else. She kept calling me Hester and I could see she was spoiling for a fight, heaven knows why. She went on at me about my weight and my mousy hair, can you believe? I know I'm no Miss South Africa, but she was downright, bloody rude. Badly brought up, my mother would say.'

Dani was indignant. 'The nerve, anyone with eyes in their head can see that you're gorgeous. She's just jealous of your Rubenesque stature, that's what it is. I suppose she's one of those waif-thin women with cheekbones you could slice bread on and no boobs to speak of who thinks that anyone with a bit of flesh on their bones and bigger than a size eight is grotesquely overweight.'

Hannah laughed. 'I'll take that as a compliment. She is very skinny and looks like a strong wind would blow her over, but there's something else about her that I can't quite put my finger on. She plays the ditzy helpless female but I have a sneaky feeling it's only a role she adopts for her family.'

'And what did the sexy Tom Maartens have to say about that?'

'Absolutely nothing. I couldn't believe it. Jack, the son, seemed more embarrassed than Tom was. He just sat there like a great lummox and let her insult me. It was quite unnerving. But he did apologise later, in a way, says she has a 'condition'. The son's quite sweet though, and is even capable of talking in full sentences, unlike my teenage nephews who communicate by means of grunts and animal noises.'

'Did anything you heard from Tom convince you that he's not involved in something nasty?' asked Dani.

'No. He's a bit of an enigma is Tom. I think I'm going to have to be a touch more wary of him, just in case he's only cultivating me to make sure I don't discover anything too horrid. He's powerful enough to make me vanish if I step over the line.'

'Oh, don't,' said her friend, 'I couldn't bear it if anything happened to you.'

In the distance she heard Dani's doorbell ringing.

'Hannah, there's someone at the door. I'll call you back later, okay?'

Hannah sipped lukewarm coffee and went over her notes on the murders once again, positive that she had overlooked some clue in them. She knew for certain about the connection between at least two of the killings. Looking at the others, she found too many common denominators for them to be dismissed. She once again began to wonder about dissidents and who would want them dead. A trip to the archives was called for, and at night when it was quiet was the best time to go. She slipped on her shoes, picked up her car keys and headed out the door.

***

The sniper lay observing the next target, a gardener innocently mowing the lawn of a deserted golf course for his white masters, unaware that someone was watching every move from the shadows. The sun hung low in the sky like a ripe melon about to burst and vomit its messy pulp on the earth below. As it sank lower and lower, the gloom began to distort the edges and outlines of the surrounding vegetation and the clubhouse in the distance.

Before the man knew what was happening he would be dead, and the traitorous scheming thoughts in his head would dribble out into the grass, never to see the light of day or come to fruition in a violent attack against those that paid his wages and gave him succour.

The killer felt no compassion. The gardener deserved to die. Parasites had to be exterminated so that the infestation of society could be stopped. Those that had thoughts of equality, of revenge and violence had to be obliterated. And those that did the purging had to be paid.

The target pushed his mechanical growling beast across the green grass, his black skin gleaming with sweat, and the odour of ignorance and inferiority polluted the air.

The sniper stayed hidden in the sand trap, covered in biscuit and fawn-coloured fabric, face, neck and hands distorted by bands and splotches of beige and brown, indistinguishable from the ground. Then, breathing deeply, holding the lungs empty, the shot was lined up and in an instant between heartbeats a finger squeezed the trigger and the bullet sped from its snug home towards the gardener. It sunk into his skull, shattering bone, pulverising grey brain matter destroying every memory, every thought, every morsel ever learned in his short life.

On the front of his head a cherry hole disfigured the black skin, on the back a ragged exit wound the diameter of a grapefruit ruptured the peppercorn curls. The bullet vanished into the undergrowth. The target's bowels loosened and a trickle of yellow urine spread downwards, but he was unashamed. His lifeless body slumped to the ground and he was gone into the vast expanse of eternity from which there was no return.

It was done. One more enemy of the state eliminated. Retrieval and disposal of the body would now take place.

CHAPTER

Ten

A ghostly blue light and the whining buzz of the air conditioner disturbed the peace in the nearly deserted building. A few night staff and other zealous reporters working on stories drifted about ghostlike, their shadows floating ethereally across grey walls. The sharp odour of industrial disinfectant lingered in the cheerless linoleum-floored corridors as Hannah went into the basement where the newspaper kept its files and started digging through the dusty records and microfiche. What she found made her head ache and left her tongue dry.

A veritable plethora of information about dissidents and activists both black and white existed. What amazed her was the propensity they had for disappearing or going into exile. She wondered how many of them had gone into exile in worm-ridden graves in far-off mountain ranges.

Hannah discovered lists of names she had not seen or heard before, including many that had not been in the police's missing persons files. Someone in the past had gone to a lot of trouble to detail incidents about disappearing agitators. She recognised a scrawled signature at the bottom of one of the pages, the name of a reporter that had unexpectedly left the paper and gone to live in the United States.

It was long before her time, but everyone heard the rumours about how Henry Spencer had annoyed the bosses with his insistence that they try to report as much of the truth as the law allowed, and if possible, more. An incident in one of the black townships where Spencer had gone to cover the story occurred that caused the offices to be searched and put under surveillance. Nothing incriminating was found, but the police picked Spencer up, detained him for a week and raided his home. There they found 'subversive material' and other evidence that he was in league with the black consciousness movement and thus an enemy of the state.

He became a banned person under the law, unable to travel beyond a certain radius or to meet with more than one person at a time, and constantly under police surveillance. Shortly thereafter, he escaped in the night and left the country. Speculation flourished about why exactly he'd left, but it didn't take a genius to figure it out.

Hannah's notepad began to fill up with scrawled notes that only she would be able to decipher and her mind began to swell with ideas and thoughts that she knew would keep her awake at night. There was a leaden feeling in her stomach and a stench in her nostrils from the carcasses of supposedly dead stories. She wondered why it was that no one had smelt them before. Maybe they had, but had disguised the stench with the political perfume so liberally distributed by the government.

She slipped out of the building and drove home, watching behind her to see if she was being followed.

Hannah was summoned to Frik van Niekerk's office the next morning. Until recently he barely acknowledged her existence, and when he did it was to leer at her while trying to look down her blouse, and to wonder what such a sweet young thing was doing in the male-dominated world of journalism. His attitude did little to improve her already jaundiced view of men.

Van Niekerk's watery blue eyes squinted at her. He spat into a cup and picked at yellowed teeth with the end of a pencil. Hannah suppressed a shudder as she was forced to watch him delve around in his mouth for the remnants of his lunch. A sour smell crept up on her so she leaned back and surreptitiously put her hand over her nose. Finally he managed to tear his thoughts away from the treasure in the crevices between his molars and focused on Hannah.

'You've been digging around in the files in the basement? It might not be healthy for a cute young thing like you to go excavating in certain areas, you know.'

'I'm only researching a story,' said Hannah. Her voice squeaked as it always did when she found herself backed into a corner.

'Some stories are better not researched too thoroughly. Those files are buried down there for a reason. Because they are dead, like the people they are about and sniffing about corpses can be dangerous, especially for sexy young things like you. You never know what you could catch, skattie.'

He used the term of endearment sarcastically and Hannah felt a flutter in her chest as she realised that this man was far from harmless. She was definitely being warned off.

'I'm not now, nor ever will be, your darling,' she said. 'I was only interested because I'm investigating that murder last week. I thought there might be a connection with some other cases but I was wrong so I'll have to pursue another line of enquiry. It was most likely a robbery gone wrong anyway.'

They both knew he wasn't fooled, but Frik had cautioned her now and she would have to take responsibility if she chose to ignore the warning. She went back to her own desk with wet armpits and sticky hands.

Hannah decided to make copies of the files as soon as possible and take them home out of range of scanning eyes. She busied herself with routine work for the rest of the day, trying not to draw any attention to herself and left with the herd as they all walked out into the sunshine and headed back to their safe families and well-ordered domestic lives.

Hannah went for a swim in the pool at her flat, ate and spent a few hours at home, waiting until she was sure the most diligent workers would have left, then headed back to the office.

The city streets were clear of the rush hour traffic and she could see bulbous dark clouds gathering in the buttermilk sky above the tall buildings. The scent of rain in the air urged her onwards as she didn't want to be caught in a thunderstorm on her way home. She drove down Charles Street, past Magnolia Dell, a popular park where bronze statues of Peter Pan and Wendy kept eternal vigil over the children playing in the pond. The tranquil scene of youngsters sailing boats and frolicking about playing catch, blissfully unaware of the politics of the nation, only served as a bleak contrast to the events she was uncovering.

The night watchman barely acknowledged Hannah as she ran over to the lift to take her up to her office on the fifth floor. Only she didn't stop there.

She moved briskly down the fire escape, takkie soles squeaking on the tiles, into the file room and even though she was entitled to be there, she knew that if Frik found out she would be in trouble.

Something crunched underfoot and she stifled a scream, telling herself sternly to stop being an idiot. She made her way over to the filing cabinet she had left the previous night and opened the drawer that held the activist files. It was empty. Hannah closed the drawer and made sure it was the right one. It was, and when she opened it again, it was still empty. She searched through the other drawers but the files that she had been looking at earlier were definitely gone. She leaned against the cold steel filing cabinet and thought hard. She sniffed, noticing a smoky smell. It smelt like burnt paper...or files. She peered into a nearby dustbin and saw a disturbing pile of black ashes.

Hannah picked up a piece of charred paper, which crumbled in her hand. On a remaining corner she was able to make out the name of an activist who had disappeared from his home in the Eastern Cape six months before. She crushed the piece in her blackened fingers and left the file room silently, her disquiet increasing by the minute.

CHAPTER

Eleven

Hannah stopped off at Dani's to fill her in on the latest development. She pushed the door open and called, 'Dani?'

'Come in, I'm just trying on the T-shirt you sent me,' shouted Dani from the bedroom.

'What T-shirt?'

Dani appeared in the doorway, swaying her hips and walking in an exaggerated manner like a model on a catwalk. She was pulling a baggy shocking pink and green T-shirt over her head, not at all her usual style.

'Well, no chance of you getting lost in the dark, is there?' said Hannah, wondering what on earth her friend was thinking wearing such a garment.

'No, there certainly isn't and I believe I have you to thank for this fetching creation. Very generous of you as usual, but I must admit I'm a bit worried about your taste...'

'What?'

'It arrived by post yesterday while we were on the phone. From you, there was a card with it, look.' Dani picked up a small white card with the words 'Thanks, your friend Hannah' typed in the centre, and handed it to Hannah.

'Dani, first of all, I would never pick something as revolting as that for you and secondly...' She froze and then spoke urgently as Dani began rubbing her eyes.

'Dani, take it off! Take it off now!'

Dani pulled the offending garment over her head and dropped it on the floor, looking at it in fright.

'Hannah, what...' She rubbed her eyes again and then started screaming, 'My eyes, my eyes - ' She sprinted out of the room followed by Hannah and ran to the bathroom where she began splashing water on her face. Her eyes were red and swollen shut, her face covered in livid blotches.

Hannah dashed to the phone and called her doctor who arrived speedily. While he attended to Dani, Hannah called Tom and told him what had happened.

'I'll collect the T-shirt and send it for testing.' he said. ' Can you stay with Dani for a while just in case?'

'Yes.'

Hannah put the phone down and went to check on Dani. Her friend was asleep so she closed the door and went into the wood panelled study. She picked up the phone and called Themba, explaining succinctly what had happened.

'Sounds like the kind of trick the security police would use to try and scare someone. You have not noticed any parked cars outside your flat, have you?' he said.

'No, I don't think so, none that look suspicious anyway. You think I'm being watched?'

'Perhaps your buddy Detective Maartens is not as innocent as you think. I have done a bit of checking up on him and he seems clean, but you can never tell.' said Themba.

Hannah felt the hairs on her arms standing up at the thought of what could happen if she was wrong about Tom. If she was, it wouldn't be the first time she had allowed her emotions to prevent her from seeing the truth about a man. She leaned forward in the chair and rested her elbows on the large oak desk.

'Okay, what did you find out about him?'

'As you would expect, he was brought up by strict Calvinistic parents, and a career in the SAP was the natural progression following two notable years of National Service in the army. Just think what fun he must have had being indoctrinated twenty-four hours a day.

'Then it seems he found himself in that nebulous geographic place, known by us other South Africans as 'the border'. I suppose he should be proud to be remembered as one of the brave that risked their lives holding back the red invasion.' He snorted.

'He could, if he doesn't keep waking at night in a sweat after having nightmares about dead friends and burning flesh like my cousin Richard did. And the government still has the gall to deny being involved there. At least Tom came home alive.' She sighed, feeling a deep-seated pang at the futility of her cousin's death.

'When he finished his National Service he married Laurel, although there is a note in his file that his colleagues thought that she was not a suitable wife for a policeman,' continued Themba. 'There is not much information about her background though. She was also in the army, and even played netball for the national team but was discharged on medical grounds, some kind of mental breakdown following an accident.'

'She's not important. From what I saw the other day she needs a strong man to protect and care for her, and Tom seems quite happy in that role. That might explain why he puts up with her rudeness, not to mention the jealousy,' said Hannah, still smarting from Laurel's comments.

'She must fulfil some need of his or he would not stay with her,' said Themba.

'If you ask me it's all a bit one sided. She relies on him totally, but I know what you men are like, one look from gorgeous eyes and you forget how to think, with your brain at least. Heaven knows how she would cope if something happened to him,' she replied. 'But her poor son, to have a mother that's as dippy as she is can't be easy. She's so vague. Apparently she gets lost regularly.' She was annoyed that she still felt irked at Laurel's behaviour. 'Maybe he's learnt to adapt and perhaps her oddness is just what Tom needs to counter-balance the structured life he leads as a policeman,' she muttered.

'Sounds to me like you have a soft spot for the policeman,' said Themba.

'Don't be ridiculous,' said Hannah, suppressing the burgeoning feelings she had for Tom. 'I just think it's better to keep as close to him as possible, in case he is involved in some way.'

'Okay, if you say so. Now, I have got something else here, just a second-'

The sound of Themba shuffling papers rattled down the line.

'You know you're amazing the way you get information, don't you? said Hannah.

She picked up a pen, doodling on a piece of paper and pictured Themba in his little house in the township. Dani's study was large and airy, the furnishings expensive, the stationary all part of a matching set. Themba lived in a one-roomed house with a rickety second-hand desk that he had found at a dump. He kept his documents in a child's school suitcase that didn't lock and was held together by a piece of white elastic. He had a number of pens and pencils that Hannah had taken from work and wrote his notes on paper embossed with her father's name.

'There is a police report in Tom's file that is interesting. When Jack was about five weeks old, some teenagers found him screaming in his pram in a park and handed him in at the local police station, which just happened to be the one where Tom was stationed. It says that Laurel 'forgot' him.'

Hannah snorted. 'You'd think that the birth of a child would shake some responsibility into her.'

'Or,' said Themba, 'she might have been suffering from post-natal depression and if she was already mentally fragile, it is easy to see how motherhood would tip her over the edge.'

Hannah grudgingly acknowledged that this might be a possibility. 'That would certainly account for why Jack and his dad are so close. But I don't know, there's something about that woman. Most of the time she acts like she's from another planet, but sometimes the look in her eyes made me think she isn't the complete bubble-brain she appears.'

'Well, you are pretty good at reading people, I just think you might be a bit biased as far as Laurel is concerned,' said Themba.

'I'm not, the women is nuts,' said Hannah annoyed that Themba was able to see through her so well. 'I'm going round to see Tom at the station later on. He was taking Dani's T-shirt to be tested. I think for now I'll just have to trust him, until we can come up with something definitive about him being dirty,' she said.

'From his file and the word on the street, I think he is okay but I am going to do some more checking on him. These guys are experts at hiding their true motives and agendas from prying eyes. If he is one of them he will have hidden his tracks. But if he is innocent it must be a bit of a nightmare trying to work out which of his colleagues he can trust. If he is any good, he will already have a multitude of questions. You said he does not think it is the guys from Vlakplaas.'

'I'm pretty sure he thinks that someone knows more about what's going on,' said Hannah.

'One thing is for sure, the disappearances and murders involving political activists cannot be written off or brushed aside for much longer, not with reporters like you asking awkward questions. There is a lot of speculation about a third force involved in the ongoing political violence and we all know that it is only a matter of time before the wheels begin to fall off the National Party machine,' said Themba, 'They will do anything to keep control.'

'I wonder how long they'll resist the change,' said Hannah. 'Despite the laager mentality of the men in command and the loyal volk, something has to give and all I can do is pray that the country doesn't erupt into a bloody civil war like our neighbours to the north.'

'You and me both.' replied Themba. 'Let me know how you get on tomorrow, and Hannah, keep your eyes open for innocent-looking Mercedes Benz cars driven by men in dark glasses, okay? And one more thing, I would be careful about what you say on the telephone. Chances are a large insect has made its home in your flat.'

It had never crossed Hannah's mind that her flat might be bugged.

CHAPTER

Twelve

When Hannah arrived at the police station the next day, one of the men, a tawny-skinned Afrikaner with halitosis and acne scars on his cheeks, grabbed her arm as she walked past.

'Hey, Hannah, long time no see,' he said.

She pulled away, nodding tersely. She'd been rejecting his advances for months now and had hoped he'd given up.

'Ag, don't be like that, man. Everyone knows you and Detective Martins have been screwing like rabbits for weeks. What's he got that I don't, hey? Come on skattie, how about a kiss? Don't be so frigid.'

Hannah tried to move away but he leaned in close and pinned her against the wall, thrusting his hips against her, obviously enjoying the jeering and egging on he was receiving from his colleagues.

Tom came out of his office and reacted instantly. In one swift, fluid movement he grabbed the man in a chokehold and flung him backwards, slamming him into a filing cabinet, his muscled arm across the man's throat.

She couldn't hear exactly what he said, only the sibilant hissing sound of the words he spat out. Her attacker's face blanched and he coughed, unable to breathe. Tom grabbed the man by the collar and frog-marched him down the corridor. They went round a corner, she heard a thump and then a door slamming shut. Tom appeared a few minutes later tucking in his shirt and wiping his hands. The watching men were silent.

'Sorry about Immelman, the man's an idiot,' he said and led Hannah into his office, ignoring the stunned faces of his colleagues.

She was relieved Tom was not the kind to try and prove his manhood with lewd jokes and dirty language and grateful he didn't think that the mere appearance of a female in the male bastions of the SAP was an excuse for degeneration into a pit of sexually charged suggestion and innuendo. He picked up a folder and spoke calmly, although she detected gruffness in his voice that she'd not heard before.

'You've definitely stirred up something with your investigations, Hannah. I had some tests done on the shirt your friend received and it was impregnated with ninhydrin.'

'You're kidding. Ninhydrin?'

'It's an acid-based powder supplied to police forces all over the world to trace fingerprints on paper,' said Tom.

'I know what it is. It's used extensively by our Security Police. Don't look so surprised, Detective, I'm full of useless information. Actually, I did some research on it for the paper once. Donald Woods was a reporter too and the same thing happened to his daughter.'

'How's your friend?'

'She's fine thanks,' replied Hannah. 'She still has some violet patches on her face, but they'll fade.' She sank back in her chair. Tom fixed a baleful eye on her.

'You're going to give up your investigations now, aren't you?'

Hannah sat up straight. 'If you think I'm going to let bully-boy tactics like these scare me off, then you don't know me very well at all. If they, whoever 'they' are, think sending me a picture of a dead cat and hurting my friend is going to make me give up on my hunt for the truth, they better think again.'

'I don't like the idea of you pursuing this line of enquiry.'

Hannah ignored him and continued, 'You know I told you I found some files about missing activists? Well, Frik van Niekerk warned me off so I went back to photocopy them when he wasn't about, but they were gone.'

'What do you mean gone?'

'They'd been burnt. I found the ashes in a wastepaper basket.'

'And you're sure it was the files you were looking at earlier?'

'Yes. It must have been Frik. I've always been a bit suspicious of him so I was wondering if you could find out if he's a spy for the state or an informer or something? And if he is, maybe he has links to someone high up that might be connected to these killings. Why else would he try to sink my investigation? I've made a list of the names I remembered, hopefully you can get more info on them. I have a feeling you might identify some of those unidentified bodies. If the names in the files were important enough for Frik to prevent me finding out about them, surely the police will have similar dossiers too. What do you think?'

'I think that you are a problem in more ways than one. You have an uncanny knack of sniffing out the truth no matter how well it's been hidden. I'm getting scared for you, and I'm afraid yesterday's episode is only the beginning. One day you're going to discover something that will land you in trouble you won't be able to talk yourself out of.'

'I'll be okay. You know me, never at a loss for words,' Hannah replied, hoping it wasn't too obvious that she was badly shaken at the attack on her friend.

'You know, Miss Smith, those curves and come-hither eyes of yours can get you access to places inaccessible to me and it's only because you're able to obtain information I can't, that I'm letting you continue along these lines.'

'I wasn't aware that I needed your permission to pursue my enquiries,'

'I can only protect you up to a point,' he said. 'I have too healthy a respect for the system and I value my job and life too much. I'll see what I can find out about van Niekerk and the names on this list. But, Hannah, be alert from now on. You've definitely rattled someone's cage.'

With a brief goodbye Tom turned back to the work on his desk and Hannah left, avoiding the glare from Immelman, who was holding an ice pack to a black eye.

Hannah drove away, automatically checking her rear-view mirror. Behind her she saw a beige Datsun pulling out of the car park of the public swimming pool near the police station, but never gave it another thought until she was almost home when she noticed that it was still there, hanging back slightly. It was probably nothing, but she couldn't take any chances.

She turned left at the next junction and the beige car followed, so she stopped at a café, went inside, bought a newspaper and a loaf of bread, watched through the window for a few minutes and when she came out the same beige car was parked on the other side of the road; two men in the front and another in the back. Her pulse quickened. Trying to act relaxed, she reversed, drove off and continued down the road, wondering where else she could stop that would look like a pre-planned errand. The beige car stayed behind her, never getting too close but always in sight. When she turned right and then a quick left, the car dropped back, but was still visible in the rear-view mirror.

Hannah put her foot down and swung her car round a corner, the beige car sped up too and she began to panic. Going home now was out of the question, there was no telling who was tailing her or what their motive was but they weren't friendly, of that she was sure. Stopping off at Dani was unthinkable, she couldn't put her friend in danger. For a moment Hannah considered going to her parents', but that would only expose them to the mess she'd landed herself in too.

Hannah took off at speed, zigzagging across the eastern suburbs, mind spinning as she tried to figure out who her pursuers were. The quiet roads they were racing down were almost deserted, barely a car in sight, ideal for an assault of some kind. She had to find somewhere busier and decided that Lynnwood Road, a busy route in and out of town, was ideal. There was more traffic and they were less likely to attack her in public.

At the next set of lights Hannah turned into the traffic, so distracted she almost collided with a taxi. The driver hooted loudly, swerving into the path of an oncoming car. It was a close call and the crunch of fenders colliding behind made her jump but Hannah was too intent on out manoeuvring her pursuers to care and didn't even look back to see what had happened.

Down Lynnwood Road, past the University of Pretoria's Men's Residences and the Afrikaans high school further along, and still Hannah couldn't shake her tail. By the time they'd reached the next junction and an on-ramp to the highway, Hannah was getting desperate. When the lights changed she turned onto the Johannesburg highway, hoping to lose them in the fast moving traffic but no such luck. If she sped up, they did too, when she slowed down, so did they. She weaved dangerously from lane to lane, cutting off other drivers who hooted and flashed their lights, but no matter how fast she went it was no good.

It must have been quite obvious to the men by now that Hannah knew she was being pursued, but the beige car was dogged. Wherever she went it followed and she was running out of petrol. Driving endlessly wasn't practical. There was only one solution. Hannah hit the brakes, and the beige car slewed to the left with a frantic manoeuvre to prevent hitting her and the nearest car, which hooted furiously, a rude hand gesture appearing through the window. A quick, illegal, u-turn, bumping across the central barrier, flattening the trees and shrubs that divided the two sides of the highway, she careered into the opposite lane, ignoring the blaring hooters and squealing brakes as she nosed in front of the oncoming traffic. Hannah thought she'd lost them for sure and once she'd taken the off-ramp for Atterbury Road, she headed towards the police station once more, a different route from before but just as busy.

One thing was evident; they'd been waiting for her at the station, maybe Tom had sent them after her himself, but they could hardly attack her in full view of the police, could they? A quick look in the rear-view mirror and Hannah smacked the steering wheel in frustration. The beige car had re-appeared and was following her as she back-tracked towards Hillcrest Swimming Pool and the Brooklyn Police Station, but as she pulled up next to a police van with two officers in it, the beige car kept going and disappeared down the road. Hannah waited for a good forty five minutes before feeling confident enough to try going home again.

By a circuitous route through the Jacaranda-lined streets, paranoid every time a car got too close, Hannah returned to her flat, circuiting the block four times before she was certain no one was lying in wait for her. She ran inside quickly, desperate to call Themba, but as she reached for the receiver, she pulled her hand back as if it was a black mamba, and eyed the telephone suspiciously. Feeling slightly foolish she switched on the radio louder than normal and inspected every inch of her flat looking for bugs. It was clean, and safe to phone her friend.

Themba answered immediately, almost as if he'd been waiting for her call. Hannah told him what had happened, trying to make light of it.

'This is a serious development, Hannah,' said Themba. 'You've got to be more careful about who you talk to.'

'I know, but I can't just give up, not now that I know for sure I'm on to something big.'

'It will not matter how big it is if you are dead, Hannah. We need to find some way of keeping you safe. Let me think about it and please, take care. If you see that car again, you should tell Maartens, and perhaps make some copies of your documents and findings so far and put it somewhere safe, just in case...'

'In case I get killed,' said Hannah. 'That's a good idea. I'll give it to my dad's lawyer, to be opened in the event of my death or a nasty accident.'

'It is not a joke, Hannah.' Themba was grave and she apologised before ringing off.

Although she was exhausted, Hannah made copies of all her notes and documents, put them in an envelope, addressed it to her father's lawyer and dropped it in the post box outside the flats. Sleep eluded her. She spent a fitful night going over and over the last few weeks in her mind.

***

The hunt was over. The killer looked down at the slaughtered prey in the car boot and felt the familiar prick of tears. It was still a human life and there was always a feeling of momentary melancholy for the families, the wives and children left behind, but they would get over it in time.

As the car travelled out of the city a slight drizzle began and the killer wiped a hand across the misty windscreen, turning down a deserted road in an isolated area. The veld was dry and dusty and as the rain continued, droplets of water dripped down the long blades of grass and plopped like muted drum beats in exploding circles on the earth. Grey-green mountains nearby were silhouetted in the haziness of the falling moisture.

Swiftly, carelessly, a hole was dug, the body deposited and the killer was away, leaving no discernible trace of ever having been there. The rain fell harder and the dirt covering the victim began to wash down the hill in muddy rivulets.

Now the waiting would begin again and there would be time to spend some of the hard-earned money for this job and anticipation of the next. People always needed to die. Especially here, in this sun-scorched land where people with blood on their hands lived as if there was no tomorrow.

CHAPTER

Thirteen

It was rush hour three days later. The streets were congested, car hooters blaring, pedestrians too impatient to wait for the lights to change skipping between queues of traffic. Large buses and dilapidated minivan taxis belching smoke and disgorging workers blatantly disobeyed the traffic rules. A large black woman with no evident concept of road safety stepped out onto the kerb, raised her arm and yelled piercingly and a passing taxi, already bulging with passengers, pulled across two lanes of traffic, nosed in front of a waiting car and driving halfway up the pavement, collected the new fare.

Hannah tapped her fingers on the steering wheel in irritation. It was only half past seven in the morning, but the sun was already blazing and shining straight into her eyes no matter how she angled the sun visor. She wound the window down but a blast of hot air and car fumes made her cough and wind it up again. The lights ahead changed to green and she started edging forward, hoping she wouldn't end up being late for her meeting with Tom and wondering if any of her informants had responded to her enquiries about the missing activists. Radio Five switched to a traffic report.

There was a reverberating boom and the world rocked. With a strange roaring, the back window of the Volkswagen Beetle in front of her disintegrated. The air inside her car seemed to be sucked out and as she struggled to catch her breath the alignment of the scene shifted but it took a couple of heartbeats for the reality of what was happening to sink in. Time crawled as Hannah watched everything unfolding in curiously slow motion.

Vehicles all around seemed to be involved in a macabre ballet, spinning and turning and leaping into the air gracefully before plunging to earth with a dull thump. A passing *bakkie* with blackened sides whirled by out of control, crashing into a red mini and shunting it across the road into the path of an oncoming bus. Brakes squealed and the bus slid elegantly into the side of a building, which shuddered at the impact.

Hannah opened her mouth to try and equalise the pressure in her ears and was struck by a dreamlike realisation that an explosion had taken place nearby. Her car was soon covered in drifting dust and debris. The traffic ground to a complete halt, hooters blew and she became aware of muffled screams and moaning.

She sat in numb stillness before opening the door and getting out shakily, her feet crunching on the ground. The radio continued to play cheerful drive-time music as she inhaled acrid smoke and coughed, running her tongue across gritty lips.

Hannah stared in awe at the devastation confronting her, noticing with a jolt that a large bus, packed with commuters from the townships had shielded her car from the blast and taken the brunt of the explosion. A few survivors spilled out onto the pavement, but inside the wreckage of the bus it was ominously quiet.

A mangled car laid in the middle of the road ahead, the tyres melted, smoke pouring upwards in a thick black column. Shop and office facades were shattered, shards of glass strewn everywhere. Hannah flinched when the heavy metal door of a nearby building fell with a tired moan. A gushing fire hydrant spewed water into the street soaking a charred naked mannequin lying stiffly on the pavement. The street was filled with dust and confusion and not far from Hannah the gory remains of a man.

An Indian woman wailed, clutching a burnt sari round her scorched body and a small boy, eyes wide with shock, clasped her leg. A white woman sat down in the middle of the road and held a tissue to her face, mopping a stream of blood. The door of a nearby car opened with a crash and four coloured men spilled out onto the pavement, coughing and gasping for breath. One of them held a handkerchief to a gaping wound on his forehead, another had serious lacerations on his arms, his face was contorted in pain.

Hannah's ears were ringing as she ran over to a young black girl dressed in the uniform of the OK Bazaars lying amid the rubble on the ground, eyes closed, legs badly burned. Hannah took her wrist with a trembling hand. The girl was breathing, her pulse weak but steady.

Hannah touched her gently. 'Can you hear me?' The girl moaned. 'The ambulance is on its way. It's going to be fine.' Hannah tried to comfort her, stroked her face tenderly and muttering comforting words. She tore the sleeve off her shirt and used it to bandage a gaping wound on the girl's arm.

In the distance she could hear wailing sirens and as the girl had lapsed into unconsciousness she stood up to see if anyone else needed help. An unrecognisable body lay nearby, only the trunk remaining. Hannah turned away, eyes burning, bile rising.

A dazed middle-aged man clutching his bleeding head staggered towards her. Hannah took him by the arm and helped him over to the solitary remaining chair of a popular Italian Restaurant. He sank down and groaned.

'It was a bomb. Looks like it went off at SAP HQ.'

Hannah limped down the road towards the headquarters of the South African Police. Through the settling dust, she could see a pile of shattered concrete and mangled metal where the entrance once was. She sent up a quick prayer that Tom had not been inside and wondered again why he had sent her a message asking her to meet him there that morning instead of at his local station.

While she waited, helping the injured wherever she could, emergency personnel and police began to appear, starting shepherding the walking wounded towards the gathering ambulances. A young nervous policeman tried to usher the stunned survivors out of the area, Hannah amongst them.

'*Kom, kom, mense! Vinnig, los die karre, laat waai....*'

Hannah stopped listening as he continued yelling in Afrikaans that anyone whose car was parked in the street and who could still drive should get their vehicle and follow the traffic officers away from the scene. He also instructed them to present themselves to their local police station as soon as possible to give a statement about what they had witnessed.

It was chaos, the city would remain gridlocked for hours, but eventually the traffic around the sight of the explosion began to dissipate as officials cleared the way for fire engines and other emergency vehicles. Hannah made her way towards work, relieved to see that the area round the blast had already been sealed off, and that the traffic was flowing sluggishly out of the centre of town.

She arrived at the office block where the newspaper had its offices and made her way to the lift and up to the fifth floor. The antiseptic calmness inside after the madness she had witnessed in the streets took her by surprise and she began to shake, a rushing noise echoing in her ears.

Time went by in a daze and she was barely conscious of Dani rushing over and ushering her to a seat. Someone else appeared with a glass of water, another ensured she wasn't injured and wiped the dust out of her eyes and mouth. Distant muted voices asked what had happened, if she was hurt and if she needed a doctor. They'd heard the explosion, but couldn't see much and were relying on those staff members that had witnessed it personally to give an account. Hannah managed to reassure them that she was unharmed but still disorientated.

Frik van Niekerk watched impassively as the ladies clucked around Hannah and the steady stream of incoming staff that had also been caught up in the disaster outside. They were all bemused with varying descriptions and theories of what had actually happened. One thing they agreed on though, was that a bomb had been detonated in or near SAP Headquarters.

Finally, tapping his foot, Frik van Niekerk said, 'Glad you aren't hurt, skattie. Lucky for us, we get a firsthand account of what happened. I hope you aren't too shaken to write an article for us? I'm sure you realise this is a major news event. Or are your delicate sensibilities so upset you need to go home?' Dani spun round, but Hannah put a restraining hand on her arm.

'It's okay. He's right. It isn't often we're involved in the news like this. I'll be fine.'

The remainder of the day passed in surreal tones of blue and grey with sounds muffled like they were under water and an annoying tickle in the back of her throat. Hannah forced herself to concentrate on writing and by mid-afternoon was able to deliver what she believed was a reasonable report of what had happened. Van Niekerk read it cursorily then glared at her.

'You can't seriously expect me to publish this.'

'Why ever not? It's the truth,' she answered, her voice barely audible above the noise in the office.

"Acts of terrorism and sabotage have become almost daily occurrences now. The armed wing of the African National Congress, Umkhonto we Siswe-The Spear of the Nation commonly known as MK, have abandoned their futile attempts at a peaceful resolution to the country's problems. Previous refusals to resort to aggression have been interpreted by the government as acquiescence and an invitation to use armed force against the people without any fear of reprisals. It does not surprise anyone in the media that the government policies of repression and brutality were today met with violent retaliation." He read it aloud, mocking her and her words with every syllable.

Before she could defend herself he continued in a sneering tone.

"Over the last few years MK has struck at several strategic targets, blown up railway lines, power plants, military bases and recruiting offices. Today's bombing in central Pretoria is only one in a long line of acts of terror perpetrated against a population who, for the main part, have no say in the actions of the government and who also suffer under the restrictive regime and it's policies."

By now the office had fallen silent and aware of the audience van Niekerk continued.

"The ANC's decision to resort to armed conflict aimed at civilians and innocent bystanders may not gain them much sympathy from the white people, who because of censorship and the clandestine nature of the government are ill-informed about the true extent and effects of apartheid on the vast majority of the population.

"It is no secret that those whites speaking out are persecuted, banned, jailed or worse. Is it any wonder that so many of the government's detractors have been forced to flee abroad?

"It's all very well for the international media to condemn the country and all its white inhabitants as complicit, but as I and my colleagues very well know, most information about the true extent of the government's policies is kept hidden from them and it is only through the efforts of the international media, aided and abetted illegally, that anything about what is truly happening in South Africa is ever revealed.

"Today's tragedy has impacted the lives of hundreds of South Africans of all races. The question must be asked if armed resistance is serving any useful purpose at all or if it is merely hardening the hearts and attitudes of those that have the power to bring about change. While South Africa has managed to evade all out civil war similar to Rhodesia, I wonder how it can be avoided much longer. Bombings, strikes, riots and general unrest only serve to further infect the festering wounds that apartheid has inflicted on the people, and yet there is still such hardcore resistance to the idea

of a truly democratic country. The escalation of the armed struggle does not seem to be softening anyone. If anything, it is making the ruling minority even more adamant to hang on to the power.

"Politicians continue to make placatory noises while staying firmly behind the lines they have drawn in ink. Legalised racism will never be accepted by the world yet they continue along this path as if it is the only way forward. Meanwhile, as the common man struggles with day-to-day life, factions on both sides of the political spectrum continue their bloodletting, killing and maiming in the name of freedom, all believing they are right, all unwilling to back down.

"Is it possible peaceful negotiation will ever succeed? It is going to take brave men, both black and white, to negotiate the maelstrom and bridge the chasm that exists in our fractured country.

"After witnessing the devastation of today's events, I for one, would welcome the resumption of peaceful talks. I do not think I am alone in hoping that one day true democracy will be possible in South Africa."

Van Niekerk pointedly dropped the article in the bin, yelled at the silent onlookers to get back to work and then turned to Hannah with a pained expression on his oily face.

'You still look a bit dazed, so I suppose it's too much for me to expect you to remember that annoying little thing called the law, which very specifically prohibits publication of such writing as this. I need reporting on the facts, not inflammatory rhetoric, therefore I'm going to ignore this article and put it down to the shock you've suffered. You can go home now, Hannah.' He dismissed her tersely, turning back to another reporter before she had even said a word.

Dani insisted on driving Hannah home where she gratefully had a quick shower and lay down on her bed, her head pounding and every muscle in her body aching. A cut on her leg began to throb. She took a couple of painkillers and closed her eyes again, trying to forget the images of what she had seen that day.

They all knew who had perpetrated this act of terrorism and even though the country was on high alert for just such eventualities, the reality of such an attack so close to home was particularly sobering. She made a mental note to ask Themba about any MK cadres that might be operating in the area.

***

Nationalism was an important emotion. It could not be explained or defined, that surge of pride and belonging. The daily singing of Die Stem at school assemblies for twelve years had helped to stir up and embed the emotions already swirling through the killer's unformed body. In the still innocent child, emotion was a stranger, and the new strange swelling tightness in the chest and throat was foreign and frightening. But it was real, undeniable. It was one of few things that made sense; a rare moment of genuine passion.

Childhood was spent watching other children mewling and wailing and overwhelmed by sentiment, and it became a game, trying to understand the swift and free passions that seemed to flow out of them, making them laugh and cry and fight. To be devoid of any of those feelings created a sense of detachment that didn't go unnoticed. After the first few reports containing words like 'does not socialise well', and 'needs to participate more in class', the young killer had formed a strategy, a plan that was infallible and easy to maintain, a strategy that would keep the adults from asking too many questions.

Acting the part of 'normal' was easy, and it gave unseen, hidden pleasure and a sense of superiority that was easily concealed. Pretending to be like the others was a skill that grew easier with passing time. The knowledge that everyone else was clueless created a warm sensation, a stirring of something primal, unidentified.

Then into a bland and horrible pre-pubescent world had come the first ray of genuine feeling, a welling up of blood lust that couldn't be explained, that had to stay buried. But it was remembered and given voice from time to time over the years, and all the time it grew stronger. Secretly, hidden. It was the driving force for every consequent action that the killer took, the only element of being that truly made sense and enabled life to continue with the smallest vestige of hope for a better tomorrow. And it jelled so perfectly with what was taught about nationalism.

Yes, national pride was useful. It kept out the red tide that threatened to swamp them all. It held back the atheist communists who coveted the country and her abundant riches. It mobilised the true believers, motivated them to fight back and not surrender the land they had built up themselves by the sweat of their brows. It helped keep the baying wolves of humanism and agnosticism away, and it created a perfect platform for someone with aspirations to kill.

The killer would gladly die for the country, but the act of creating death was so much more fulfilling, so much more effective, and so much better paid.

CHAPTER

Fourteen

To Hannah's intense irritation, Frik filled up her week with endless trivial matters that he needed 'instantly'. He had her running all over the city interviewing survivors of the bombing, the ambulance and fire-engine drivers, the shop owners who had lost their businesses, anything to keep her busy and stop her from working on the dead activist story. By Friday, she was ready to impale him with her pencil and it was only Dani that prevented her from attacking him with a loaded stapler when he made her go to Pretoria North, the other side of the city, to interview a woman that had lost her legs in the blast.

'He's only doing it to annoy you. Don't let him get under your skin like this, it's just what he wants.'

'I know, I know. And the bombing is a big story, but he's such a *poepall*. There are plenty of other reporters that can do these interviews.' Hannah dropped the last piece she'd written in Frik's pigeon-hole. 'Come on, let's get out of here. Thanks for playing taxi for me this week, I could just as easily drive myself but... I'm getting neurotic in my old age.'

'Jislaaik, Hannah, if it was me that was chased like that I wouldn't leave the house without an armed police escort,' said Dani. 'Why don't you stay with me this weekend? Just in case.'

'Mmm, no, I'll be okay.' Hannah tried to sound confident, but once Dani had dropped her off and she was alone, she was unable to concentrate on anything, jumping at every noise. After a shower she took out her notes and spread them on the table, studying them again, linking names, dates and places, desperate to find the missing clue that would solve the case or tell her who was after her.

Well after midnight, her body aching, Hannah went to her bedroom. She went to draw the curtains and stopped, her skin going icy when she saw the red-yellow pinprick of light in the garden of the house across the street. She switched off her light and watched from the darkness, occasionally seeing the bushes move and the glow of a cigarette. Someone was hiding in the bushes watching her flat. And that put an end to sleep for the night.

She lay in her bed wide awake, flinching at every creak and noise, convinced someone was breaking in to slaughter her but no one broke in, no one tried to get in through the windows; there was no attack of any kind. Eventually Hannah dropped off to sleep at four in the morning.

The next day she dozed on and off, checking the street outside constantly. The hider in the bushes had gone, but every half hour the beige car drove slowly past her flat. The phone rang and Hannah jumped, dropping her mug of coffee in fright. It was Dani, checking up on her. Hannah didn't tell her about the man in the street or the cruising car, trying to act relaxed but refused to leave the flat for a shopping trip.

'No, I'm fine, I've got stuff to do round here, I haven't vacuumed for ages and I have a load of washing to do. I'll see you at work on Monday.'

Hannah rang off and sank onto the couch, where she stayed for the remainder of the day and night. Weighed down by a sense of her own mortality and an inexplicable compulsion to see the yellow-eyed policeman, Hannah decided to call on Tom, Sunday or not. She hoped he didn't go to church.

Her own faith had taken a pounding recently as she struggled to reconcile the message preached from the pulpit with the reality of life in South Africa. She resisted the urge to attend a service at the Methodist church, for once unable to seek solace in the brick and glass building.

Nonetheless, she drove past the church as the morning service was coming to an end, slowing down to avoid the pedestrians and church members dribbling into the street. It was hot and the car windows were open, allowing her to hear the familiar strains of 'Ode to Joy' played badly on an out-of-tune organ assaulting the congregation chatting in the sunshine. A group of smartly dressed women huddled in a group, no doubt discussing something vital like the flower arrangements for the following week, and two little girls in frilly dresses hopped up and down the church steps giggling and singing 'Jesus Wants Me for a Sunbeam' at the tops of their voices, while their mothers watched indulgently.

The church was situated opposite a green children's playground and Hannah hid a smile at the sight of five teenagers emerging from the trees and sidling back across the road in the hope that their parents wouldn't notice they had spent their collection money on cigarettes and sweets and their devotional time smoking and chatting to girls in the park instead of on the hard chairs of the Junior Church. One of the boys surreptitiously stubbed out a cigarette and took a swig of Coke to disguise the smell. During her adolescent years Hannah too had spent illicit time in that park while her parents innocently imagined she was listening to the story of Jonah and the Whale in the small building next to the main church.

She was unsettled, the events of the past week and the months of investigation weighing heavily on her mind. Her instincts screamed at her to avoid Tom, to put space between them, but she found herself driven by an uncontrollable inner force that she was unable to resist.

It was a sleepy weekend in Tom's tranquil neighbourhood and Hannah wondered again how it was that the world seemed so normal here, when all over the country were pockets of violence and despair.

The area the Maartens lived in was a fine example of the social engineering perfected by the Nationalist government. The Group Areas Act very effectively kept the different races apart and the exclusively white-owned areas free of what were considered undesirable elements. The government had the power to forcibly remove people from regions not designated for their particular racial group, entrenching its policy of segregation. Land ownership was inextricably linked to the apartheid system that, with its excessive restrictions and controls, enabled the privileged white classes to function in a legally protected environment.

Blacks were excluded by law from participating in the economy and as a result lived in deprived areas. While the street Hannah was travelling down was smooth and the pavements well maintained, she knew that in the townships not far away, the roads were little more than dirt tracks and those that were tarred were in disrepair. The system of nationalist socialism was manipulated in favour of the whites, with state funds being allocated in disparate proportions in different racial areas. She clenched her jaw and tried to focus on the matter at hand.

***

Many stories were told about co-operation between warring factions and it wasn't unusual for pacts to be concluded between those on opposite sides of a war. Intelligence gathering occurred everywhere and this information was helpful to everyone, so despite their primary objective being elimination of the enemy, it had been a lucky coincidence discovering that MK was planning an attack on SAP HQ.

It could have been so simple and solved many problems for them all. No one would have suspected that the woman's death had been planned; she would simply have been collateral damage in an ongoing conflict.

But this was what came from trusting someone from a sub-specie of low intellect, someone without the prerequisite training and skills. They'd lured her there with a perfectly feasible note and all he'd had to do was wait for Smith to park her car in the underground parking garage and then place the bomb in the strategic spot clearly marked for him. No reasoning or thinking was required, no wires to connect, no timer to set, it was all done for him. They'd allowed plenty of time for her to get upstairs into the building before it detonated but the terrorist had been sloppy. He'd overslept and missed his bus and the mission failed when he tripped and fell over in the street, because he'd been rushing, the one thing they had told him not to do.

His punishment was that he was now no more than a stain on the pavement. Their frustration was that the woman was still alive and they'd have to think of something else to get rid of her. But how many accidents and near misses could one woman have? The police were starting to take notice, the very thing they had tried to avoid.

It was providential they had someone on the inside, someone close to the woman who could observe her, record and relay her every move.

CHAPTER

Fifteen

The carnage of the week distracted Hannah from her primary objective, but no more. Though she was eager to hear the official police line on the bombing, she was more interested in how Tom's other investigations were going. She was starting to cobble together a picture in her mind of exactly what the murders might mean and she wanted to check out her theory with him.

No one answered her knocking so she walked down the path to the back door, impressed once again by the tidiness of the garden, where even the compost heap was organised, and peered in through the window.

Tom and Jack were drinking coffee in the kitchen. Jack was still in his sleeping shorts and when she knocked and entered hesitantly, Hannah was afraid that the look in his eyes indicated he was about to have a cardiac arrest. He stuffed a piece of toast smothered in peanut butter and syrup into his mouth, burped and wiped his lips with the back of his hand, his father grimacing at his Neanderthal manners. She turned to Tom who raised an enquiring brow. A blushing Jack retreated.

117

'Sorry to barge in on you like this, Tom, but I did knock,' she said in a nervous rush. 'I wanted to check you were okay after the bombing and also, I had an idea about the case and I wanted to know what you think. I'm sorry I missed our meeting, but just as well in the circumstances.'

Tom indicated that she follow him into the lounge.

'No, it's fine. Laurel's away collecting butterflies for a few days, so we can talk uninterrupted. Thank God she wasn't around this week. She doesn't cope with violence very well. Jack's been badly upset by the bombing. The father of a boy in his class was badly wounded and may not survive. He hasn't been able to concentrate on a word I've said all morning.'

'He seems like a sensitive kid,' said Hannah. 'This kind of thing is bound to have an effect.'

For a moment Tom was pensive. 'What meeting did you miss?'

'The morning of the bombing. You sent a note asking me to meet you at police HQ at seven o'clock. I got stuck in traffic and was late, that's why I wasn't inside the building when it blew up.'

He frowned. 'I never sent you any note.'

Hannah sat down with a jerk and her hands began to shake. She licked dry lips and stared at Tom, eyes wide. 'But-'

It didn't make any sense. Surely the people that were after her hadn't destroyed an entire building and killed countless people in an attempt to silence her? She didn't know enough. All she had were theories and suppositions. She had no concrete evidence, no names, no real picture of the truth. It seemed so dramatic, overkill when surely an accident that involved her alone was easier to arrange. She wasn't that important, what she was investigating couldn't be that cataclysmic.

'It's no use trying to work it out now,' said Tom and she was grateful for his calmness. 'I suppose you want to know what our thoughts are on the bombing.'

She took out her notebook, ever the reporter ready for a story, even if this one had come at an inconvenient time for her. She put aside thoughts of why she had been lured to the building shortly before it was blown up and who was capable of doing such a thing. Tom cleared his throat and she forced herself to concentrate on him, watching his face closely to see if he was as distressed by this latest attack on her as she was, but he seemed unmoved.

'Officially it was a briefcase bomb planted by terrorists, probably Umkhonto we Siswe. Unofficially I can tell you that it seems to have detonated early, that's why it went off during rush hour outside the building. We think the plan was for the briefcase to be left inside and set off sometime during the morning, but apparently it exploded before it could be planted. That's why so many civilians, black and white, were killed and injured. But this isn't why you wanted to speak to me, is it?'

'The bombing is a whole other story, Tom, and I'm sure you're looking into MK cadres in the area. I believe there's one operating out of an abandoned warehouse in Pretoria North, but you probably know that already.'

Tom folded his arms and she could see he was disconcerted. Perhaps he didn't know about the cadre Themba had told her about. She changed tack abruptly.

'I can't get distracted now because I need to concentrate on my primary investigation. What happened is terrible, but it's just another one of the acts of violence we're getting used to and there are enough people scrutinizing every aspect of it.'

She walked over to the large glass sliding doors that led into the garden and nearly screamed when the gardener, who was crouched over a flowerbed, turned and grinned at her before bowing his head respectfully. He stood up, tossing a handful of weeds into a wheelbarrow. His face and overalls were muddy and the scar on his lip was almost healed.

Hannah turned away and spoke rapidly, her voice unsteady, as she wondered how the hell Themba had ended up working as Tom's gardener.

'You know there's talk of a third force out there, stoking up trouble in the townships? Well, maybe it's one of these 'agents provocateurs' that we're dealing with. It's not only black agitators and dissidents that have been killed. A number of anti-establishment whites have also died. Is it too much of a stretch to think there's someone out there being paid to bump off assorted people, not matter what their political affiliation? My question is this, who would want both sides dead and why?'

Tom joined her at the door and she heard a hissing noise in her head, sure he would notice at once that something was wrong, but he didn't and waved to Themba, who doffed his cap politely.

Then he lapsed into silence for a while before turning to face Hannah.

'You want to know what the psychology behind the killings is.'

'Exactly. It could be purely functional, they're getting rid of people that are in the way for monetary gain and that fits the political angle and in my opinion is the most likely. It could be sadistic, and motivated by the enjoyment the killer gets during the act, in which case it's an individual on a killing spree, or it's a psychopath – someone with an abnormal perception of violence who fails to see murder as unpleasant or wrong, and that fits too, because whoever we're after certainly doesn't think they're doing anything immoral. Who knows, it could even be a combination of all three, and based on the number of murders and the geographic locations and timescale of those that have gone missing, I'm inclined to think it's a group rather than an individual.'

'You're talking about a pack of killers, all with the same ideology, hunting and killing right across the country. It could be anyone in any level of society and what their true agenda is, I shudder to think. If it's purely financial, which makes the most sense, it means no one is safe,' said Tom.

'Even if the assassins themselves are in it for the money, there's someone behind them pulling the strings, someone who needs these people dead,' said Hannah. 'I can't think of any reason for killing dissenters other than political.'

'And if we're right, this country is in a hell of a lot more trouble than we could ever imagine,' said Tom.

'Okay, what now?'

Hannah noticed a movement out of the corner of her eye and saw Jack, dressed in jeans and scruffy rugby jersey, watching them from the doorway with an anxious look on his face. She had a momentary surge of regret that he had heard, but then reasoned that perhaps it was time he knew a bit more about the country he lived in.

Hannah returned home and sat in the lounge reflecting on everything she knew thus far. The three recent murders that had grabbed her initial interest were only the beginning. Who knew how many more bodies were lying undiscovered? The burnt files had listed over a hundred black activists and dissidents that had disappeared or were suspected dead.

The police missing persons files named whites that had vanished in suspicious circumstances and she'd dug up the appropriate newspaper reports about them at the time. It was a sad reflection on the state of media reporting when a missing white took up columns of space, whereas a lost black man or woman wasn't mentioned at all. Police investigations were also likely to be a lot more extensive when a white person vanished, which was why her questions had stirred something up.

It would be up to her now to find out as much as she could about how each one of the missing men and women had lived, and how they had died.

The phone rang later that evening. It was Themba with an unusual request.

CHAPTER

Sixteen

'I must be mad,' said Hannah, climbing awkwardly into the back of a blue *bakkie* with blacked-out windows parked next to a building site in a quiet street not far from Tom Maartens' house. A house was under construction, a pile of rubble falling onto the pavement, and it was behind one of these that Themba had parked. The neighbouring houses were dark, the inhabitants already settled in for the night, and the street lamps glowed yellow, casting circles of light on the road. The *bakkie* was parked near a lamp with a conveniently broken bulb and was almost invisible in the shadows.

'Do you have any idea how dangerous this is? Not only the obvious laws you're breaking like staying out after curfew, but just being here, now, like this. You're crazy.'

Themba's white teeth flashed at her and he put a cool hand on her arm. 'Relax, Hannah. This is all part of the struggle. If we are going to get results we have to take risks.'

'Maybe, but this plan of yours is insane. What are you thinking, getting a job as Tom's gardener?'

'I do not trust anyone that wears a uniform and openly takes a salary from the government,' said Themba. 'And what better way of getting to know a man than working in his house?'

'But how?' asked Hannah.

'Like I have said before, you will be amazed what people will do for money. I just offered his regular gardener a paid holiday with a bit extra for his silence and that was it, easy. The Maartens now have a beautiful new pot plant in the lounge and creepy crawlies all over the house. We should be able to hear everything from here.'

'You bugged his house? Now I know you're mad.'

When Themba called the previous evening asking her to meet him here, Hannah simply thought that he wanted to update her on his latest escapade digging up Laurel's garden. She'd no idea what he was actually up to and was terrified. If Tom found out...

Themba grinned again and put on a pair of headphones. He offered Hannah a set too and began fiddling with the knobs on a piece of electronic equipment that could have come straight out of a James Bond film.

'Where did you get this?' she asked.

'Courtesy of our friends the security police, who sadly had a break-in at one of their offices a couple of months ago. I have been dying to try it out.'

Hannah was amazed, secretly impressed but petrified at what they were doing. Themba was right about one thing however; this was certainly a good way of finding out more about Tom. The earphones crackled, and despite herself she put them up to her head and listened, holding her breath, irrationally convinced they would realise someone was listening.

Jack was speaking and sounded agitated.

'It's Mum. She won't stop crying and her eyes are all red. I never did anything, I promise. She's just lying there on the bed, not moving.'

Hannah felt a pang of compassion at what Jack had to put up with, constantly treading carefully around his mother, and not for the first time, wondered if Laurel needed professional help.

Then Tom's voice, sounding weary: 'Don't worry. I'll find out what's wrong. She gets like this every now and then. Probably that time of the month.' Jack muttered something under his breath and they heard his footsteps as he left the room, then a door slamming. Soon the muffled sounds of heavy rock music filtered through the headphones.

'This should be interesting,' said Themba. 'Might not tell us what we need to know though.'

'You bugged the bedroom too?' Hannah was aghast at this further invasion of Tom's privacy.

'People say things in the bedroom they do not say elsewhere, often before dropping off to sleep or after sex. You think the security forces respect anyone's privacy? I, for one, am only too happy to use their own weapons against them.'

'But, this is Tom, we don't know where he stands,' said Hannah.

'Exactly,' said Themba and indicated that she stop talking and listen.

They heard a door opening and the rustling of bedclothes.

'Tom,' said Laurel, her voice high pitched, verging on hysteria.

'What's wrong?' asked Tom.

'Nothing.'

'It's obviously something. Come on, tell me what's upset you.'

'I'm being silly, but I was late fetching Jack again, and he had to walk home and he was so cross with me. I know you think I'm a bad mother, always forgetting him and never arriving anywhere on time.'

'Don't be silly.'

'You should have married someone more like your mother. Not me, who's frivolous and forgetful.'

'Laurel, love – '

Hannah glanced over at Themba, hoping he would stop eavesdropping on what was an intimate moment between the couple, but he had his eyes closed and was listening intently.

Laurel's voice continued, gaining in strength and fervour. Hannah felt more and more uncomfortable and found she was sweating, her body sticky. Beads of perspiration formed on her forehead and she used the back of her sleeve to wipe them away.

'It's no wonder I was invalided out of the army. It was just that when I was injured and my friends died, I couldn't carry on and I sort of lost focus, but I'm fine now. You do understand, don't you?'

Themba and Hannah exchanged a look. This was something they didn't know much about. Not that it was useful information, but it helped build up an overall picture of Tom. Hannah was impressed with this compassionate aspect of his character.

'Even killers care about their families,' said Themba, reading her thoughts.

Tom's voice was soporific, apparently well practised in soothing his wife. 'Of course I understand. Please, it's no use getting so upset.' The bedsprings squeaked.

'It's not my fault I'm dyslexic,' said Laurel suddenly, her voice accusing.

'That is interesting,' said Themba.

They heard Tom sigh. 'I never said it was. Where is all this coming from?'

'You should have heard how Jack spoke to me when I was late. He resents me for leaving him behind last weekend. All I did was look for butterflies, you know. It's not like I abandoned him in a dustbin or anything. And he'd have hated it. He's fifteen, for Pete's sake, and I knew you were here – or were you off somewhere with that reporter woman?' The accusation hung in the air and Hannah adjusted the earphones, pushing them closer to her head.

Tom did not take the bait and it was silent until Laurel, sounding calmer said, 'I know I arrived back later than I was supposed to but we got lost coming home and had to…had to…'

She started crying again and her voice became muffled, as if she had buried her face in her pillow. Hannah was horrified and shook her head, denying the unspoken question.

'Come on, sweetie, you know you always get lost. It's the family joke. It's just one of the things that makes us love you more. I thought your butterfly group would be able to read a map,' said Tom.

Hannah chastised herself inwardly for the uncharitable feelings she had towards the poor woman, who clearly had severe problems.

'Ja, but I lost it in the veld and we spent hours driving round trying to find the way home. I'm such an idiot.' Laurel began crying again, her sobs like shots in the tinny headphones.

'Now, now, stop crying sweetie. Come on, lie down and try to get some sleep.'

They heard Tom muttering soothing words. Hannah could barely listen. Some things were too private to be shared.

Themba was motionless, face tense, then very calmly he said, 'Hannah, lie down.'

She obeyed instantly, feeling his solid body next to hers and then a tarpaulin being pulled over them. He put his arm round her shoulders, pushing her down on to the cold metal floor, the rigidity of his body the only indication that something was wrong.

She wondered what had spooked him. A vehicle pulled up next to them, a door opened and they heard voices. Then through an eyelet in the canvas Hannah saw a beam of light shining in and sweeping across the interior of the van. She squeezed her eyes shut, jerking in fright when the canopy door was shaken vigorously. The cab doors were tried next, but both were securely locked. Voices murmured, doors opened and slammed shut and the vehicle drove off.

'That was close,' said Themba, a big white grin on his face. 'But I think it means our snooping is over for tonight.'

'Who was that?' asked Hannah, still trembling.

'The cops, so you had better get out of here, they will be back, you can be sure of that. I'll take the *bakkie* somewhere and dump it. The owner will have reported it stolen by now.'

'What? You stole it?' Hannah was incredulous at the man's audacity.

'You do not think I can afford a beautiful vehicle like this myself, do you? I was planning on returning it to its rightful owner, but I have changed my mind. I think you will find that your friend Mr Frik van Niekerk will go to work by bus tomorrow.'

He let out a deep-throated chuckle. Hannah stared at him, her mouth open. He shooed her out the back and drove off with a casual wave of the hand. Hannah walked back to her own car parked a block away and went home still shaking and filled with guilt.

Heaven only knew what would have happened if she'd been caught in the back of a *bakkie* with a black man in a white neighbourhood at night. They'd broken a number of laws that Hannah had only read about and for an instant she had an inkling of what it must be like for Themba, constantly colliding with a system that tried to squash him and his rights at every turn.

CHAPTER

Seventeen

Early the next morning the police station was quiet, a pervading smell of disinfectant and floor polish lingering in the late afternoon air. A neon light flickered annoyingly in the deserted corridor, where a black cleaner dressed in long blue shorts with a red stripe round the hems, mopped the floors.

Hannah approached Tom's office and heard voices inside. She hesitated, still remorseful about what she'd listened in on the previous night. Nevertheless, she inched forward, hoping to overhear something, anything that would confirm her hopes that Tom could be trusted. Despite their recent conversation, she had lingering doubts about his trustworthiness and sneaking about was becoming second nature to her. She checked to see if the cleaner was watching, but he had moved round a corner and the corridor was empty. She took her chance.

A large filing cabinet stood outside the office and by turning sideways she was able to obscure herself from anyone coming down the passage but still had a clear view through the open door into the office. Tom was facing Kobus Le Roux, his colleague and close friend.

'Hannah thinks there's a group of hit men out there being paid to kill agitators and dissidents, both black and white, and that they're doing it for financial reasons and probably don't have any political affiliation at all. You and I already know about the death squads operating out of Vlakplaas, is it possible there's another group we don't know about? Who could be running them if it's not the police?'

From her hiding place, Hannah saw Le Roux's green eyes change and harden in an instant. The look was gone almost before it could be identified, but she could see Tom's lips blanch.

'No, man, that chick needs her head read. You can't believe anything like that, can you? You're too sensible.'

'I know, but it makes sense in a sick kind of way. You've been here as long as I have. Surely you've heard things too?'

Kobus' suntanned face was serious, his lips thin. 'Ja, I have. We've all heard things, but you're talking about it like it's fact. No one knows for sure and if they do they aren't telling. I myself don't believe it. It's too far-fetched, man, you know what these reporters are like: if they can't find the truth they invent it to sell papers.'

'Hannah's not like that. She wouldn't make anything up, she takes her job far too seriously.'

Kobus' eyes glinted and a furrow appeared in his chin. 'Perhaps I need to have a little chat with your Miss Smith.'

'She's not my Miss Smith and you leave her alone, okay? You won't get anywhere with her if you try to bully her into giving you information. I'll have a word with her. It's only a theory anyway.'

'That's good, Tom. It would be better for everyone if she forgot about it. You know what I mean?'

Tom nodded silent agreement, and Hannah was suddenly very afraid that he had unwittingly woken up a sleeping green mamba, wondering if he had ever suspected a dozing reptile under the rock of friendship.

'I know. You're right, but I thought I'd better sound you out first.'

Kobus, looking out from under heavy-hooded lids, said, 'Activists go missing for a reason. So do meddling reporters. You'll give this up now, won't you? I think it would be better if you did, because we don't want anyone to get hurt or anything, do we?'

Tom plainly didn't need to be whacked on the head with a blunt instrument to get the message. He raised a trembling finger and rubbed his twitching eyelid.

Once Kobus had left with a hard backward glance, Hannah crept out of her hiding place and after knocking lightly, entered Tom's office.

'Tom, I believe you called asking me to pop in. Can't get enough of me?'

'I've already had too much of you,' he said.

'What's wrong?'

'I think that it would be a good idea to lie low for a while. Try not to upset anyone, if you know what I mean.'

'You haven't been stirring up trouble, have you, Detective? And there I was thinking you were so settled in your comfort zone you wouldn't dare go about poking at vipers with your police baton.'

'Just for once, could you do what I ask without being facetious? I thought you'd like to know that one of those names you gave me matched a body and has been positively identified as a man called Vusi Makalele. He was high up in Poqo, the PAC's armed division, and went missing a year ago. It was being able to produce a name that helped discover who he was and that is down to you. So, thank you on behalf of the SAP. Now, about keeping your nose out of other people's business for a while, I'm not kidding around.'

For one breathless moment she thought he was referring to the bugs in his home and the instant before betraying herself realised he couldn't possibly know.

'You do understand, don't you, that someone exposing a covert hit squad is just as likely to be in danger as those that are the hit squad's primary objective?' said Tom. 'You need to back off for a while.'

'Okay.' Having run out of things to say, Hannah stood awkwardly for a moment feeling a strange tension in the air between them. Tom stared out of the window in silence, his shoulders rigid.

'I'll see you later,' said Hannah and left. Of course she couldn't tell him that she had overheard his conversation with Le Roux, but reassured herself that if Tom had been warned off, it was improbable that he was involved in any kind of death squad. She dismissed the warm sensation flowing through her as relief that one of her leads had paid off and that a family somewhere would finally be able to officially say goodbye to their father or husband or brother.

Delving round in her handbag for the car keys, Hannah noticed a sudden burst of activity. She stopped and watched as men in blue bustled out the building, talking loudly and holstering their weapons, on a mission to prove they were still in control. She could hear dogs barking and the engines of yellow vans revving. Something was up.

Tom walked towards her holding a sheaf of papers. Kobus, looking decidedly bad tempered, followed him.

'I never met anyone else with your luck of being in the right place at the right time. There's been another murder. Some hikers found a body in the Magaliesberg Mountains about an hour and a half from Pretoria. It looks a lot like the last one. This is getting to be an epidemic. Perhaps you aren't so wrong, Miss Smith,' said Kobus.

Tom jogged his elbow. 'Come on, let's see what it's all about then. You'd better come too, Hannah, you know you want to.'

Kobus gave her a filthy look and muttered something to Tom, who grunted a response in irritation and climbed into the car.

Hannah followed them in her own car, aware that Kobus' eyes were watching her constantly in the rear-view mirror.

She was preoccupied as they drove towards the murder scene and on the way had a fleeting thought that was gone before she could quite grasp it. It paddled about on the edge of her mind and when she finally remembered what it was, she dismissed it instantly as ludicrous.

The Magaliesberg mountain range, lying between the highveld savannah of the Witwatersrand and the African bushveld, had once been of great tactical importance to Boer and English forces during the Anglo-Boer war, both vying for control of the range with its access routes to Pretoria and Rustenberg. Its rocky ridges rose before them, the red sediment disturbed by the recent rains. Mountains that had once tested the military skills of Boer leaders like De la Ray and Smuts, experts in guerrilla warfare, were now a crime scene.

The array of fauna, flora and geology was of little consequence to the official-faced men poking through the grass along a popular hiking trail, bagging anything they thought might shed light on the killer. Forensic experts sifted through the mud next to the corpse, looking for clues that would help in their investigations, and earnest teams of men combed the richly wooded slopes searching for evidence. A medical examiner was bent over the body.

Tom and Kobus stomped off to assess the situation, commanding Hannah to wait some distance away from the cordon. She shifted slightly to get a better view and ambled as close as she could, but regretted the impulse immediately.

A swollen body coated in blood mingled with slime and mud sprawled inelegantly, legs dangling in a shallow river, the marbled skin on the hands and face a fetid ghastly reminder of a savage act. Hannah tried to breathe through her mouth to prevent herself from gagging and wiped a hand across her clammy brow as the smell of putrid flesh reached her.

Despite the studious activity of the police, only the occasional cooing of a dove and the shriek of a raptor broke the eerie calm. A large foot in a brown boot overturned the rock a dung beetle was sheltering under and it scuttled into the grass. A cinnamon-coloured snake slithered out of a hole and slipped away into the khaki veld with a swift wiggle. Nature objected silently to the intruders who had but one thought: to find any remnants of identity the killer might have left behind.

Hannah tried to focus on what was happening on the hill but had to consciously keep her gaze from returning to the rotting corpse. Her breathing was shallow and she was beginning to feel light-headed, unable to get the stench of the marinating body out of her nose. She gave Tom a wan smile and stared at the area to the left of his shoulder, unable to forget the exchange she had overheard between him and his wife.

'You look like a buck caught in a truck's headlights. Is anything wrong?' Hannah was jittery and flexed her neck and shoulders, trying to relax.

'No. Sorry. I've had a rough week, and too much coffee. Any idea who it is?' she asked.

'Good grief, woman, you've seen the corpse. It's barely human. You can't expect us to identify him just like that. We aren't miracle workers, surprisingly enough.'

'No, but isn't there identification? A wallet or passbook, something like that?'

'If there was I wouldn't be telling you about it, would I? There are official procedures that I have to adhere to,' he said. 'Just because I let you come along doesn't mean I'm going to allow you to compromise the investigation in any way. You do realise you can't write anything yet, don't you? Not until we give you a proper statement.'

'I know. Sorry, but you will let me know who it is as soon as possible, won't you? There might a link to the other killings.'

'It could also be the remains of a cheating husband and for all we know it's a muti killing, there have been a lot of them in this area.' said Tom.

'You don't seriously think this is a human sacrifice by a sangoma, do you? It doesn't look like any body parts are missing.'

'How can you tell from over here? Look, we know local witch doctors believe human body parts make their muti more powerful, and until we know better, we're open to all eventualities,' said Tom.

Kobus walked over and glared at Hannah. 'You shouldn't be here, Miss Smith, I can't think why Maartens invited you to join us. You could be tramping all over vital evidence. Tom, we need you.'

'I'll be in touch, Hannah,' said Tom.

Hannah muttered goodbye and left, taking one last look at the crime scene where men and butterflies collided, getting in each other's way.

CHAPTER

Eighteen

It was approaching midnight and Hannah was sitting on the floor of her lounge with the cat on her lap looking at a pile of tapes that had arrived from Themba that morning. They were marked by date and she sorted them into the most recent recordings, took a sip of lukewarm coffee, hesitating for a moment before putting a tape into the cassette player and pressing play. It was strange hearing Jack's disembodied voice in her home.

'My mom will have a cow if she sees you in the house, Themba. I thought she told you the servant's plates and cutlery are kept in a cupboard in the garage,' said Jack.

'Yes, she did, and she said she would leave some pap for my lunch but I cannot find it, so I thought it might still be on the stove. I am sorry I came into the house. Please do not tell her.'

'Don't worry. Look, I don't think there's any mealie meal, but can I give you bread and jam instead?' asked Jack. 'Or what about baked beans on toast like I'm having. Have you ever had baked beans before?'

'Do not go to any trouble for me, *baas*,' answered Themba with a note of sarcasm in his voice.

'My dad's the boss, not me,' said Jack. 'I'll do beans on toast for both of us.' Pots clattered.

Hannah leaned forward, turned up the volume and picked up a notepad, ready to make notes if anything unusual was said. For all that he was so innocent, Jack could very easily know something important without knowing it.

'I should not be in here,' said Themba. 'If your mother finds me here she is going to fire me,'

'No, she won't. Why are you so scared? My mom's harmless.'

Themba grunted. Hannah found that she was clenching her teeth, holding her breath in case Laurel arrived home and caught Themba. She was quite sure the woman wasn't as harmless as Jack seemed to think.

'Ag man, it's fine, don't worry and I've never talked to a black man before. Not a grown-up one anyway. But I'm not scared of you. Is that weird?'

Themba laughed, 'Yes, it is actually. Most people are scared of me for no specific reason other than that I am black. I am used to it now.'

They chatted a while longer with Themba entertaining Jack with tales of the hardships of his life and gently probing for any information he might have about his father and any suspicious activities. Jack seemed surprisingly well informed but frighteningly naïve about the state of the nation. Like she'd been at his age. But as far as his father was concerned, Tom was a saint who could do no wrong, apart from neglect his family due to work.

A door opened followed by the clack, clakc of heels on linoleum. Hannah leaned forward.

'What *exactly* is going on here?' Laurel's voice broke in, abrasive and rattling in her chest as if she had a cold.

'Hi, Mum. You forgot to leave lunch for Themba so I made him some and we started chatting and he's been telling me a few things I didn't know.'

'Jack Maartens! We do not chat to the servants, especially the new garden boy. You hardly know him and if you ask me he is far too familiar.' Her voice dipped to a stage whisper as if she was trying to make sure Themba couldn't hear. 'He looked me straight in the eye yesterday and told me to wait when I asked him to clean the pool. You can't trust them, Jack. No matter how long they've worked in your home, you never know if they're going to rise up and murder you in your sleep, do you?'

'Mum, he can hear you,' said Jack.

Laurel snorted. 'Take your lunch outside, Themba. You are not to come inside again, do you understand?'

'Yes, madam,' said Themba. 'Sorry, madam. I will not come inside again.'

'You bloody better not!' snapped Laurel.

Hannah listened for a few more minutes and then switched the recorder off.

Try as she might to explain it away, her gut instinct was still that Tom could be involved in something nasty, but despite her suspicions, she didn't feel comfortable spying on him. What if he found the bugs?

Nevertheless, she decided to listen to the final two tapes before going to bed. The first contained nothing more than the every day comings and goings in the Maartens house and nothing even vaguely interesting was on them, apart from emphasising the fact that Laurel was a most peculiar woman indeed. Then, just as she was about to give up, something on the final tape caught her attention.

The phone rang and Tom answered, ' Maartens,'

A man's voice spoke, 'We've been hearing some rumours about that journalist woman,'

'She's not a problem, I assure you. I can take care of her,' said Tom.

'You'd better. My boss isn't happy about her enquiries. She's finding out things that are supposed to be over and done with. If she keeps it up she's going to get into serious *fokken* trouble, understand?' said the man.

'I told you, I can take care of her. She trusts me. Tell him to relax.' He hung up.

Hannah switched off the tape, skin tingling, thought for a moment then switched it on again. All she heard was Jack and his father heading off for school and then Laurel leaving too. Lost in thought, Hannah left the tape playing, a gentle hissing the only sound, but then a noise made her sit up straight. She heard a key in the lock and someone entering the house.

'Hannah.'

She almost jumped out of her skin.

'Hannah, I know you are listening so I am going to give you some commentary to liven up your day.'

It was Themba, who had obviously broken into the house. She went cold.

'Now, stop panicking. I did not break in. I used the key Master Jack thoughtfully gave me so I could go in to get lunch and tend to the indoor plants. I am sworn to secrecy though, because apparently his mother would not approve.' He laughed and Hannah bit her lip in anger. He was so frivolous, so cavalier about his own safety.

'I have not seen any mysterious men entering the house in the dead of night either. And now, I am going to have a good poke around while they are out. Take a breath Hannah, it is all going to be fine.'

Hannah was livid, but couldn't stop listening to the sounds of Themba searching the house with a mocking commentary accompanying his felony. He went systematically through the house, opened every drawer, every cupboard, and looked under all the beds and behind all loose furniture. He went into Jack's room, and made noises of disgust at the mess, then continued his search. She could hear him opening doors and moving furniture and was on tenterhooks, waiting for him to be sprung by a returning Laurel, or worse, Tom.

'And now, I am in the master bedroom. Plenty of frilly pink stuff, not at all what I would expect from Detective Maartens. The cupboards are too neat, obviously a very efficient maid, nothing hidden at the back, there are no vials of poison or caches of hidden weapons in here. Although, to be honest, he would not exactly hide those kinds of things in his family home, would he?'

Hannah couldn't believe her ears.

'I am now checking the bathroom, nothing in the toilet cistern, nothing in the…ah hah, and what have we here?'

She listened to him grunting, then banging and his small intake of breath.

'There is a loose panel at the back of the bathroom cupboard. I will remove it….so…' She heard a thump, 'What I have is a small metal case and if I just open it like this…good gracious, this is a serious weapon,'

Hannah was dismayed.

'It is a gun, and I suppose not all that suspicious as the man is a policeman. Eish, but it is a beautiful creation, one I have not seen before, and I am pretty sure it is not standard issue. Hmm. I will have to try and find out more about it. I will just write down the details and then I think it is about time I got out of here.'

Hannah waited until he said a mocking 'I bid you goodnight,' turned off the tape and padded into the kitchen to make fresh coffee. Her mind was whirling and she knew she'd be unable to sleep. Was it possible she was wrong about Tom? All she had heard tonight pointed to him being involved in something dodgy. Why would he have a gun hidden in his home and who was the man on the other end of the phone?

She stood at the window looking into the night, waiting for the kettle to boil and almost had a heart attack when a face appeared in front of her. She opened her mouth to scream, then realised it was Themba. She opened the door and ushered him inside.

'What the hell are you doing lurking about out there?'

'I was not lurking, I was waiting for you. I did not want to disturb the neighbours by knocking on your front door.'

'Coffee?'

Themba nodded and sat down at the kitchen table. She could see him eyeing a jar of biscuits and wondered when he'd last eaten. She offered him a biscuit, then made a ham sandwich and put it in front of him. He devoured it without a word. She used the rest of the loaf to make more sandwiches, which she wrapped in foil. A couple of pots of yoghurt, three apples, two tins of tuna, an opened tin of jam, half a packet of cream crackers and a handful of tea bags went into a plastic bag along with the sandwiches. He nodded his thanks when she placed it in front of him. Themba hated taking charity so Hannah refrained from asking if he needed money.

'Tell me what else you've found out about Tom,' she said.

Before he had a chance to tell her anything else, there was a loud knocking on her front door. They both froze.

'Who on earth could it be at this time of night?' said Hannah. She looked at Themba anxiously. He was poised to flee. The knocking became more insistent.

'Hide in my room.' Hannah pushed Themba towards her bedroom, grabbed a dressing gown and put it on over her clothes before walking to the front door. She opened it a crack and peered out. To her consternation two large policemen were on her doorstep.

'Yes?'

'Nag, mevrou. Good evening, missus. Is everything all right here with you?' said an enormous dark-skinned officer. He took his cap off respectfully.

'You mean apart from being woken up in the middle of the night by you nearly breaking my door down?' she replied, without thinking.

The other smaller man pursed his lips. 'Your neighbour said she saw a black man entering your home and was worried for your safety.'

'Oh? No, she must be imagining things. I've been asleep.'

'Your lights were on when we arrived,' said the small man.

'I know, I fell asleep reading in the lounge,' said Hannah, silently cursing her nosy neighbour. 'Seriously, why would I have a black man in my flat in the dead of night?'

'There are many things in this country that can't be explained,' said the big man. 'There are even respectable white reporters that consort with the black criminal element. Perhaps we should come in and have a look around, just to check that you're safe?'

'Don't you think I'd know if I had a man in my flat? But if you insist…' She opened the door wider, inviting them in, hoping they wouldn't notice the sweat on her brow or the tape recordings lying in full sight on the table. It was obvious they knew all about her and she wondered if a neighbour had actually called or if this was a spot check because they were suspicious of her activities.

They came in and took a cursory look around. She watched as they went into her bedroom and when they looked under the bed and opened her cupboard she clenched her lips together, but her room was empty. Themba had slipped away into the night, an expert at blending into the shadows and becoming invisible.

The police left and Hannah wondered again who had sent them and if their visit had been as innocent as they'd made out. It was not beyond the realm of possibility for Tom to have sent them along in an attempt to intimidate her.

CHAPTER

Nineteen

The week following Laurel's butterfly collecting trip and the discovery of the body in the Magaliesberg had escalated out of control before Hannah knew what was happening. At the office she was eager to see if the sticky webs she'd put out had yielded any trapped insects and stood transfixed, rubbing her icy hands together, when she read the scrawled note someone had left on her desk. She'd found her whistleblower. Trying to slow her breathing, she sidled out of the office making sure no one saw her leave.

Hannah waited impatiently, drumming her fingers on the waist-high wall enclosing the car park. The Pretoria train station buzzed with commuters and harassed families lugging luggage. The smell of diesel fuel and car fumes mingled with hot tar, engines revving, a car backfiring and a child screaming nearby, added to her already pounding headache. A taxi hooted, the driver yelling something in Sotho at a prospective passenger, and she jumped. Uncomfortably hot with damp patches under her arms and perspiration running down her back, Hannah fanned herself with a rolled-up newspaper. She remembered the trips back and forth by train to university in Johannesburg and wondered if the station had always had the same tatty and slightly seedy feeling about it. Perhaps in the glow of youth she hadn't noticed it, had mistaken it for romance.

A slim brunette wearing a khaki suit with orange epaulettes, an unflattering peaked cap and a worried look on her face approached, her heels crunching in the warm gravel. A half-smoked cigarette dangled from fingers with untidily chewed nails. Her eyes darted from side to side and she sniffed. Greasy lank hair was scraped severely off her face, secured by an elastic band.

'Thanks for coming, Marie.'

Marie put up a quivering hand and pushed damp tendrils of hair off her forehead. She sniffed again and spoke hoarsely.

'I can't talk long, Hannah. If anyone sees me with you...I only have half an hour for lunch.'

'Come on,' said Hannah. 'Let's sit in my car. We'll be less noticeable. You don't look very well, are you okay?'

Marie Jooste worked in the admin department of the South African Army and was one of Hannah's most loyal informants, but seeing the look in her eyes today, Hannah wondered how much longer she would receive information. Fear that had not been there before was evident on Marie's face.

Marie took a nervous drag on her cigarette. The tips of her fingers were yellow, the nicotine from the ever-present cigarette a reminder of her vice.

'Only a bit of flu. Look, I found something by accident. I don't know if it's true though, but I hope it isn't and like I said in my note there's a piece that I knew you'd be very interested in. The general was out of his office and I needed a file off his desk but I bumped a stack of papers on to the floor and when I was tidying them up I saw it.'

'Saw what?'

Marie pulled a crumpled wad of papers out of her bra. She shrugged when she saw Hannah's face.

'No one would look in there, would they? I must go now. You can't tell anyone I gave you this – promise me. I don't think I'll be able to speak to you again because I think the general is getting suspicious. He nearly didn't let me come out for lunch.'

Marie left, looking over her shoulder in case she was being followed. Hannah sat in her car poring over the photocopied document and then stared into space, her eyes filling with tears at what this new information meant to her and to the lives of people she cared about.

The document Marie had copied from her boss's desk read like a spy novel. All countries had their dirty tricks department and she knew better than most that South Africa was no exception, the death squads at Vlakplaas being a prime example, however even though she had suspected this reading it in black and white was enough to make her sick to her stomach. Knowing her suspicions were based on fact gave her no feeling of triumph but left her feeling bereft and isolated, harbouring a secret she could share with no one.

By the time she had read the last crumpled page, Hannah's palms were sweaty, the paper wet. She felt as if her chest was being squeezed by a giant hand and for a moment felt faint so she opened the car door to let in some air and the world stopped spinning.

Her theory had been mostly right, especially concerning the financial incentives she had speculated about, but contained in Marie's files was an element of information that she had not seriously considered and she realised she would have to keep what she'd learned to herself until she could find confirmation.

The list of names and bank accounts Marie had photocopied held a name she recognised. How could something like this happen? And how could her instincts be so wrong about someone? Maybe it was a coincidence. And yet, the harder she tried to convince herself that any number of people named Maartens could be involved in a covert unit run by the Defence Force, a creeping coldness told her she was wrong and that Tom was not to be trusted.

Hannah headed home, automatically driving out of the airless concrete city centre, towards the cooler leafier neighbourhoods. The sun was blazing and she wound down her window even further, allowing the fresh air to blow across her face and body.

She drove past a small shopping complex and on spotting a public telephone had a sudden inclination to call Themba. She parked outside a men's clothing store and pondered the document Marie had given her. She needed help and he was just the one to give it.

Safely inside the phone booth, Hannah glanced round to ensure no one was taking undue notice of her and rang Themba. He answered immediately, surprised to hear from her so soon. They spoke succinctly, constantly aware of the danger they were in if anyone intercepted the call.

'I just had an interesting meeting with my contact at Army HQ and she gave me a document that you need to read. I've underlined a couple of names, one in particular, and I wondered if you could get me some background information?'

'Anyone I know?'

'Maybe. Look, I can't talk now. I'm not sure how safe I am. Someone could be watching. I'll drop it in the usual place.'

'Fine. I will get back to you as soon as I know something. Be careful.' Themba put the phone down while Hannah hesitated for a moment, realising she had forgotten to ask him if he intended removing the bugs from Tom's house any time soon.

She returned to her car, drove to the nearby library, made a photocopy of the document and placed it in a brown envelope. She then drove to the greengrocer's.

Lucky Kristopolous was an immense Greek who owned a popular fruit and vegetable shop not far from where Hannah lived. He was full of the joys of life and had a booming laugh, known and loved by all who knew him. He was also part of Themba's underground network and was used as a safe drop by Hannah and Themba along with others in the movement.

'Hello, Hannah, apple of my eye!' Lucky grabbed Hannah's hand, squeezing it enthusiastically, his double chin rippling with mirth. 'What you want today, my dear? Some nice pineapple? I have lovely apples just for you.'

Hannah allowed him to steer her towards the back of the earthy-smelling shop. She inspected the display of colourful fruit, surreptitiously dropping the envelope into the conveniently placed shopping basket. Lucky moved remarkably swiftly for a large man and had the envelope tucked under his apron almost before she realised it. Themba would have the document before the end of the day. She selected a couple of crisp apples, paid and exchanged a few more pleasantries before leaving and heading for home.

A small group of local maids, dressed in floral uniforms with matching headscarves, sat under a tree on the side of the road. As the parks in the area were exclusively for white use, they gathered on the roadsides and open areas of veld. A couple of the maids, including her own, were wearing a silver Star of David on a piece of black felt pinned to their lapels, indicating that they were members of the Zionist Christian Church. It wasn't uncommon for Hannah to see a group of men and women dressed in the uniform of the ZCC holding an informal service on the roadside, since they had no church buildings of their own to meet in. She waved to Grace, who was sitting cross-legged talking to her friend Doris.

Rounding the corner, deep in thought, Hanna noticed a green car parked outside her building. She glanced up at the window of her modern flat, looking as usual for the cat, which liked to sit on the windowsill and watch the traffic. The drawn curtains instantly caught her attention. She liked to leave them open to let in the sunshine.

Hannah frowned. Perhaps Grace had closed them. She parked in the underground garage, pleased to be out of the claustrophobic car and went inside deep in thought. A group of terracotta pots were arranged outside her front door and she made a mental note to water the plants. She plucked off a few dead leaves and was about to put her key into the lock when she heard a faint sound inside the flat. She stopped and put her ear to the door. There it was again, a faint thump. Her cat, portly though it was, never made that kind of noise and she had seen Grace outside.

Hannah stood still, listening, an uneasy feeling crawling up her back. Then she saw a faint muddy footprint made by a large man's shoe on the grass welcome mat. She stared at the door, perplexed, and noticed scratches around the lock.

She backed away and started making her way out of the building, her mouth dry. When her flat exploded, Hannah was halfway down the stairs leading to the garage, feeling slightly foolish and reprimanding herself for over-reacting.

CHAPTER

Twenty

Hannah watched a team of men meticulously going over the ruins of her flat. The terrified cat clung to her shoulder, claws embedded in her skin, teeth bared. Hannah stroked her, burying her face in the soft, ash-covered fur. Shattered crockery and one charred shoe lay among the debris. The walls were blackened, the curtains torn. A tap spewed water into the air and the smell of burning and petrol was everywhere, leaving a burnt-toast taste in her mouth and making her eyes smart.

She turned at the sound of running footsteps comingnup the stairs and was taken aback when Tom burst in. He pushed past the firemen and glared at Hannah.

'I warned you that you were in over your head and you ignored me, you stupid bloody woman.' Hannah blinked. 'God, when I heard that there'd been an explosion in your flat... it's more obvious than ever now that your life is in jeopardy and when whoever did this finds out you survived...'

153

He put his hand to his neck as if he was suffocating and said so quietly she wasn't quite sure she had heard correctly, 'I am becoming far too attached to you, Hannah Smith.'

Pieter Du Plessis, the head of the forensics team, was sifting through the wreckage and he came towards them tossing a piece of melted plastic that Hannah recognised as her portable radio, onto the floor.

'You had a lucky escape,' he said. 'It was definitely a petrol bomb and if the fire brigade hadn't arrived so fast, the whole building could have gone up.'

'Let me know as soon as you get any leads, please,' said Tom. He turned to Hannah. 'You'd better come with me. You can't possibly stay here. But you'll have to leave that animal with a neighbour. Jack's dog would have it for lunch.'

'No thanks, I'll stay with my friend, Dani,' said Hannah.

'Don't be ridiculous. Whoever is after you will be watching all your friends and family. For a supposedly intelligent woman you make the most pathetic decisions. You'll stay with me and that's final,' he snapped.

Hannah nodded meekly and allowed him to lead her to his car, where she sat in silence, wondering if getting her alone was all part of his plan. For all she knew, he had bombed her home himself, or at least organised it. Her head was drubbing and for now it was easier to go along with him. Perhaps being in his house would be fruitful. She could do a bit of prying if the opportunity arose, but she'd also be at his mercy if he truly did want her permanently out of his hair.

When they arrived at the Maarten's home, Jack was in the garden bouncing a tennis ball against the garage wall, each bounce leaving a round brown patch on the white surface. His dog Dudley yapped at his heels, desperately darting backwards and forwards trying to catch the ball. Tom careened down the road and swept into the driveway, clipped the curb and narrowly missed the post box.

Jack walked towards them and then frowned as Hannah sat frozen, clutching the dashboard, unable to get the vision of her wrecked flat out of her mind. He opened the car door and asked, 'What's wrong?'

Hannah blinked. 'Um - I...'

Jack peered at her. 'You look like someone microwaved your cat.'

She couldn't help herself and laughed aloud, shakily getting out.

'Someone blew up her flat so she's going to stay with us for a while,' said Tom, striding towards the house. Jack stood transfixed, his mouth open.

Hannah followed Tom inside gratefully and sat amazed as he efficiently made a pot of tea and produced some coconut biscuits on a plate. He grinned when he saw her surprised face.

'Yes, I know, I'm surprisingly domesticated for a South African male. I've had lots of practice pacifying hysterical females.'

'I'm hardly hysterical, thanks,' she replied.

'No, not yet, but you had that look in your eyes. I've seen it often. Every time my wife gets lost trying to find her way to the latest loony cause she's into.'

'Does she often get lost?'

She already knew about Laurel's propensity for misreading directions, but Tom didn't know that. She felt another pang of guilt at how much information she had gained illicitly about him and his family.

He sighed. 'Only once a month or so. Can't take her anywhere. I'm always afraid we'll lose her for good one day. We went on holiday once and I let her drive but I fell asleep and we ended up lost in the mountains of Swaziland instead of at the hotel near Mbabane. I don't let her drive much any more.'

Hannah saw the weary look on his face.

'Must be hard for you, Jack, having a mother that needs constant supervision.' She blurted this out without thinking and wondered again if Laurel was on something. Jack looked at the floor.

'He can handle it,' said Tom. 'I need to make a phone call. Jack, look after our guest please.'

Jack led her into the lounge and took a biscuit.

'Who do you think blew up your flat?' asked Jack.

Hannah shrugged. 'Could be anyone.'

'My dad says you should find yourself a man and stop putting yourself in danger like you do,' he said.

'He does, does he?' she said. 'And what else does he say?'

Jack blushed.

'Well?'

'He says you're the best damn journalist he's ever met, but don't tell him I told you.'

'Wouldn't dream of it.' She was pleased. High praise indeed.

Jack took a bite of biscuit and flicked a crumb off his T-shirt.

'I was wondering, isn't it a bit hard being a journalist and trying to write about things that are happening when you aren't allowed to write about them, the things that are happening?'

Hannah laughed. Jack grinned and flapped a hand at her.

'You know what I mean.'

'It's virtually impossible, actually. But we manage to get round some of the restrictions as best we can. The English press has a bit more freedom than the Afrikaans press, thankfully. Hopefully journalists will one day be allowed to print the truth even if it isn't what the government wants to hear. Perhaps in the future someone that was involved will be brave enough to relate the facts and not the propaganda. I've tried, but a smelly scorpion called Frik van Niekerk has his eye on me. It's probably due to him that I'm now homeless. So much for trusting your colleagues, hey?' She couldn't exactly tell him that she suspected his father might be involved too.

Hannah took a sip of tea and noticed Jack studying her from under his fringe.

'But, if you go against the government couldn't you get into trouble?' he asked.

'That's what makes it so much fun. I mean, where's the challenge if there isn't any danger?'

'Danger like someone blew up your flat?'

Hannah suddenly lost her good humour.

'Yes, exactly.'

Somehow the reminder that the danger was genuine was more scary than boasting about it to impress a teenage boy.

Hannah sat on the couch watching Jack, who was propped up against the piano languidly picking out the theme tune from The Pink Panther. She could see her own feelings reflected on his innocent face.

They sat in companionable silence for a while, drinking tea and eating cookies until Tom returned looking sombre.

'Jack, will you make up the bed in the spare room for Hannah please?'

'Why can't Priscilla do it?'

'It's her day off,' replied Tom.

Jack stood up and glared at his father

'You aren't going to discuss anything interesting while I'm gone, are you?' he asked.

'Go on, Jack.' Jack shot him a resentful glance over his shoulder. Hannah's hands began to shake.

'Righto, Hannah, why would anyone want to bomb your house?'

Hannah clasped her hands together, deeply distressed by the knowledge that someone wanted her dead because of her investigations.

'You okay?' asked Tom.

'I'm fine.'

She could see that it was no good trying to feign innocence.

'I have a contact in the Army, Marie Jooste, and she –'

'Hang on a minute, Marie Jooste? We had an incident at Defence HQ this afternoon, that's where I was when I received the call about your flat. I had to go down there because it was kind of sensitive. This Marie woman, she fell out of a window.'

'No!' Hannah leapt to her feet.

'The official story is that she committed suicide, but to be honest it all seemed a bit weird to me. She left a note but it didn't ring true, and it wasn't signed. Anyone could have typed it.'

'It's a load of bull! I don't believe it. Marie would never jump out of a window. She was frightened when I saw her this morning and now we know why. They killed her. They *killed* her, Tom. It's my fault, it's all my fault.' She flopped back on to the chair and tried to quell the rising panic.

'I think you'd better tell me what she told you,' said Tom.

Hannah told him about Marie and the documents she'd copied but she didn't tell him everything, only enough to keep him quiet, and she resisted the urge to confront him and ask if he had something to do with the destruction of her flat and the death of her friend. She hauled the document out of her bag and hoped he wouldn't notice that the last page was missing. Showing him the document couldn't harm. Better to play along and give him the impression she didn't know he was implicated at this stage.

Tom took it and read it in silence, then sat back and closed his eyes. He didn't speak for so long that Hannah was sure he'd fallen asleep. When he opened his eyes she noticed a slight tic at the corner of the left one.

'Okay, Hannah, what now?' he asked.

'I need time to think. My brain is all fuzzy at the moment. I'm going outside for some fresh air.'

Before he could reply she was out of her chair and pushing open the garden door.

CHAPTER

Twenty-one

Hannah cast a quick glance up and down the street, and not seeing any suspicious vehicles, walked into the garden towards the man bent over the rockery. Since the real gardener was still away, they'd agreed that Themba would continue working at the Maartens to avoid looking suspicious. She went up to him and put her hand on his shoulder. He sprang to his feet, alert and ready for instant flight.

'What are you doing here? If Laurel sees us she will have me carted off in a police van faster than you can say 'terrorist'. And you are not exactly popular with the madam either, let me hasten to add.'

'I had a bit of an incident at my flat today; well actually it was petrol bombed. No, I'm fine,' she reassured him as he swore.

'I hope it is not because of me. If someone has found out about our relationship - ' He appeared worried, although Hannah knew being in jeopardy was nothing new to him.

'No, it's not that. It's the investigation. That information I sent you is political dynamite. I know you haven't received it yet but when you do you'll see what I mean and obviously somebody out there wants to make sure I don't do anything about it, like publish it. Tom insisted I come here and I suspect it's so he can keep an eye on me. I'm very much afraid I've put myself at his mercy. He…'

'Hannah?' called Tom, coming towards her and Themba, who wiped his hands on his overalls and flashed a smile. Tom was disconcerted and his hand moved automatically to his gun.

'Tom, you know Themba Ntini. He's done some work for my parents and I was surprised to see him here now.'

'Afternoon, Detective,' said Themba, shrinking back momentarily before holding out his hand. Tom took it hesitantly.

'Themba's had a quite a lot to do with the police in the past,' said Hannah.

Themba inclined his head slightly, 'Yes, I have had plenty of opportunities to get to know some of your colleagues first hand. I realise that in any police force there are men that find the undiluted power a kick and use it to make themselves feel superior,'

Tom blinked, clearly not used to hearing such sentiments expressed so eloquently by his servants. He studied Themba for a moment and Hannah was afraid Themba had overstepped the mark.

'Or it's how they get their kicks. What's it they say about absolute power corrupting absolutely? Some of the guys I work with have become real brutes because they have too much power,' said Tom, taking both Hannah and Themba by surprise.

'I have spent most of my life trying to stay out of the clutches of sadistic cops – black and white, I hasten to add. Did not always succeed.' Themba licked his cut lip instinctively, an action that wasn't missed by Tom.

'Who did that to you?' he asked, subdued.

'It does not matter now. There is always someone eager to cross the line and misuse his authority.'

The two men eyed each other warily, opposite sides of a system that had taught them from birth to mistrust and fear each other. The air was charged with a bizarre sense of unreality as they considered one another and in those few timeless moments were impelled to rethink and dissect the ideologies of a lifetime. Hannah waited, unsure of how to proceed.

Tom abruptly broke the unsettling ambience that had engulfed them all. Hannah realised he was worried that someone would see him and Themba talking in what could only be called a familiar manner. He was firstly a policeman and knew enough about how things worked to know that prying eyes were everywhere. After the warning he had received from Kobus Le Roux he was right to be more concerned than usual about being compromised in any way. Holding a serious discussion with the gardener in the company of a reporter was sure to raise a few eyebrows and they never knew who would see them and pass the information on.

He picked up a spade and pointed at the rockery. Themba realised instantly what Tom was doing and knelt down as if studying the area. The two men dug up the ground without enthusiasm while Hannah took up a watering can and tried to look involved too.

'Themba, perhaps you can help. You haven't heard anything in the townships about activists being killed, have you?' asked Tom. Ever the detective looking for a new informant, thought Hannah. What would he think if he knew the truth?

'The townships are full of rumours and innuendo and the police and their death squads feature highly. I have heard talk of a third force that stirs up problems at mass gatherings like soccer matches and funerals. Trouble seems to erupt out of nowhere and afterwards no one is ever sure how it started, but the police are always conveniently nearby to brutalise the troublemakers. Perhaps there is a group of, shall we call them vigilantes, who are out there bumping off activists and dissidents purely for financial gain. It is a scary thought.'

Hannah held her breath. Themba savagely ripped out one of Laurel's prize plants thinking it was a weed and threw it into the wheelbarrow.

'Yes, it is, because it means that no one is safe, not even a reporter,' said Tom. The inferred threat hung between them and Hannah shivered, though the sun was scorching.

'And there's serious money behind it,' she said. 'This isn't a bunch of hoodlums looking for kicks. There's too much organisation for that. They know who to target, where to find them and how to dispose of the bodies. I think we've only scratched the surface as far as finding corpses is concerned. I wonder if someone has become careless?'

'You mean because of the bodies that have been found?' asked Themba.

Tom frowned and studied Themba again. Hannah could see he was suspicious and made a small movement to the black man, indicating that he remain quiet.

'Yes. It seems odd that remains have started turning up, almost by accident. Or maybe because someone has been sloppy,' she said, turning away as if she wanted to prevent the gardener hearing anymore.

'Perhaps your investigations have put extra pressure on the killers,' said Tom. 'I mean, think of it like this; for who knows how long, these murders have been taking place and gone undetected. Then you pitch up and start asking questions about the victims. Suddenly missing activists become important and you're demanding answers about the possibility of death squads. Now, whoever it is has to either stop the killings or change tactics and maybe they've become careless or too rushed or something…' He trailed off.

Dudley, the dog, sped into the garden chasing a ball. Jack followed and stopped short when he saw his father, Hannah and the black man at the rockery.

'What are you doing, Dad? You hate gardening.'

'Yes, I do, thanks for reminding me. Well, Themba, you just keep up the good work and let me know how your brother is and when he'll be able to come back to work. Thanks for the help, Hannah, but I don't think drowning the flowers is particularly beneficial. Let's leave it to the expert, shall we?' He dropped the spade and turned towards the house.

Hannah winked at Themba, who picked up the ball and threw it across the lawn for the dog. Jack, a perplexed expression on his face, ran after his pet. Themba walked off pushing the wheelbarrow, slipping easily back into his role of servant.

'I think,' said Tom, 'that it would be a very good idea for us to keep quiet about your actual reason for being here. I mean, I don't think we should tell my wife, it would distress her too much. She's already having sleepless nights about my involvement in your investigations.'

'I bet she is,' murmured Hannah and Tom shot her a sharp glance. She kicked a clod of earth.

'I know she can seem a bit unfriendly, but it's only because she's shy,' said Tom to her surprise. 'She's never been very good with people, doesn't have much confidence, which is strange for such a beautiful woman, don't you think?'

'Mm,' said Hannah. What on earth did he expect her to say?

'I met her while I was in the army, but we got married anyway and before we knew it, she was pregnant. She went into the army when Jack started nursery school and was one of 'Botha's Babies'. She did her training down near Cape Town, at the South African Army Women's College in George.'

'Interesting career choice for a white woman from a good background,' said Hannah.

'Well, unfortunately she couldn't afford to go to university and the army offered her an excellent opportunity. She was quite something, you know. She more than met their criterion of 'presenting the image of women in uniform positively' and being a mother already made her even more perfect. She played netball for the

Defence Force and you've never seen anyone shoot like she could. I mean shoot the ball into the net. She has an amazing eye. I never challenge her to anything that requires hitting a target, because she beats me everytime. When she was a child the other kids wouldn't let her play marbles with them because she was such a crack shot, so she resorted to climbing the tree in her garden and shooting nuts at passing blacks with her catapult. Then she discovered netball and that was it for her. Although being in the 'A' netball team doesn't have quite the same prestige as being in the First rugby team, does it?' he said, with a smile, 'She still gets wound up about that. She's a bit of a feminist is my Laurel, can't understand why women are still considered second rate citizens in this day and age.'

'Why did she leave the army?' asked Hannah, not caring in the least about his answer.

'She was injured during manoeuvres. She's hopeless at reading maps, has no sense of direction and she got lost in the mountains and fell into a ravine. A couple of members of her team died while searching for her. When they found her she was almost dead from exposure and she took ages to get over the trauma. She blamed herself for her friends' deaths. That was when they realised she's dyslexic. How she got through school without anyone noticing is a mystery. She became depressed and has never been the same since.'

Hannah felt a pang of pity for Laurel. Now that he had opened up, Tom seemed incapable of stemming the flood of justifications for his wife's odd behaviour. Hannah listened uneasily, trying to feel something more charitable towards Laurel, but all she could focus on was the way Tom's hair curled into the nape of his neck. A downy intimacy had wrapped itself round them and she was loath to break its spell. Even though she heard his words, he seemed to be talking on autopilot, the words he was saying conflicting with the message in his eyes.

'Laurel had a bad time when Jack was born. Now, we realise it was post-natal depression, but back then they just called it the baby blues and told her she'd get over it in time. She never did, completely, that's why I was happy for her to go to George, I thought it would help her focus on herself for a while, but it all ended badly and now...'

He looked at his wristwatch and frowned. 'I wonder where she is? She should have been home ages ago. I think I'll give her aunt a ring.'

Hannah watched his retreating back and sighed. Life was becoming far too complicated. And despite her emotions getting the better of her, she knew Detective Tom Maartens wasn't to be trusted.

***

A new strategy would have to be developed. By now the reporter should be dust, her remains blowing across Pretoria, or at the very least she should be horribly disfigured, ruing the day she had begun her investigations. But the operation had been a disaster and she had escaped the blast. It should have been so simple to get rid of her and they had started small, not wanting to draw undue attention to themselves, but she blundered on, refusing to surrender to their scare tactics, edging ever closer to discovering something vital and exposing them.

It was a sad state of affairs that even their own could not be trusted. The traitor had ended up smashed and bloodied at the foot of a building and though the files she'd stolen had been destroyed there was no doubt that she had divulged their contents to the Smith woman, and they had to prevent her from sharing this information with anyone else. In the beginning she had been an irritation, now she could bring them all down and sabotage their mission and it was imperative that she be silenced. It was a matter of national security.

They would have to increase their efforts to make sure the reporter kept her nose out of business that didn't concern her. The homes of her parents and her friend were already under surveillance as was her office, and Van Niekerk would let them know the minute she showed her face. She had nowhere to hide. When they caught up with her there would be no mercy, no compassion. They would stop her. For good.

CHAPTER

Twenty-two

Tom and Hannah were deep in conversation again when Laurel returned home. Jack was listening nearby with a rapt expression on his face.

'Hello,' said Laurel. Tom jumped to his feet, irrational guilt showing.

'Laurel, honey, Hannah's in a bit of trouble. There's been an accident at her flat so I said it would be okay if she stayed here for a while.'

Laurel barely missed a beat. She smoothed her flawless tresses and smiled a smile that somehow stopped short of her eyes.

'I'll get the spare room ready.'

'I already did,' said Jack.

'Oh, good. It's Priscilla's day off, now I'll have to put away the shopping myself before the ice cream melts. Come and help me, Jack.'

'Actually, I'd rather not,' said Jack. 'I want to talk to Hannah and Dad.'

'Very well,' said Laurel.

Hannah knew it was not very well. 'I think I should go. Laurel obviously isn't happy with my being here and I can go to Dani or my parents. You've already done too much for me.'

'Whoever bombed your flat is no idiot and going to your parents or your best friend would be asking for trouble. No, you'll stay here, the one place they'd never think of looking.'

Hannah agreed reluctantly and resolved to stay out of Laurel's way, but the tension in the house could not be ignored. She offered to help make supper and Laurel watched her closely, constantly shaking her head and making noises in her throat.

'No, Hester, it's very kind of you to offer to cut the vegetables, but I prefer to slice them into thinner pieces. Tom is quite fussy about his food, but you wouldn't know that,' she said finally, taking the knife out of Hannah's hand as if she was a child.

Hannah made her way to the dining room where she laid the table, determined to win her hostess over. She folded the serviettes creatively and placed a bowl of flowers in the centre of the table. When Laurel bustled in and swiftly removed the flowers, refolded the serviettes and rearranged the place settings, she held her tongue, but could feel her cheeks burning and her pulse racing. Laurel made a small moue of regret as if to apologise for wanting things a certain way, but Hannah wasn't fooled. She recognised a power play when she saw one and wondered why on earth Laurel thought a chubby reporter like her was a threat to her perfect domesticity.

Supper was eaten in silence, with Jack squirming in his chair uncomfortably. Tom tried in vain to make small talk and Laurel simply looked confused, as if the extra guest was too much for her. Hannah excused herself early, pleading a headache. She was sitting in bed making notes when there was a knock on the door. It was Laurel.

'Sorry to disturb you, but I noticed you forgot to clean the bath and I do always like the bathroom to be spotlessly clean. You probably didn't notice the cleaner in the cupboard so I've put it out for you. I know Priscilla could do it tomorrow, but she wasn't expecting a guest either and she has a very busy day ahead of her.' She stood with her hands on her hips, waiting. Jack's door opened and then shut.

Hannah stared at her, speechless, and realised that Laurel was waiting for her to get up and attend to the bath. She got out of bed, put on the dressing gown borrowed from Jack and went to the bathroom. The bath was spotless, but she made a big show of cleaning it, while Laurel watched over her shoulder. When she'd finished, she put the cleaner back in the cupboard and turned towards her room.

'I hope that meets with your approval, but Laurel, just so you know, I didn't use the bath. I had a shower. Would you like to inspect it? I'm quite sure I cleaned it and hung up the bathmat.'

Hannah knew she was asking for trouble and she was a guest but the audacity of the woman stirred up a primitive feeling in her. Laurel muttered something under her breath and scuttled off down the passage. Hannah went to bed seething, tossing and turning, only falling asleep as the sky began changing colour.

The next morning an exhausted Hannah went downstairs to find that Jack and Tom had already left for school and work. Laurel was seated in the kitchen drinking a cup of coffee. She looked at her wristwatch and then at the clock on the wall.

'Gracious me, I thought you'd never get up. I was just about to come and wake you,' she said.

'It's only seven, isn't it?' said Hannah. 'I don't start work until half past eight, there's plenty of time. I had a bad day yesterday and I didn't sleep very well.' She forced a laugh but Laurel did not respond and swiftly washed her cup, fastidiously wiping up every drop of water in the sink.

'Were you still hoping to have breakfast? I never eat in the mornings myself, that's how I keep so slim, but you look like you're the type that insists on a hearty breakfast every day.' Laurel's lips twisted in what was obviously supposed to be a smile.

Laurel was spoiling for a fight but she had chosen the wrong person. Hannah was in a foul mood and made a swift decision, determined not to retaliate. She was not going to stay around to indulge her hostess's bad manners.

'Actually, I have a ton of work to do, don't worry about breakfast, I'll pick up something at the canteen. See you later.' She left a bemused Laurel standing in the kitchen, and wondered how this incident would be reported to Tom.

After a busy day trying to juggle work, speak to her insurance company and make a report to the police, Hannah reluctantly drove towards the Maartens' house. Approaching Jack's school she noticed a forlorn figure standing at an empty bus stop. It was Jack and as she approached he shook his head and kicked a stone, before slinging his rucksack over his shoulder and heading towards home. She hooted and pulled off the road.

'Hi, want a lift?'

Jack opened the door and climbed in. 'Thanks. My mom was supposed to pick me up three hours ago after rugby practice, but she must have forgotten.'

'Perhaps something important came up. Lucky for you I was passing this way, isn't it?' she said. Jack opened his rucksack and took out a sandwich, which he scoffed in an instant. Hannah grinned.

'About my mom, I heard her going on about the bath last night. Why didn't you tell her you showered?' he asked suddenly.

'I don't know, didn't want to make a fuss, I suppose. Is she always so…tense?'

'No, most of the time she's not altogether with it and wouldn't notice if the house caught fire, if you know what I mean.'

Hannah resisted the urge to snort. Laurel had been altogether with it that morning. 'Maybe having an unexpected visitor upset her.'

'No, she likes having guests. It's you she doesn't like….I mean…sorry.' He put a hand over his mouth like a child.

'Don't worry. I have a knack of rubbing people up the wrong way. Just ask my brother. I'll try to stay out of her way.' He was reassured and stared out of the window.

To Hannah's relief Tom was already home and reading the newspaper on the stoep. Laurel appeared from the garden clutching a handful of flowers and gave a moan when she saw Jack with Hannah.

'Oh, Jack, I did it again, didn't I? I was supposed to fetch you but Auntie Beryl had a nasty fall. I had to take her to the hospital and I simply forgot all about you. I'm sorry.' She put her arms round him and hugged him. Jack gave Hannah a pained look over his mother's shoulder.

'I need a lie down, it's been a mad day.'

Before anyone could protest, Hannah took herself to the spare room and flopped on the bed. She dozed for a while but was woken by raised voices coming from the room next door. Tom and Laurel were having a row and it didn't take a genius to figure out it was about her. She opened her door a fraction and heard Laurel.

'I don't trust that woman, Tom. She's far too sexy to have round here with an impressionable boy in the house, not to mention you can barely keep from drooling. The way she's bursting out of her clothes, it's, well, it's vulgar, that's what it is. Plus I simply can't cope with all the extra work. She makes an awful mess, you know.'

Hannah closed her door and decided she would have to go to Dani, despite the danger. She thought about Tom's revelations concerning his wife's life and tried to recall what she knew about the role of women in the army.

Some years earlier, before transferring to the crime section, Hannah had written about what were euphemistically referred to as 'women's issues' and had investigated career options for women, including in the Defence Force. She had stayed in George at the South African Army Women's College conducting her research, where she spent time with the women and attended some of their classes including those designed to help them make the most of their femininity, such as how to skilfully apply make-up, lessons quite clearly given in an attempt to prevent any possible contradiction between the traditional idea of femininity and serving in the SADF. Butch, brown-clad women with muscles and cropped hair were not encouraged.

She'd written a derisive attack on the way women were portrayed in *Paratus*, the official South African Defence Force magazine, where physical attractiveness, outstanding cooking skills and the mastering of other domestic pastimes were lauded. She had argued that emphasising a female soldier's ability to competently perform her job while combining it with the traditional domestic responsibilities of wife and mother was one way of reinforcing the stereotypical philosophy that men were dominant and women were, and should remain, feminine and subservient.

Working in a male-dominated profession that reflected the culture and society they lived in, Hannah was fully aware of the pressure women were under to maintain the natural order and support their men ideologically, even if this meant ignoring the violent acts of repression that were carried out by these men. For those women that volunteered to serve in the armed forces, it was imperative that they in no way detracted from the strength of the men they were supporting. As the weaker sex, women were to be protected and defended by the men who had a monopoly of power. War was considered a totally male affair and the military was the last bastion of male power, a patriarchal institution from which women were excluded.

Laurel's helpless female act made sense now. She had obviously been so indoctrinated and brainwashed during her time as a 'Botha baby' that the woman was incapable of thinking for herself.

When it quietened down, Hannah went in search of Tom to tell him of her decision to leave. He and Jack were sitting in the lounge in silence but before she could explain, Laurel appeared carrying a suitcase and announced that she was off to stay with her Auntie Beryl for a few days. Hannah and Jack exchanged a guilty look of relief. Hannah was tired and didn't have the energy for another power struggle with this woman who knew exactly how to get her own way with her husband and child.

'If that's what you want, Laurel,' said Tom.

Hannah wondered if it was her presence there that prevented another full-scale argument.

'No, no, don't try to stop me, Tom dear,' she said, as if he'd been about to try. 'She needs me to help out while her hip heals and she's been wanting to teach me to use her knitting machine, now's as a good a time as any, don't you agree?'

Tom wiped his palms on the arms of the chair. Jack sniffed and patted Dudley. Hannah stood awkwardly, sensing a family moment that did not include her, and when no one spoke, escaped to her room with a garbled apology. She lay on the bed and ten minutes later heard the front door open and then the car starting up outside. She went over to the window in time to see Laurel turning into the road with Jack and Tom watching her retreating back. She couldn't suppress the feeling of victory that the woman was gone, reasoning with herself that it was Laurel's own decision to leave and that nothing she herself had done had precipitated this. Perhaps they could have a relaxing evening.

***

The new target was just ahead, unaware that he was being stalked silently through the darkness. Conditions were perfect. The air was still and the night gave excellent cover to the figures creeping stealthily through the veld. They were no longer individuals but a cohesive military unit that had become one with the earth, merging, invisible. Pale skin was unrecognisable beneath the skilfully applied camouflage paint, stripes and blotches covering exposed areas of skin, the face, the hands, the back of the neck. Parts that formed shadows had been lightened, those that shone darkened.

Approaching the quiet village, they were indistinguishable from their surroundings and crept closer and closer to the target. A barking dog was swiftly silenced, one jerk breaking its neck. Brown-black garments with soft floating edges, irregular patterns and strips of muddy netting broke up their silhouettes as they surrounded the hut.

This was not the time for a well-placed shot to shatter the man's body like the last one. They had to be silent predators, subdue their natural inclination to yell and whoop in victory. This time there had to be interrogation, the man had to be taken alive. That was why they'd come in a group instead of sending in their lone sniper. He would die, but not now. His life would be extinguished in a far-off place where no one would find him, his body returned to dust without ceremony.

The pack closed in on its prey. The unsuspecting man was urinating in the bushes, pants down around his ankles. He was unprepared for the savagery of the shapes that leapt on him from the blackness, could offer up only a token resistance as he was overpowered. Before he could scream or cry out, protest that what they doing was wrong and illegal, they were upon him, pressure was applied to just the right spot and the man fell unconscious, was swept up and bundled away like a carcass of beef bound for market.

They arrived in silence and left without trace. The man's family would search for him when he did not return. They would hunt through the bush, scour the veld and if they were stupid enough they would call the police.

CHAPTER

Twenty-three

Hannah settled remarkably comfortably into the Maartens' household. Tom and Jack were on their best behaviour and Jack, despite the occasional lingering look, was the model of decorum. He even managed to hide his disgust at her spaghetti bolognaise.

Laurel was still away at Auntie Beryl's and phoned daily pretending to be relieved that Tom and Jack had someone to care for her family while she was offering succour to her injured relative. They fell into an easy rhythm while Hannah tried to rid herself of the nightmares about being inside her flat when it blew up. Her neighbour kindly agreed to care for the cat that had long since made itself at home on her bed.

After a hard week of following leads about missing activists that led her nowhere, Hannah decided on an early night. She went to bed in a spare room that seemed to be trapped in a 1970s' time warp and read a dreary magazine about macramé before finally turning off the light. She lay in the soft rose-scented bed, mentally reshuffling her notes, but could reach no conclusion as to what she should do next. She turned over, pummelled the pillow into shape and closed her eyes.

Three hours later Hannah sat upright in her bed, her chest hammering, hearing shots and the sound of voices. Dudley was pawing at the back door barking angrily. Footsteps came thundering down the passage and the door of her bedroom burst open. It was unlit in the room and the light from the passage behind the man prevented her from seeing more than his silhouette but she couldn't mistake the gun in his hand.

Hannah was unable to move. All she could do was look at him in terror and pray that it wouldn't hurt too much. Dudley burst through the door, teeth bared, and leapt at the intruder but he threw the dog off and aimed his gun at her. In the instant before he pulled the trigger, Hannah threw herself sideways. She heard the loud report and saw a spurt of yellow as he fired, then felt a hard punch in her shoulder as she landed with a crash on the floor.

It didn't hurt at all and she thought she must have banged into the bedpost when she fell. Stunned, she noticed the man's brown lace-up shoes with thick rubber soles covered in mud. The foot crunched viciously down on her wrist and she cried out, looking up at the shadowy figure of a man with a scarf partially covering the lower half of his face. He gave a wry shrug, as if he was vaguely sorry that it had come to this, and raised his gun. Hannah closed her eyes and waited for death, intensely annoyed that she was going to die in her pyjamas.

This time there was no shot, only a grunt as someone tackled her assailant low and hard from behind. He fell sideways and landed on the bed with a loud curse. The two men wrestled furiously and then, after another flash, the struggling stopped.

Hannah lay half under the bed, clutching the corner of a pink sheet, and didn't move. A dull throb was spreading over her shoulder and she put her hand up to rub it, thinking it was bruised from the fall. When she took her hand away she saw it was red, she stared at it in fascination. She had never been shot before.

A figure loomed over Hannah and she sighed. Death would have to wait.

'Come along. We need to get out of here,' said Jack, as if he was inviting her to join him for a drink. She gazed at him in disbelief.

'No.'

He grabbed her arm and she winced, stabbing pain shooting down to her fingers.

'I don't have time to argue with you. We have to get out of here. Now.'

Jack pulled her resisting towards the door and she caught a glimpse of a man spread-eagled across the bed.

She stumbled down the passage leading towards the lounge at the front of the house, clutching at Jack's shoulder to stop from falling over. Scarlet drops were falling on to Laurel's lovely clean carpets. She would not be amused. Hannah realised with a start that it was her own blood and stood in a trance watching each slow splash.

'Come *on*!' said Jack, giving her a shake. Hannah followed him because she didn't know what else to do.

She was relieved to see Dudley sitting in the hallway. The dog wagged his tail. Hannah patted her thigh and Dudley came to her obediently, pushing his damp nose into her trembling hand. She patted his head, his warm hot breath on her skin a small comfort.

'Wait here,' said Jack, and crept towards the lounge.

He disappeared into the shadows and she sank down on a chair with Dudley at her feet. Her shoulder was throbbing wildly by now and she could feel the blood running down her arm and on to the floor. She wondered vaguely how much lifeblood had to drip out before she would lose consciousness.

She pushed herself up and made her way to the kitchen where she turned on the cold tap and put her hand under the icy water. Priscilla had been in and the counters were deodorized and disinfected with not a thing out of place. The patterned linoleum was cool on her feet as she rummaged through the cupboards looking for some kind of first aid kit.

All she could find was a pair of kitchen scissors and a couple of clean yellow dishtowels covered in huge sunflowers. She cut them up and wrapped them round her shoulder. They would have to do.

She went back into the hall and met a stony-faced Jack coming out of the lounge. He was clutching her car keys and handbag.

'Where have you been? I told you to wait.' He had turned into a stranger.

'I preferred not to bleed to death, if you don't mind. I was getting something to wrap around my shoulder,' she said. The boy at least had the grace to look ashamed when he noticed the blood-soaked makeshift bandages.

'My mother isn't going to be amused when she sees what you've done to her tea towels.' He gave his head a little shake. 'We must get out of here, I saw at least two more men outside. This is what we're going to do.' He sketched his plan in a tight voice.

On the way to the back door Hannah glanced into the lounge. The coffee table lay smashed, the pink couch was overturned, cushions scattered and Tom's body was horizontal on the floor. She faltered in a panic. Jack stared straight ahead, his face and lips colourless. In dismay she saw the patch of crimson soaking the carpet round Tom's tousled head. Dudley whined.

Forgetting her own pain, Hannah ran to Tom and took his wrist, searching for a pulse. Tom groaned and opened his eyes.

'Hannah,' he murmured. 'Take Jack, get out of here. You must save my boy - please? Go. Go now...' his voice faltered and trailed off, his head lolled to one side and blank eyes stared at her.

'You can't do anything for him now. He's dead and we will be too if we don't get out of here,' said Jack, grabbed her hand and pulled her away. He stopped at the hall cupboard and pulled out a tracksuit top. He tossed it to her.

'Here, put this on, you'll die of hypothermia out there.' Pity he didn't notice her feet were bare, she thought.

CHAPTER

Twenty-four

Jack stood at the back door. Hannah pulled aside the wispy cottage curtain at the kitchen window and tried to detect any suspicious shapes in the darkness. Jack made a move as if to open the door, planning to run out of the house to her car. She darted across and grabbed his arm. She was supposed to be the adult here, wasn't she? She had to pull herself together.

'Wait, there might be someone else out there. Our only chance now is to get to the car another way. We'll try the side of the house.'

'But - '

Hannah shook her head and took his hand. He wrenched it away.

'We can go through your neighbour's garden. It will take us round the block and we can get to the car from the street. They'll never expect us that way.'

She stumbled weakly against the door and Jack put his arm round her waist to support her, half carrying her as they made their escape. Hannah forced herself to put one foot in front of the other, her legs curiously detached from the rest of her body.

'Don't say anything. Come on.'

They crept along the side of the house with Dudley close on their heels, waiting for shots and shouts, but nothing happened, the only sound was a cricket in the bushes.

A low fence divided Tom's house from the one next door. Jack climbed over and lifted Hannah over too. She gave a small groan as he inadvertently grasped her wound. With Jack once again supporting her, they made their way along the neighbours' wall until they came to the end of the building.

Hannah glanced towards the house and saw a pale face at the window, someone woken by the sound of shooting. Keeping low, they tiptoed across the front lawn and out into the street. Their bare feet made scarcely a sound, only a gentle pattering on the damp tar as they staggered down the deserted grey street past the silent watching trees, round the block and then turned back towards the Maartens' house where Hannah's car was parked in the driveway.

Through the partially open curtain in the lounge, Hannah and Jack saw the beam of a torch and knew Tom's killers were still there. A dark car was parked down the road but it seemed empty. They took a chance and dashed to her car, keeping low.

Jack unlocked the door, lifted Hannah on to the passenger seat and slid into the driver's seat. The damp leather smell embraced Hannah like a familiar friend. Dudley jumped in panting, and gave her a comforting lick as if to say, 'Don't worry. Everything will be fine now.' Jack shoved him into the back.

Hannah hoped the neighbour would have the sense to phone the police. At any minute she expected them to be discovered and she wanted to scream at Jack to hurry up and get them out of there. Her shoulder was on fire and she drooped against the dashboard, weak and light-headed. Jack was clutching the steering wheel in white-knuckled hands.

'Can you drive?' she asked him.

Not answering, Jack started up the car, reversed out of the driveway and with a squeal of tyres raced off into the night. Hannah felt him beginning to shake.

'Where's your mom staying?'

'She's…I can't remember.'

The strength he had summoned when he stormed to her rescue had vanished, leaving a frightened, shocked boy.

'Think, Jack. Where's your mom?'

'Auntie Beryl. She's staying with Auntie Beryl. She lives in Joburg.'

'Well, we can't go all that way. It's the middle of the night. We'll find somewhere to hide until morning and I need to find a chemist to fix this shoulder.'

Jack drove through the sleepy streets, tall trees profiled against the night sky. Silver surrealistic moonlight streamed across the landscape and a sense of being trapped in a Hitchcock thriller filmed at a tilted camera angle enveloped Hannah. A few dogs barked as they drove by silent monochrome gardens and a solitary light burning in the window of a peaceful house.

Jack stopped at an all-night emergency chemist.

'I need cotton wool, gauze, bandages, painkillers and a large bottle of Dettol antiseptic. It will have to do. If they ask questions say your mom cut her hand on a broken bottle,' she said and tossed him her purse.

Finally, after what seemed a marathon journey in a bumpy car driven erratically, Jack found a secluded park and pulled off the road, stopping with a jerk behind a tall tree in the parking area. He turned to Hannah, shuddering, his jaw clenched.

'Jack, you have to help me. I think the bullet only grazed me but you'll have to dress the wound.'

'It's all bloody,' he said, his nostrils flaring.

'Come on, it hurts like hell.'

He pulled aside the sodden tracksuit top. She winced. Jack clamped his lips together, removed the tea towels and picked up the Dettol and a wad of cotton wool. Her shoulder was a mess of blood and scored flesh but Hannah was right in thinking that it was only a glancing blow. Thankfully no bullet was lodged in her. She looked with interest at Jack's lips, which had turned a very striking shade of green, and felt the sharp smell of antiseptic burning her nostrils as the car began to tilt sideways.

When Hannah woke she was snugly wrapped in bandages with her head on Jack's young shoulder. A smelly blanket that he must have found in her boot covered them both.

She sat up groggily. 'Jack,'

He turned towards her and her chest tightened at the anguish on his face. She had never experienced true grief before and tried to put her arm around him but he turned away with a stifled sob. Hannah was hopeless in the face of his sorrow. She cried with him for his father, knowing that what she felt about Tom couldn't compare in even the smallest way to what he must be feeling. She waited in silence until he stopped crying, but the boy had such despair on his face she could barely breathe.

'We should have tried to help him. We shouldn't have left him there all alone,' he muttered.

'We couldn't do anything. We had to get away. He wouldn't have wanted you to stay there in danger. You have to think of your mom now.' Even as she said it she felt like a traitor.

'My mom. Can you imagine her now? She's always been so lost. I don't know what's going to happen to her. I suppose I'll have to take care of her.'

Poor Jack, catapulted into manhood overnight.

'You saved my life, you know. Regular knight in shiny pyjamas you are.'

He turned away again. All Hannah could do was leave him to cope as best he could and try to understand his immovable grief.

CHAPTER

Twenty-five

'Jack dear. Is your mum with you?'

Jack's Auntie Beryl smiled at them through glasses with thick lenses that magnified her eyes to alarming proportions. Perhaps the glasses stopped her from noticing that Jack was wearing a pair of woman's jeans and a cerise sweatshirt with *Université Sorbonne* printed on the front. Hannah always carried a suitcase of spare clothes with her in case she was sent away on business at short notice. She dug her fingernails into Jack's arm before he could answer.

'No, she sent me to ask if she left her jersey here. This is our friend, Hannah.'

'Hello, Hannah. No dear, it's been quite a while since I saw your mother. When did she say she left her jersey here?'

'Um, last time she visited you,' said Jack, his voice starting to sound distant.

'Well, I'll have a look, but I don't think so. Do you want to come in for some tea?'

Hannah shook her head. 'No, sorry, but we have to go.'

'If you find her jersey will you hang on to it until we come back, please?' said Jack with a grimace that was meant to be a grin.

'Of course, dear. Drive safely and give your parents lots of love from me.'

They drove off in silence. Jack was breathing heavily and Hannah could feel him trying to squash down the panic that was threatening to overwhelm him. She rubbed her shoulder and tried to distract him.

'I think we should buy you some decent clothes. Can't have you going around looking like a transvestite escaped from the nut house.'

Hauling out her credit card, Hannah directed him to stop at the nearest clothing store and bought Jack clothes, underwear and shoes. She grabbed a pair of jeans and a shirt for herself, popped a couple of painkillers in her mouth and pondered their options.

They drove back to Pretoria in silence.

Finally he said, 'Where the hell do you suppose she is now?'

'Are you sure you have the right auntie?'

'I'm not a complete idiot. Anyway, there aren't any other aunties. Hannah, what if they…if she's - ?'

'Relax, Jack. I'm sure she's fine. Maybe she changed her mind and went somewhere else instead.' She thought this highly unlikely, but it seemed to reassure him.

Hannah wasn't sure what to do next. The logical thing would be to go to the police, but somehow that didn't feel right, especially in the light of what she knew. They headed off the highway in silence and stopped at a junction.

Hannah glanced across at the people in the car next to them. Jack made a throttled sound and sank down in his seat.

'The driver, he's the guy that shot dad,' he whispered. Hannah felt a clunk deep within and inhaled sharply. She and Jack exchanged looks and without need of any discussion, followed them.

CHAPTER

Twenty-six

Hannah drove at a leisurely pace behind the white Toyota, not wanting to attract attention. It headed out of the city and to the highway, heading north. She turned to Jack.

'Keep going.'

Hannah was relieved. It would have taken more will power than she had to stop now. They'd barely had a minute to fully absorb everything that had occurred the previous night, and now they were heading God knew where, utterly clueless as to why. What awaited them at the end of their journey couldn't be imagined at this stage, but the sense of imminent danger was growing stronger and stronger. The further they travelled away from Pretoria, the less hope there was of someone coming to their rescue should the need arise. All sensible thought told her she should turn round immediately and take Jack back home, but at that moment she was anything but sensible, impelled by a force stronger than herself and impossible to resist.

They drove steadily through the Transvaal and then began the climb towards the Escarpment. The road was straight and free from traffic, this being the lesser-travelled route with little to see but monotonous flat yellow veld. Shrugging off the feeling of disquiet at taking Jack into danger, Hannah flexed her muscles and stretched her aching shoulder. Jack folded his arms and slouched down, staring out the window.

On and on they drove, past the numerous guest farms popular for trout fishing that peppered the route up to the Eastern Transvaal. The white Toyota stayed ahead, never out of sight for more than a few seconds, and Hannah began to fear they would be spotted.

Jack murmured something under his breath.

'What? I didn't quite catch that,' said Hannah.

'I said all this is your fault. If you hadn't come to stay no one would have broken in and killed Dad. It was you they were after, wasn't it? They tried to kill you at your flat but missed and you led them straight to us. I wish they'd shot you instead.'

Hannah said nothing. He was right. It was her fault. Jack twisted in his seat to face her, the seatbelt catching him across the neck, leaving a red welt. His voice was slightly hoarse.

'Did you hear what I said? Don't ignore me.'

'You're right, Jack. It is my fault. My brother's right, I'm a disaster. If it wasn't for me you'd be happily living your life and your dad would still be alive.' The road blurred and she blinked. 'About your mother...'

'I don't want to talk about her.'

He turned away. Dudley sat upright on the back seat panting, his eyes keenly taking in the unfamiliar surroundings. Hannah focussed on the road ahead, avoiding getting too close to the car ahead. When an overloaded taxi overtook her, she allowed it to settle between them and the white Toyota. The battered blue minivan had goods piled high on its roof and the assortment of mattresses, suitcases and bundles of blankets wobbled from side to side. She watched it fearfully, certain it would topple off at any moment. Thick clouds of black noxious smoke streamed out of the taxis' exhaust pipe making her cough as a puff blew in her open window.

'Why don't you pass?' said Jack irritably, 'those things are going to fall off the next time we go over a bump.'

'It shields us from the guys up ahead,'

The taxi turned at the next junction and she slowed down to ensure that no one in the car in front would see them when they too stopped. They waited at a stop sign for a truck to pass and Hannah uneasily noticed the driver looking in his rear view mirror. She leaned forward as if to adjust the radio, turning her face away. Jack didn't need any explanation and put his head in his lap. The car drove off and she followed once more.

The traffic built up and Hannah allowed several cars to pass her, hoping that the Toyota wouldn't turn somewhere without her noticing. It would have been very useful to have Jack keep watch from his side, but he was leaning back with his eyes closed.

The petrol gauge was hovering dangerously close to red and they would have to find somewhere to fill up soon or they would be stranded. To Hannah's relief the Toyota pulled off the road at a liquor store in the sleepy rural town of Dullstroom, which was practically deserted.

'Thank goodness. We can fill up and get something to drink,'

She drove into a garage on the other side of the road. Jack tied a piece of rope round Dudley's neck and let him out of the car.

'Stay here and watch them,' she instructed Jack, who shrugged, glowered and leaned against a pole.

While the attendant filled up the tank, Hannah darted inside the butchery-cum-café and bought supplies. Anxiously keeping an eye on the other car, she handed Jack a couple of chicken pies, which he wolfed down while she took some painkillers, hoping they wouldn't affect her driving. Jack poured water into a tin for his dog, which lapped it up gratefully. They stood hidden behind a rubbish skip, waiting.

An autumnal freshness was in the air and the aroma of waffles and honey floated down the street. It was so quiet it was almost possible to imagine they were on their way to a lovely holiday, except for the gnawing worry in the pit of her stomach and the fear that they could be captured if they made one careless move.

Hannah watched the bottle store entrance and when the driver and his passengers came out laughing raucously and the white car pulled away, Hannah and Jack emerged and followed discreetly once more.

She glanced over at Jack with a frown. The events of the last few days were clearly gnawing at his mind and there seemed little she could do to help. She could practically see the pressure building up inside him and wondered what she would do when he finally exploded. He was obviously beginning to reassess his decision to go with her on what was prospectively a life-threatening journey.

They continued their journey, easily trailing the car in front and the countryside sped by. Soon they found themselves winding through the breathtaking scenery of the Eastern Transvaal and Hannah had to make a concerted effort to concentrate on her driving. The car ahead stuck diligently to the speed limit as it began to climb up the treacherous Long Tom Pass.

'What a stupid name, Long Tom, what's it mean, anyway?' muttered Jack. 'My dad's called...was called Tom...'

'I think it's named after the cannons that were used during the Anglo-Boer War.' Hannah glanced over at the boy and saw the gleam of a tear on his cheek.

'Huh,' Jack closed his eyes again.

The rolling hills and sweeping valleys traversed by rivers and rocky gorges were awe-inspiring but Hannah kept her gaze fixed on the road ahead, unable to drink in the splendour for fear of plummeting over the edge. She wished she could pull off the road at a rustic stall selling pottery and other African crafts to exercise her legs and massage her shoulder, which was thumping as she navigated the steep gradients and hairpin bends. She expelled her breath in a sigh when they began the descent down the other side.

It was a pity Jack couldn't drive legally, but she didn't want to risk being pulled over, though they could both have used a break. He was very keen to give it a try and sulked for the next hour when she declined his offer to take over. Every so often he sighed and glared at her, but she didn't have the time or the inclination to deal with his brewing temper, and ignored his small protests. Despite the fact that none of this was his fault, it didn't make her feel any more charitable towards the boy and she had to bite her lip to prevent herself from saying something that would only ignite the situation.

A wide expanse of mountains spread before them. Majestic peaks loomed mysteriously behind the softer hills clad in vast verdant forests and the horizon stretched as a jagged hazy line in the distance. The air was crisp and clean as she opened her window to allow it access to the car, which was beginning to smell of adolescent boy and sweaty dog. It was peaceful, only the gentle hum of the engine disturbing the silence as they had long since turned off the radio due to poor reception. How was it possible that her life was in such turmoil?

Her mind was brimming with thoughts and images and suppositions. How had she managed to land up in this mess? Dragging a boy who had lost his father across the country in pursuit of who knew what, and all because she couldn't stop to think before acting. How was it possible Tom had died, like that, when he was part of it all? Was it simply an accident, had the killer shot him by mistake or had they decided to get rid of him because he wasn't as committed to their cause as they hoped? Surely his involvement with her had nothing to do with it, or was she the reason he'd been killed? She thought she'd go mad trying to figure it all out.

The Toyota ahead turned on to a dust road cutting through a Eucalyptus plantation. Hannah stopped.

'Why are you stopping? Follow them,' said Jack.

'No, they'll see us if we also turn off the main road. We'll wait awhile and then go after them. It'll be easy, this road doesn't go anywhere, it's for logging trucks.'

They sat on the side of the road and never once mentioned the reason why they had followed the white Toyota for the last four and a half hours.

CHAPTER

Twenty-seven

Finally Hannah was sure their quarry was far enough ahead not to spot her dust. She drove down what was little more than a dirt track and rounded a bend. The white car was parked on the side of the road. It was empty.

She pulled over and climbed out of the car.

Jack scrambled out after her. 'Stay, Dudley,' he ordered the obedient dog, which lay down on the back seat then he headed towards the Toyota before she could stop him. The boot was open and they looked in, recoiling in disgust at the smell of urine and faeces.

'Do you think they had a prisoner in here?' whispered Jack.

Hannah nodded, the same thought had occurred to her. Voices could be heard not far away. Hannah started towards them. Jack followed closely, gripping the hem of her shirt with icy fingers. The voices became clearer. She winced at the tone being used and hesitated, but the stifled cry that came next drove her on. She didn't understand what it was that impelled her forward but her emotions were in overdrive and she didn't stop to think.

They made their way beneath the rustling canopy of trees, fearful of crunching leaves, until they saw a clearing a few metres ahead. Patches of blackened charred grass after a recent fire made the ground crunchy underfoot, new green shoots forcing their way up through the dryness. It was eerily still, a few random birdcalls breaking the motionlessness of the plantation.

Hannah stopped to confer with Jack. He was wide-eyed and his face was pale with sweat droplets on his upper lip and dark wet circles on his shirt. The corner of his mouth was red and raw.

'You don't have to come, you can go back if you want,' mouthed Hannah, pointing towards the car. Jack scowled. He started forward doggedly and Hannah followed.

They inched closer, hoping they wouldn't be heard, until they had an unobstructed view of the clearing from behind the large trunk of a fallen tree. They stopped. Hannah could see three people standing in a group and as they watched one of them moved, revealing a black man crouched on the ground. His hands were bound behind his back and he was stripped to the waist, fear evident in every muscle.

'*Asseblief, baas*, please master, I will not talk, I have a family...'

The man tried to bargain for his life but his captors were having none of it. One of them slapped him across the mouth. Gleaming sweat covered the prisoner's almost naked body, the rolling whites of his eyes standing out bleakly in his despairing face. Even from their hiding place, the two watchers could see the welts and bruises across his back and the stains on his trousers. Three intimidating figures surrounded him, balaclavas disguising their features. One of the faceless figures, holding a gun, suddenly turned in their direction and seemed to look straight at them.

Hannah hit the ground, barely an instant before Jack, and lay trembling in the sunshine. She could hardly breathe and every muscle clenched as she tried to merge with the bare earth. Stones dug painfully into her flesh and dust caught in her throat but she dared not move. She could hear the trees rustling above, threatening to betray their presence, and the menthol fragrance biting into her nose made her want to sneeze. She shivered, certain they could hear the banging of her heart.

The killer seemed to look directly into her eyes for a few moments before turning away. Jack was wide-eyed and staring, his whole body juddering so violently she could hear his teeth chattering. He was gripping a clump of grass as if his life depended on it.

Sombre stillness had fallen over the little group. The black man seemed calmer now, resigned to his fate. His head was bowed as if in prayer. The largest of the group, a brute with a huge red beard, wearing a khaki cotton shirt and denim jeans, his belly wobbling above the waistband, walked behind the captive man and grabbed his arm, pulling him upright. He kicked him viciously in the ribs and the man cried out. The bearded man laughed and said something to his companions, who each took a turn to kick or punch the prisoner. One of them stepped forward and put the barrel of a gun up against the back of the frightened man's neck and without ceremony pulled the trigger.

The bullet made a sort of 'thwack' noise as it entered the black man's neck, penetrating his spine. He slumped forward without a sound, his body making a soft dull thud as it hit the ground and lay still. In one instant, from a living, breathing being, to worm fodder.

Shock rippled through Hannah's body, as if she herself had been shot again. Jack buried his face in the ground with a muffled whimper and Hannah realised he was being sick, retching into the dry dirt. The ground in front of him was splattered in his vomit, which he tried to cover up with soil. She put a reassuring arm across his shoulders, desperate to still his scrabbling hands and signalled to him to stay immobile and quiet.

The killers heaved the body into the freshly dug grave, talking all the time, poured petrol over him then set the body alight. Hannah and Jack lay there, the sickly sweet smell of charred flesh mingling with the dust in their nostrils, the African sun searing their skin, and watched the man burn.

CHAPTER
Twenty-eight

'Slow down, and tell me again what happened, lady.'

Hannah took a deep breath and spoke in her special voice, the one she reserved for the particularly dense people that seemed to have a monopoly on positions of authority. They'd been there for going on an hour now and were no nearer to receiving any help than when they'd arrived.

The little policeman sat watching her from behind his desk. He was about eighteen and quite visibly thought she was deranged. Perhaps their dirty clothes and her shaky voice helped convince him of this. The fact that Jack was slouched against the wall scowling, surrounded by a very pungent smell, didn't help.

Jack was furious and had begged Hannah to get them as far away as possible but after considering everything she decided that, despite her misgivings about their trustworthiness, going to the police was the best thing to do.

'Up to now I've done everything wrong, Jack, this time I'm going to do the right thing. I'm a journalist and I have a responsibility to the public. I also have a duty to that poor man and his family, and to you and your father. I can't drive away with a clear conscience and leave him there until some unfortunate hiker stumbles across his body in the distant future. I know why you don't want to get the police involved, but I'm sorry, we're going to report what we saw to the proper authorities.'

Hannah drove to Graskop, the nearest town with a police station. Fat lot of good it had done.

She took another deep breath and explained, again, what they had witnessed. The policeman peered out from under his thick steel-rimmed glasses and shook his head.

'Jus' wait a minute here, lady,' he said in a thick Afrikaans accent and disappeared into the gloomy recesses of the Graskop police station.

Having driven directly there, Hannah expected them to spring into immediate action. They were met instead with barely concealed scepticism at their story. Paralytic fear had now given way to rage.

She propped herself up against the brown functional charge desk, trying to calm her jangling senses. It was like any other police station she had ever been in. Recently polished red floor, serviceable but uninspired furniture and Wanted posters lined the walls next to other placards designed to help the discerning South African citizen identify land and limpet mines. An impressive array of sundry weapons of terror was on display in a glass cabinet on the wall. She squinted closely at the display, breaking out in a sweat as she remembered the gun the killer had used.

Jack sat on a hard wooden bench. Hannah observed with concern that he was clammy and seemed unable to stop shaking. He raised a trembling hand to wipe the sweat from his forehead and noticed his blackened fingernails, an expression of disgust on his face.

Someone sniffed behind Hannah. This burly, dark man was undoubtedly in charge and why he had not been called earlier she did not know. He, his whole demeanour said, would not allow a manic female to intimidate him. The little constable cowered behind him and smirked.

'Tell me what you saw, lady,' he said in a tired voice reminiscent of her brother's tone, determined to get rid of her as soon as possible. Being called 'lady' every five minutes did not improve her already severely taxed sense of humour. She bit back a biting tirade about the incompetence of the SAP and patiently told the man what he wanted to hear.

'And where did this happen?'

'I told you, my brother and I are on holiday and we took a wrong turning through a plantation. It's about thirty kilometres from here. I'll take you there.' No point in telling them the whole truth.

'That won't be necessary.'

Perhaps tired and dirty journalists and sulky teenage boys often wandered into their little bastion of law and order and told them tales of murder in eucalyptus plantations. His owl eyes blinked at her, and his expression told her that this interview was over. Hannah stifled her temper rather admirably, she thought, the years of icy control in the face of a belligerent parent standing her in good stead.

'Good, we'll be on our way then and leave it in your capable hands,' she said brusquely and beckoned Jack. He stood up to follow her, but froze when Owl Eyes called after her.

'Not so fast, lady.'

Hannah turned in time to see the knowing glance passing between the two policemen.

'I'd have thought that a journalist like you would know you can't just come in here and make a report like that and then leave without filling in some kind of official statement,' said Owl Eyes. Hannah smiled sweetly and flashed her most charming smile from behind clenched teeth.

'Of course not.'

The last thing she wanted was to go giving out her personal particulars to anyone. Breathing loudly, Owl Eyes slid a buff form across the sticky counter.

Hannah painstakingly filled in the form and then an account of the murder they had witnessed. She signed it with a flourish and returned it to him, willing him to challenge her. She was in the mood for a fight.

'By the way, I heard that a senior policeman was murdered in Pretoria last night. Do you know anything about that?' Jack shot to his feet, an action not missed by the policeman, whose demeanour suddenly became a whole lot less sluggish.

Owl Eyes shuffled a few papers in front of him and his voice deepened.

'Now how would you know about that up here, lady? It hasn't been on any of the news bulletins yet. Maybe you should stay here and answer a few questions, hey? Like, why didn't you try and stop them?'

Hannah took a deep breath and thought fast. Jack looked as if he was about to faint.

'They would have killed us and I'm not ready to die yet. Secondly, I'm a reporter, Sergeant. I have my own sources and I keep in touch with my office even when I'm away. One of my colleagues mentioned something he heard, I wondered if you knew anything, being the police and all, I mean. If it's true it's a good story and that's just what I need if I'm going to get ahead in my job. Help me out here.' She gave him her most captivating smile, somewhat lacking its usual charm because of her filthy face.

'Ja, well, that's all very fine, I must say, but I think it would be as well for you to answer some questions anyway.'

'Look, my brother is extremely upset at what we saw and I need to get him back to the hotel. You have my details if you need to contact me again.'

She hoped that he wouldn't ask for the name of the hotel but he didn't have any reason for keeping them there. What was he going to do, arrest them?

Reluctantly Owl Eyes let them go but Hannah had a bad taste in her mouth realising she had possibly made one of the biggest mistakes of her life. While she was convinced the killers were not policemen, she couldn't be sure, and perhaps even this sleepy backwater was within reach of the tentacles of the state.

Jack trailed along behind her with an 'I told you so' expression on his face.

'Now what? The cops are going to find out everything. I told you we shouldn't tell them. But no, Miss Smith knows what's best for everyone, doesn't she? Who cares about one more dead black man anyway?'

Hannah stopped and grabbed his arm, resisting the urge to slap him.

'I'm going to pretend I didn't hear you say that, Jack, because I know that you're upset at what we witnessed and also because it's obvious you don't know any better. It's what you've been taught your whole life. And surely you don't think I'm thick enough to give them my real name and number?'

Jack mumbled something rude and headed off to the car, pulled the door open with fury and slammed it. He sat with his arms folded over his chest in silence until Hannah joined him. She rubbed her shoulder, and hoped it hadn't become infected.

'We'll be okay if we don't panic. I *am* a journalist and there's no reason I couldn't have heard about your dad before it was on the news. But who knew they'd react like that? I don't know what I was thinking. It sort of spilled out. I've never seen a man executed in cold blood before, I just followed my first instinct. You're not the only one that's upset.'

Jack didn't need to open his mouth to say what he was thinking. She shivered at the new impenetrable flash in his blue eyes.

'I'm sorry, Jack. First your dad and then this.'

He shrugged, as if it was the kind of thing that happened every day, but Hannah didn't miss the slight quiver of his hands.

'What now?'

'Now I think we should find ourselves a secluded hotel and lie low for a while. For one thing, one of the car tyres is making a funny noise and we can't get it fixed until

Monday. The last thing we need is to get stranded on a country road. And I need to think.'

Jack started unbuttoning his shirt. 'No, I don't want to think.' He turned away, wiping a grubby hand on his jeans.

Hannah started the car and drove cautiously, looking for somewhere to stop. She followed the signs to a secluded B&B up a dirt track, hoping it had two spare rooms. Dudley would have to sleep in the car.

She stopped gratefully when she saw the name on a plank declaring that this was Toad Hall. It seemed like a sign, The Wind in the Willows was one of her favourite books. It was a charming green-roofed white building with a well-tended garden, a wide stoep running the length of the house.

A tiny wrinkled lady almost hidden behind a large bunch of proteas adorning the oak reception desk smiled when she saw them.

'Good afternoon.'

'Hello,' replied Hannah. 'We need somewhere to stay. Do you have two free rooms? Please.'

'Come in, my dear, you look exhausted.'

She cast an inquisitive look at Jack, who, despite his best efforts and a change of shirt, still smelled strongly.

'Sorry about our appearance, we got lost and then got a flat tyre and Ja…John's been feeling unwell in the heat and has been car sick – sorry about the smell.'

Jack glared at her and put a trembling hand over his mouth.

'Claude, we have guests.'

Claude, a grey-haired man with a stern expression, came ambling into the room. His mouth was shrivelled, the edges drawn together as if a thread had been pulled. Hannah realised with amusement that he wasn't wearing any teeth. Jack's jaw slackened. Hannah nudged him and he closed his mouth. Claude nodded his head and Mrs Claude ushered them into an immaculate reception area.

'I have two lovely rooms for you. How long do you think you'll be staying?'

'I'm not sure,' Hannah replied.

'Well, never you mind. You're welcome to stay as long as you wish. We don't have many guests at this time of the year. They all seem to prefer the big hotels. My husband and I run this place by ourselves, although we have a girl in the kitchen and a garden boy. Claude, take their bags up to the blue room for the lady and the yellow room for her brother.'

Claude made a slurping noise, muttered something incomprehensible and walked out.

'Don't you worry about Claude. He acts like a bear, but actually he's very gentle.

'I have a dog,' said Jack suddenly. 'Dudley.'

'We love dogs. Dudley's welcome to stay in your room with you,' said their hostess. 'Our cat's as thick as two planks and won't even notice. Silly kitty.'

Jack disappeared and returned swiftly with a grateful Dudley. Claude came back into the room and growled. Mrs Claude led them up a narrow staircase. In every nook and cranny and on all conceivable shelves were statuettes and figures of frogs. It was like walking through a vast cartoon-swamp. Jack giggled as he came face to face with a large green frog-lady sporting a pink bonnet and carrying a purple parasol. Hannah caught his eye and stifled a laugh. He remembered he was still angry and scowled.

The old woman opened a door and led them into a pretty room. The walls were covered in bluebell print wallpaper with matching curtains and duvet cover. The gentle fragrance of lavender hung in the air. Mrs Claude showed Hannah the gleaming white-tiled en-suite bathroom. A small basin and a writing desk completed the furnishing. The room had a huge bed with large feather pillows that began to look more and more enticing.

'I'll leave you alone now, love. If you need anything ring the bell.' Mrs Claude indicated a small knob next to the bed.

'Thank you. Would it be too much to ask for a cup of tea? We've had a long trip.'

'Would you like something to eat?'

Hannah shook her head. 'I'm not very hungry, thanks. Tea will be fine.'

All she wanted was to bath, take some painkillers and sleep. Jack was about to fall over. He gave her a weary look and followed a chattering Mrs Claude.

CHAPTER

Twenty-nine

Hannah lay on the bed thinking over the day's events. The room grew dark and with a start she realised it was night and the hotel had fallen silent. Her legs were chilled and her shoulder ached, so she changed the dressing and took a few more painkillers. She heard a gentle knocking and Mrs Claude entered with a tray of sandwiches with a thermos flask of hot water, some tea bags and a plate of sandwiches. Hannah was most grateful, realising how hungry she was.

'Thanks very much. This is just what I need,' she said.

'No trouble at all. You just let me know if there's anything else you need.' Mrs Claude patted her on the arm and left.

. She poured herself a cup of tea and stood at the window looking out on the soulless night, and pondered their predicament. The stars above twinkled gaily, unaware and uncaring of the melancholy wrapped around her. She should never have left Tom alone like that. She should have stayed with his body and notified someone. Running away made them look guilty. They would think she had killed him and kidnapped Jack. This was a totally irrational conclusion to reach, especially in the light of all that had gone before, but in the heat of the moment and in her precarious state of mind, it was the only decision that made any sense. She had to think of Jack. It was too late for Tom now but they were still alive, and in danger.

Hannah stood in the gloom, wondering what cosmic intervention had caused him to die instead of her. She kept seeing Tom's bleeding head and wondered if her friend had suspected when he woke that morning how few hours he had left, had had any inkling that he would never see his son grow up or touch his wife's face again. Poor Tom, he hadn't done anything to deserve dying like that.

Hannah was startled by Jack's voice calling her. She wrenched the door open, took one look at his desperate face and pulled him inside. He sank down on the bed, so disconsolate she wondered how he'd ever be able to recover.

'Can I stay with you?' A smaller darker shape whined, and Dudley appeared next to his master.

Hannah put an arm round Jack and pulled him closer without a word. He shrugged off her arm crossly and lay down, curled in a foetal position. She could see his body shivering and covered him with the thick duvet before lying down next to him and staring at the ceiling, unqualified to help him overcome his grief. After a brief hesitation, Dudley jumped onto the bed and curled up on Jack's feet.

The next morning they woke to a grey rain-soaked world. Hannah's head felt thick, like she'd been asleep for a year.

An insistent pain pulsed behind her eyes and her shoulder was stiff and sore. The hotel seemed deserted, isolated by the fine fog drifting outside the window. Her body felt as if it was filled with cement and every movement took immense effort. She opened the bedroom door, careful not to wake Jack who was still asleep, and slipped out of the hotel and into the fresh air.

The gentle rain caressed her cheeks when she angled her face upward, mouth open, allowing the moisture to settle on her tongue. Lacy mist swathed the countryside, and ethereal trees and buildings lurked in the drizzle. Only the soft dripping of water off the roof broke the stillness.

While the night had brought rest, it had not brought peace and the thoughts that had plagued her returned with renewed vigour. She stood outside in a frozen daze, the rain soaking through her clothes, running down her skin, cooling her feverish body. She began to shiver but was loath to leave the shroud of dullness into which she wanted to dissolve and disappear. A soft footfall disturbed her brooding thoughts. She glanced over her shoulder to see Jack behind her, a wraithlike apparition watching her with solemn red-rimmed eyes, taking in her damp and dismal appearance.

'What are you doing out here? Making yourself ill won't bring him back.'

Jack's face was devoid of all expression. Hannah put a hand on his arm. He pulled away.

'We have to go back and find out why this happened and you have to help me, seeing as how it's your fault,' he said.

'I know. We do, but I'm not sure it's safe yet. The men that killed your father will still be looking for us. Jack... what about your mother?'

'I don't care.'

'I do. Let's give it a day or two. I'll make some phone calls and then we'll go home.'

While Jack was watching television in the communal recreation room, Hannah went downstairs to the public telephone and called Themba. The phone seemed to ring for an age before he answered abruptly.

'Themba, it's Hannah,' she said.

'Hannah, where are you? I've been waiting to hear from you and I called Tom's but the phone was dead. I've listened to the latest recording and I heard some odd noises, popping sounds like fireworks but that seemed ridiculous. I also heard scuffling and running, but I thought it was just Jack and his dog, who kept barking. I haven't had time to listen to the whole tape yet. Is everything okay?'

Simply hearing his calm voice rumbling over the line settled Hannah's jittery nerves, and she experienced a rush of relief that she could at least rely on one person.

'No, it's not. You haven't heard, have you?'

'Heard what? Hannah? You sound strange.'

Her eyes filled with tears. For someone that had been detained and tortured numerous times for no specific reason, the deep well of compassion Themba had for others in need always amazed her.

'It's Tom - he's dead. They shot him in the head and he's dead and we ran away and left him. That's what you heard, us being attacked.'

'What? How can he be dead? Who did you run away with?' he asked.

'With Jack, I couldn't leave him there, not knowing a madman with a gun is running around trying to kill us both,' she replied.

'What madman? Hannah, try to focus and tell me what's happened.'

Hannah told him about the previous day's events and he fell silent as she recounted events in the plantation.

'We have to stay hidden for a while and it's probably best I don't tell you where, just in case,' she said.

'What do you want me to do?' asked Themba.

'Could you find out what happened to Tom's body? I know it will be difficult for you to find out much, but please try. And will you give Dani a ring to let her know what's happened too? I daren't call her in case her phone is tapped and they might be watching her hoping I'll show up there.'

'I'll do what I can,' he promised. 'As far as anyone knows I'm still the Maartens' gardener, so going to the house shouldn't pose too many problems. I'll listen to the end of the tapes of that night: you never know, they might tell me something. Just as well I haven't had a chance to remove the bugs yet. Perhaps one of the intruders said something that will shed a bit of light on who sent them. But Hannah, watch your back, okay? These guys have eyes and ears everywhere.'

'That's what I'm afraid of,' said Hannah, and told him about the reaction of the police at Graskop.

'Hmm, probably not your finest decision to date, but I understand why you did it. Let's hope they do actually look for the body because that will show they consider your story credible. Try to check in with me again in a day or so. That will give me time to do some investigating of my own. Be careful.'

Hannah rang off feeling less fraught and wandered round the beautiful landscaped gardens pondering their next move. The champagne clear mountain air and the warm sunshine unclouded the thoughts in her head. Feeling more focussed, she began to dissect what had happened.

For the moment, her priority was keeping Jack safe. She decided they should stay at Toad Hall for another night while she considered their options and to enable Jack to come to terms with his father's death.

Mrs Claude was only too delighted to have the two travellers another night, and assured them it was no trouble at all.

'Claude caught some lovely trout in the dam this morning. I'll make that for supper. I hope you eat fish?'

'Sounds wonderful,' said Hannah. 'He eats anything that isn't nailed down.' Jack shrugged.

Mrs Claude nodded and shot an anxious look at Jack, who'd fallen asleep on the couch, his face drooping in sorrow. Mr Claude volunteered to give the car a check up and change the tyre, Hannah gratefully left him to it.

They spent the remainder of the day playing Scrabble and watching television and avoided discussing the things that were uppermost in their minds. Jack was surly and ill tempered and by the end of the day cooped up with him, her patience was beginning to fray. Mrs Claude's kind suggestion that he take a walk was met with a bad-tempered snarl and a scowl that made the old woman retreat towards the kitchen.

Hannah smiled apologetically and muttered, 'Teenagers, hey?'

Jack slept in her room again that night and the look he gave her forbade any comment. He kept rigidly to his side of the bed, moving irritably out of reach whenever Hannah accidentally touched him. Neither of them rested much that night. Jack had a nightmare and woke drenched and moaning. Hannah put a hand on his taut shoulder until he stopped whimpering and fell asleep again.

***

The traitor was dead, his body reduced to ash, and the unit could now return to safety. But just as they reached their lair, a phonecall with the velocity of a bullet fired from one of their own guns, shattered their euphoria. All the planning, the precautions, the intense hours spent trying to wring the last ounce of information out of the man's stubborn flesh and it had come to this. The endless days enduring the man's pleading and crying, his denials and pleas and offers of co-operation were time wasted. The news could bring about a cataclysmic end to life as they knew it.

It paid to have spies everywhere and information about the reporter had trickled though the filters. The ripples the latest news caused, however, could be felt by each one but most keenly by the leader of the pack, whose icy rage was more terrifying than anything they had seen before.

A team was sent racing through the night to intercept and silence the woman before she could do any more damage to them, to their plans, to their being. It was time they succeeded in shutting her up for good. Mistakes would not be tolerated.

CHAPTER

Thirty

The sun streamed through the window, glistening off a spider web spun across the corner of the glass. Hannah rolled out of bed, muscles protesting, and staggered over to the mirror. She groaned. Her eyes were red and puffy, her face was swollen and her hair stuck up from the top of her head.

'Charming,' she muttered to her reflection and ran a hand through her hair. A thought struck her.

She dressed and went downstairs, leaving Jack asleep. Mrs Claude greeted her gaily, ushering her into the empty wood-panelled dining room. The smell of freshly made toast and bacon made her tummy rumble. Hannah wasn't inclined for idle chatter, she had too much to think about, but tried as politely as possible to make Mrs Claude realise she wanted to be left alone.

She ate some toast and jam and sipped freshly squeezed orange juice. Mrs Claude poured a cup of fragrant coffee and hovered nearby.

'There are some lovely walks along the river. You look like you could do with a bit of fresh air,' she said

'Thanks. I'll certainly take a look around,' said Hannah

Claude shuffled into the room and gave her a surly nod. Mrs Claude slapped him on the shoulder.

'Claude, some courtesy for our guest.'

'Morning,' he said, without looking at her. 'Car's done.'

'Morning, and thank you. Add the cost to our bill.' Hannah replied, more breezily than she felt.

'Don't mind him, the silly old fart.'

Claude sat down at the table and opened his newspaper pointedly. Hannah finished her coffee and stood up. Mrs Claude, who had been waiting nearby, put a hand on Hannah's arm and ushered her to one side.

'I'm sorry, dear, I hope you don't mind, but I can see you and your brother have been through a tough time and it's none of my business, but earlier this morning when I was in town at the farmer's market, I saw a big blond man asking people if they'd seen a young lady and a teenage boy anywhere. He said he was your husband and from the description he gave I knew at once it was you.'

'You didn't -?'

'No, no. To be honest, I didn't like the look of him and well, you seem like a nice girl and it's nothing to do with me, but I thought that if you'd run away you wouldn't want me telling him where you are, would you? I hope I did the right thing.'

Hannah squeezed the old woman's hand.

'Thank you. Will you tell my brother I've gone out for a bit? And please, don't tell him that anyone is looking for us. I don't want to worry him.'

Hannah drove into the small forestry town of Graskop and found the chemist. Perched on the edge of the

Drakensberg Escarpment, the town was already springing to life with a steady stream of early rising tourists idly browsing the curio shops. She looked around, afraid of being seen. No one took undue notice of her so she hurried inside, bought a few things and returned to Toad Hall.

Instinctively parking her car round the back out of sight, Hannah snuck into the hotel through a rear door, made her way through the kitchen and laundry and feeling slightly guilty, crept up the stairs to her room, hoping Mrs Claude would not hear her and come along for a talk.

Jack and Dudley were in his room, the dog watching his master, alert for any danger, but he wagged his tail when Hannah knocked and entered.

'Come with me, Jack.'

'Why?'

'You'll see. Come on.' Hannah snapped. Jack stood up with a sigh and followed her.

She emptied her packet on to the bed and set to work. After initial dissent, Jack cooperated and watched with interest.

Two strangers reflected back at them from the murky mirror. Jack's hair and eyebrows were now brown, his blue eyes more piercing than ever and she was, thanks to Clairol, a bleached blonde. Jack stared at himself, studying his new image from every possible angle.

Hannah ran a brush through her hair.

'Oh well, they do say that blondes have more fun. Time will tell. And now, to complete the disguise…'

She picked up a pair of scissors, took a deep breath and cut off her long hair, her special vanity, into a short bob that curled into her neck. She scraped together the pieces of hair in the sink and flushed them down the toilet. Not too bad, she thought, suppressing the tears that threatened. Her hair would grow back.

Jack too was given a hair cut, which made him look younger than ever.

Hannah pulled on a pair of jeans and jacket, applied heavy make-up to help complete the disguise and went down the stairs, bumping into Mrs Claude at the front door. The old lady stopped her in surprise.

'Excuse me, can I help you? Who are you and what are you doing in my house? My husband is only in the next room,' she asked. Hannah was pleased.

'It's only me, Mrs Claude. Do you like it?' She tossed her head, which felt curiously light.

The old woman barely skipped a beat before answering, 'It's very different, but yes. I think I do like it. No one will recognise you now.'

Hannah could tell she was lying and saw her giving her strange guest a questioning look.

'Is there anything I can do for you and your brother? I could call the police if you feel you're in danger? That man was a nasty piece of work if you don't mind my saying.'

'No, no, no, please, thank you, you've been more than kind. But, if anyone asks, *please* don't say we've been here. Now, I think we'll go and do a bit of sightseeing.'

Mrs Claude agreed and walked away with a slight shake of the head.

Hannah and Jack set off on a hiking trail after breakfast. The dog dashed ahead, barking in delight at this new freedom. They walked single-mindedly for five kilometres but when they arrived at The Pinnacle, a thirty-metre-high quartzite needle rising from a fern-clad gorge, Jack barely glanced at the famous natural attraction before turning away listlessly, muttering to himself. He disappeared into the bush. Hannah glanced back for one last look at the dramatic view. In all probability she would not see the area again. She had to face the prospect that, though she would take all due precautions, she and Jack might not survive their adventure.

They spent the remainder of the day hiking aimlessly around the countryside before Hannah decided it was time to call it quits and head for home. She had hoped the physical distraction would coax Jack out of his bad mood, but all he had done was whine and complain about the heat, his sore feet and his hunger, until she was ready to push him into a convenient ravine. She stifled her temper and headed back down the mountain trail towards the B&B with Jack straggling behind her, beating the vegetation with a stick as he went.

Hannah sensed Mrs Claude would tell her husband they were fugitives and she didn't want to land the kindly couple in any trouble, but the longer they stayed put in one place the more chance there was they'd be spotted. She made up her mind to pack Jack and their meagre belongings into the car and head towards Pretoria. Perhaps Themba would hide them in Mamelodi, no one would think of searching for her in the middle of a township.

They trudged back to Toad Hall and started down the long winding footpath to the rear of the hotel. As they rounded the corner of the building, Jack stopped abruptly and peered ahead, a half-eaten orange forgotten in sticky fingers. Hannah bumped into the back of him and slapped his shoulder in irritation.

'Oh, shit!' he said.

Dudley began barking, pawing at the ground, but lay down in surprise when Jack gave him a sharp slap on the rump.

'Shut up, Dudley!'

A white Toyota was pulled up outside Toad Hall. Mrs Claude was approaching, wiping her hands on a tea towel. The driver heaved his bulk out of the car, grunting, and walked towards her.

Hannah and Jack fell to the ground and watched, immobilised by fear. They had seen the man before, in a eucalyptus plantation, and once again had a perfect view. Thanks to the stillness of the countryside they could hear every word spoken.

'Morning. Looking for a room?' asked Mrs Claude.

'No. Have you had a young woman and a teenage boy staying here lately?'

Something in the set of the bearded man's face must have caught her attention because Mrs Claude took a step backwards. A tall blond man climbed out of the passenger side, walked up to her and scrutinized her; chin thrust forward, eyes narrowed. She appeared to recognise him at once and began twisting the tea towel round her fingers, eyes fixed on his bulbous nose.

'No, I don't think so, not recently. But I'll ask my husband, he's inside.' She started heading back towards the hotel but never made it, falling to the ground with a startled look in her eyes as a bullet shattered her brain, the tea towel still clasped in her hand.

The red-bearded man stepped over her body and clicked his tongue in anger.

'*Fok!*' he said, stepping in the pool of blood leaching across the dry earth. 'I don't have time for this. The boss is already pissed off that they escaped from the house that night. I can't believe we had to come all the way back when we only just got home, but dammit, what are they doing here? There are too many fucking coincidences with that reporter. The whole idea was that we could dispose of that troublemaker Ramaposa far away from Hannah Smith's meddling eyes, and what happens, she shows up in the same area. What's the point of kidnapping the man and driving him to hell and gone if she's going to pitch up everywhere we go? It's like we can't escape her, like she knows every move we make. I'll give her one thing, she's one helluva reporter.'

Claude came out of the hotel, saw his wife lying on the ground and lumbered towards her with a howl. The blond man leaped forward and grabbed him.

'Where are they? We know they're here!'

'Who? I don't know who you're talking about. Betty? What have you done…?' The blond man shook him and slapped him across the cheek.

'The lady and the teenage boy, where are they?'

'Gone, they've gone. They left this morning. Betty!'

The killer raised his gun and shot the old man between the eyes. Claude sank to the ground next to his wife, a perplexed look on his face. The two men climbed back into their car and drove off without looking back.

CHAPTER

Thirty-one

Hannah lay petrified for an instant, her extremities seized up, incapable of moving. She heard Jack exhaling in a short sharp burst. She took hold of his hand and yanked him through the garden towards her nearby car. Dudley began to whine, woofed gently, trying to figure out why his master was crying.

They clambered in, trying not to panic. Hannah was shaking so hard she could barely get the key in the ignition and stalled twice before the engine sprang to life. Her hands slipped on the steering wheel when she swung the car round towards the driveway, skidding on the dirt and away from the two desperate heaps covered in dust. Jack sat beside her in silence.

They sped down snaking roads, away from the B&B and the dead bodies but neither of them said a word, too stunned at what had happened, too relieved it was not them lying there with holes in their heads. Hannah stopped once to consult an AA map before heading south, taking back roads through rows of citrus fruit trees and banana plantations.

'They're going to wonder where I am at school,' said Jack.

'I know. But there's nothing we can do. We need to find out what happened to your dad's - to your dad. Could you try to think about someone other than yourself just for once?'

'I only meant – never mind, you wouldn't understand,' he said, sinking down even further into his seat.

They travelled at a sedate pace, stopping often to feed Jack's insatiable appetite and for Hannah to rest her still painful shoulder.

They drove through the fertile Crocodile River valley and spent an uncomfortable night in the car in a deserted caravan park near Nelspruit before heading out again. Hannah planned on taking at least three days to complete the five-hour trip, reasoning that wandering the country for a while would throw their pursuers off the scent.

At about five thirty they stopped at a grimy roadside café for coffee and something to eat. Jack went inside and when he came out he reached into his back pocket, pulled out a rolled-up newspaper and put it silently into her hand unable to meet her eyes. The large black headline splashed across the front page made her numb.

'Local hotel owner and wife brutally murdered! Claude and Betty Marais of the Toad Hall Bed & Breakfast were found dead today outside their home near Graskop. The couple had both been shot in the head. Police are looking for a young woman and teenage boy they believe had been staying with the dead couple. Anyone with information...'

Hannah shook her head, trying to shake out the image the words conjured up.

'We should never have stayed with them. They would be alive if it wasn't for me. If I hadn't gone blabbing to the police like that no one would even have known we were anywhere near here and now…'

'There's nothing you can do about it. It's not your fault,' said Jack, but his eyes showed no compassion, there was no warmth or comfort in his words and she knew he was only saying what he thought he should.

'It *is* my fault and it doesn't make any difference what you say, it's obvious what you think and you're right. We should never have stayed there and as for going to the police, what the hell is the matter with me? How could I ever have thought following that white Toyota was a good idea? You're not the only one that's selfish and self-absorbed, are you?' she said.

'Can we go now? It's starting to rain,' said Jack.

Hannah stared up at a sky like lumpy porridge wishing she could disintegrate in a puff of smoke and blow away in the wind. She had never felt so utterly desolate and alone and knew she would spend the rest of her life remembering Mrs Claude's kindness - and her death. It would haunt her dreams for years.

Jack had had time to brood during the journey and was once again simmering.

'Now what? We can't run around the country for the rest of our lives. Someone will miss me even if no one misses you. I have friends, you know.'

'All right, Jack, I'm fully aware that this road trip has turned into an abortion. We'll find a phone and I'll call my friend Themba, he'll find us somewhere safe.

'Safe? You seriously think we'll ever be safe again? None of this makes any sense. I thought you were so cool but actually you don't have a clue what the fuck you're doing, do you?' He stopped and stared at her. 'Themba? Do you mean the garden boy? Now I know you're nuts.'

Hannah sighed, deciding to let his rudeness go. It wasn't her job to discipline him and it was obvious that like her, he only used profanity when he was under considerable stress.

'Actually, Themba's not a gardener. He's a journalist and I've worked with him for years. I trust him.'

'Well, I don't. As far as I'm concerned he could be terrorist. My mother thinks he is. Why can't I go to Joseph? I trust him.'

'Jack, we can't involve anyone else in this, especially your friend. The more people that know, the greater the chance there is we'll be found and we don't want to put anyone else in danger.'

Jack leaned back in his seat and they travelled in silence for the next two hours until finally Hannah spotted a phone box at a large roadside farm stall. She left Jack seething in the car.

Hannah called Themba, hoping he had managed to find out something about what had happened to Tom, but his news filled her with muscle-paralysing dread.

'I don't know quite how to tell you this, but Tom seems to have vanished,' he said.

'What?'

'I went round to the house and it was swarming with cops. They nearly arrested me on the spot and I had to do some quick talking to get away. A big guy, Le Roux, told me that Tom and his family are away on holiday and that my services are no longer required. Only he did not say it half so politely. It would have been too suspicious for me to hang about. As it is I think someone's been following me. My house was broken into last night and they did an excellent job of smashing it up.'

'Oh, Themba, I'm so sorry, it's all my fault.' There was no way they could stay with him now.

'A smashed up house is the least of my worries. I asked the local domestics what they knew and the maid next door said she heard shooting one night and saw two people running away from the house and driving off in a hurry, probably you and Jack. But as for Tom, no one seems to have a clue. If they do know they are not talking.'

Hannah absorbed this latest information. 'But, I don't understand. He can't simply have disappeared without a trace,' she said, trying to keep the rising hysteria out of her voice.

'No, he cannot. There has to be evidence of what happened to him somewhere, but right at this minute, he is missing. Unless – you do not think he might have staged his death do you?'

'What? No, he couldn't have, could he? I don't know. Oh my God, Themba, what if it was all a set-up, by him? What if he planned it all and it went wrong because we escaped? I can't think. What are we going to do?' She could barely stand upright as she tried to come to grips with this new scenario, which, horrifyingly, made a whole lot of sense.

'Look, do not panic yet. Give me time to do some investigating of my own. I have had Dani's phone line checked and it is clear of any bugs. I think it is best if you head straight there and lie low for a while. I will start making longer term arrangements for you.' Themba was an expert at dealing with crises and Hannah felt safe taking his advice as well as an overwhelming sense of relief that someone other than her was taking charge.

'Great, but what must I do with Jack?' she asked.

'You have to keep him with you. There is no sign of the boy's mother so I'm afraid you are his sole guardian for now.' Hannah gritted her teeth. She was about at the end of her tether with Jack.

'I suppose you're right. He's safest with me for now and I'll try not to assault him before I can return him to a relative.'

Themba gave a throaty chuckle. 'Teenagers will do that to you, but try to remember the boy just lost his father. Give him a bit of slack.'

Hannah was instantly sorry and laid her aching head on the cool glass of the phone booth.

'Call me when you get to Dani, and keep a close lookout for any suspicious cars, okay?'

'Okay. Thanks,' said Hannah and rang off, wondering how she was going to break the news to Jack that his father's body had gone astray. They had both seen what could happen to a dead body.

CHAPTER

Thirty-two

Hannah and Jack arrived back in Pretoria two days later and pulled up outside Dani's Spanish style home. Hannah was tired and dirty, her body was aching and she was desperate for a long hot soak. She'd done some thinking on the journey and had an awful sinking feeling in the pit of her stomach, a suspicion that she couldn't share with anyone. Jack as usual was hungry and in a foul mood, still annoyed that they were taking refuge with Hannah's friend and not Joseph.

Dani lived in a quiet newly built area, but taking no chances, Hannah drove round the block a few times first, eyeing every parked car suspiciously. Once she was positive no one was spying on her friend's home, Hannah used the electronic gate opener that Dani had given her previously, and drove into the spacious double garage, not wanting to leave the car in view of anyone driving past. Dani came through the interlinking door and ushered them into the house.

'Come on in. Not the dog, thanks, he can stay outside. He'll be fine in the garden. There's no way that slobbering hound is going to be let loose on my white rugs and cream sofa.' Jack shot her a filthy look.

Hannah saw her friend taking in her dishevelled appearance in a gaze that travelled down the length of her body, then back up to her gloomy face.

'You look awful, Hannah. What on earth have you done to your hair? All you need is a mini skirt and some fishnet stockings and you'd make a fortune standing on a street corner.'

Jack snorted. Hannah explained what had happened and saw her friend dart a sympathetic glance at Jack. Dani knew more than anyone else what it was like to lose a loved one, violently.

Before Hannah could say anything Dani said, 'I haven't heard anything about Tom's death at the office. That kind of thing would have been all over the news, wouldn't it? Are you sure he was dead?'

Jack's head snapped round and he stepped forward, looking hopeful. 'I don't understand,' he said fretfully. 'What reason would there be for keeping something like that quiet?'

'I heard about your flat. You know the police have been looking for you?' said Dani.

'Well yes, they would be, wouldn't they, especially since Tom is dead and his son is missing. But why would they hush it up?' Her mind was spinning and fatigue was making it hard for her to concentrate.

'Do you think he could be alive?' asked Jack, his face flushed.

'You saw his body, Jack,' snapped Hannah. 'And if I remember correctly, it was you that made me leave him there like that!'

'Hannah,' Dani reproached her as Jack's face crumpled.

'I don't know, Jack. He certainly seemed dead to me and until we hear otherwise I don't think it's a good idea to get your hopes up.' She sighed and sank onto the couch, trying to stifle the suspicion that Tom had faked his own death and was still out there somewhere intent on getting rid of her for good.

'I don't want to add to your troubles, but your dear parent has been ringing up a phone bill second to none trying to find you. You should call her,' said Dani, after a brief pause.

'No. Can't. She'll come screaming over to check that I'm undamaged and call the police.'

'Hannah, you have to. I know you two don't exactly see eye to eye, but she is your mother and she's been driving me nuts calling every hour for the last three days. You don't have to tell her where you are, just tell her you're safe.' Dani flicked something off Hannah's shoulder and pointed at the telephone. Hannah grimaced.

'Can't you do it? Tell her I'm fine. I haven't got the energy to cope with her at the moment.'

Dani disappeared to the study. Hannah glanced at Jack and was amused to see that he appeared rooted to the spot, apparently afraid to move for fear of knocking over one of the expensive vases or porcelain figures precisely placed around the room. Dani returned and stared at his dirty *takkies* and the muck he had tracked in with him.

'How long until lunch?' he asked.

Hannah rolled her eyes and grimaced an apology for his bad behaviour.

'You must be wondering how I know Hannah?' said Dani, trying to make conversation.

'Not really,' he replied and flopped on the couch, folding his arms.

'I also work for the newspaper. I'm a secretary,' continued Dani, unperturbed. 'I've known Hannah most of my life though, because we went to school together and then I married her favourite cousin Richard.'

'Oh. What does he do?'

'He died.' Jack finally reacted, contrite. 'I didn't know –'

Dani gave a swift shake of the head. 'It's okay. We married when I was only nineteen, far too young. He was doing his National Service and was sent to the Border where he was killed. What a joke, he died in a conflict where officially there was no action. We only spent nine months together before he died. Hannah never recovered. She and Richard were best friends. He was much closer to her than her brother ever was.'

'What about you?' asked Jack.

'I've learned to live without him. I had to, what else could I do? And lots of boys die up there, fighting the terrorists. That's what they call them but I'm not so sure, especially when you hear some of the things I hear at work. Don't tell Hannah I listen to the serious gossip. She prefers to think of me as a bimbo without a serious thought in my head.' Dani gazed into space for a while, a faraway look in her eyes. Then she jerked back to the present.

'After Richard died, Hannah found me a job at the paper and we discovered that I'm very good at snuffling out truffles for her.'

'What do you mean?' said Jack.

'Come on, you're a bright boy. I'm young and blonde and not bad looking they tell me, and unlike Hannah, I don't mind wiggling my hips to get what I want, no one takes me seriously. I stay as unobtrusive as possible and people forget I'm there and let things spill. I tell Hannah. Easy as that.'

'You're like a spy. Hannah's personal spy.'

Dani laughed. 'I suppose I am. And don't tell anyone, but that's the part of my job I enjoy most. Now, that look in your eye tells me you could do with a sandwich or something. Come along.'

***

Rumours and information spread like electric currents, shooting back and forth across the country looking for a place to earth. At every junction on the national grid someone could be paid to talk. There was always someone willing to betray a friend, an enemy, a family member, and the reporter had made enemies who were happy to divulge her whereabouts to the people that wanted her dead.

Setting a trap was easy. There was nowhere she could hide now, the hunter had her scent and would not retreat until she had drawn her last breath. With stealth and cunning, like all predators, the hunter closed in on the prey and when she was in sight, waited, hidden and disguised. She wouldn't realise until it was too late that she had been lured into the snare but once caught there would be no escape, there would be no pity, none of the victims received compassion, they were commodities sold to fulfil but one purpose. Money.

The reporter had to die because another mission had to be planned. One that was too big, too vital and too devastating to be foiled by a stupid woman with excessive curiosity.

CHAPTER

Thirty-three

Hannah dozed in the lounge, but could hear Jack and Dani talking in the kitchen. At least the boy was talking to someone.

'Why doesn't Hannah get on with her mother?'

'Her mother wanted a frill-covered ballet-dancing daughter but Hannah turned out to be a dirty-kneed tomboy, who preferred climbing trees to pirouetting. And she's stubborn. I remember that even as a child the more Mrs Smith told her not to do something, the more obstinate Hannah was. She has a long scar on her thigh from falling off the roof after her mother told her quite emphatically that a beach umbrella is no substitute for a parachute. But that's Hannah, has to try it out for herself.'

'Why isn't she married. She's not bad looking, not for someone so old, I mean.'

Danni laughed. 'Good grief, Jack, she's not exactly ancient. And she was engaged once, but the guy was an arsehole, sorry, but he was. He was all smiles and charm in the beginning, but the minute the ring was on her finger he turned into a monster, possessive and jealous. He hated her being friends with Richard, thought he was a rival or some *kak* like that. And then he hit her.'

'No!'

'Yes, it happened twice and she threw his ring back at him and she's been a bit, shall we say wary, of guys since then.'

'*Jislaaik*. My dad would never hit my mum, not even when she's being impossible.' Jack sounded subdued.

Hannah stood up, deciding it was time to put an end to this dissection of her life and went into the kitchen.

'Having a good *skinner* about me, you two? Dani, would you do me a favour and please let me have a long hot bath before I fall asleep right here on your clean carpet?'

'I'll even let you use my favourite bubbles because as you know, I live to please you and pander to your every whim,' said Dani, with a mocking bow, but before Hannah could make her way to the bathroom, the phone rang. She groaned.

'Now what?'

Dani's eyes widened. 'Hello, Frik. This is a surprise.'

Hannah sat up and waved her arms, indicating that Dani keep her and Jack's presence there quiet.

Dani pulled a face. 'No, Frik, I haven't seen her for a couple of days. I think she's off somewhere following a clue or whatever it is you reporters do to get a story. You know Hannah, a law unto herself. She'll pitch up when she's good and ready.'

Hannah scowled and then smiled as Dani held the receiver away from her ear and she could hear the loud squawking on the other end of the line.

'Calm down or you'll do yourself an injury. It's not like you to freak out about Hannah. No, I don't know where she is, would I lie to you?' said Dani. 'And shouting at me isn't going to make me tell you anything different, Mr Van Niekerk.' She rolled her eyes as Frik continued to berate her.

'Ask him about Tom,' mouthed Hannah.

'Frik,' said Dani, 'you know that policeman, Tom, that Hannah is friendly with? Well, you wouldn't happen to know anything about him? It's just that I thought I heard he'd been injured in an accident.' She listened for a minute or two.

'Thanks anyway, it's not important. It's only because Hannah's friendly with him that I wondered. You know what I'm like, always getting my wires crossed.'

Dani reiterated that she had no inkling of her friend's whereabouts and rang off.

'Well, first of all, Frik's in a proper strop about you disappearing without a word and I'm pretty sure he didn't believe me when I denied knowing where you are. You'd better watch out for that guy, Hannah, he's a thug.'

'I know he is, that's why I don't want him knowing where I am. What about Tom?'

Jack sat up straight, bottom lip caught between his teeth.

'He said it was strange my asking about Tom, because one of his informants, a cleaner at the police station, contacted him last week saying he'd heard a rumour about Tom being attacked, but Frik didn't take much notice because he was sure that if it was true the news would have reached him via the official channels.'

'If we can find out where this guy lives we can track him down ourselves and ask him,' said Hannah.

'We'll have to pay.'

'Yes, we will, but it's worth it if we learn anything about what happened to Tom.'

'What's the plan?' asked Jack.

'I'll do a bit of prying tomorrow and see what I can find out. Frik's sure to have the info somewhere, and if I go to work early enough, I can have a quick snoop through his desk. Now, you two look as if you're asleep on your feet. I think an early night is a good idea for all of us.'

An impatient Hannah and Jack spent what seemed an endless day waiting for Dani to return from the newspaper offices the following day. In their excitement neither of them remembered to keep an eye open for any suspicious vehicles and Hannah forgot that she had intended calling Themba to tell him of their plans.

CHAPTER

Thirty-four

Dani's snooping proved fruitful and she returned home aglow with success.

'I thought that investigating was supposed to be difficult. It took me less than five minutes to find this information on Frik's desk. The whole mission gave me such a buzz I think I might just take it up professionally.'

'You're lucky he didn't see you. He's a dangerous man and he wouldn't take kindly to you sneaking stuff off his desk without his knowledge,' said Hannah.

'Oh relax,' said Dani. 'He didn't see me and now we have these.' She produced a handful of photocopied papers that contained information about Frik's informant and a terse handwritten note about the cleaner's latest communication concerning Tom. She handed them to Hannah, who examined the notes, then found and spread out a map of Pretoria on the dining room table.

'That's Lynnwood Road, which leads out of the city, and there are quite a few plots out there that have huts on them. It looks like Frik's informant rents one of them on this farm here, *Mooiplaas*.' She jabbed a spot on the map with her finger.

'Imagine calling your home 'Pretty Farm'. Typical boer,' said Jack.

'I can't understand why anyone would want to live out there, in the middle of nowhere,' said Dani.

'*Want* isn't exactly the right word though, is it?' said Hannah.

'What do you mean?' asked Jack.

'It's not like the blacks that live on those farms have much choice about where they stay thanks to that wonderful piece of government legislation called the Group Areas Act. They aren't allowed to reside in the white areas where they work unless they live in servants' quarters and the townships are so far away that many are unable to afford the travel costs, so they just take any hovel they can find as close to work as possible. At least my parents provide a room for Grace to live in and she doesn't have to travel in.'

'Priscilla catches the bus every day and she has to leave home at five o'clock in the morning to get to work on time. My mom gets crazy when she's late,' said Jack, frowning.

'Okay, enough idle chatter. This is what I propose. We'll head off tomorrow morning when we can be sure this Silas Mhlape is home for the weekend,' said Hannah, excitement curling in her belly. She glanced at Jack. He seemed to be standing up a bit taller and had a confident gleam in his eyes. Only the slight quiver of his hands betrayed his nervousness.

'I don't think Jack should come with us. It might be dangerous,' said Dani.

Jack sprang forward and poked his finger under Dani's nose. 'No way! You're nuts if you think you're going to leave me out of this. It's my dad they killed and I'm coming with you, don't you dare try to stop me.'

Dani wiped a speck of Jack's spit off her face and with a bit more persuasion agreed to let him go along. He was probably safer with them in any event.

Perhaps if Hannah hadn't been so tired, she might have been more suspicious of the source of the information and the ease at which it had come her way, but all she wanted was to have some kind of closure about Tom. For her own sake and for Jack.

Dani and Hannah talked as they made their way out of the city to the veld on the outskirts of Pretoria. Jack sat in isolated silence in the back, fingers drumming on the back of Hannah's seat and his jiggling knee knocking her back. She reached behind her and slapped his leg in irritation.

The countryside was golden in the haze of autumn, bird calls shrill above the noise of the engine. The trees that bordered the road were bronze, ochre and yellow, creating a picture card that Hannah wished she could capture in paint. Buildings became sparse as they drove into the custard countryside, gritty Transvaal dust catching in their throats.

After a drive of just over half an hour, they spotted a farm gate with a rusted sign dangling off one hinge declaring that this was *Mooiplaas*. Hannah pulled over on to the roadside with a scrunch of tyres on dirt and surveyed the scene.

'This looks like the place. Dan, I don't like the idea of leaving the car out here. We'd come back and find it gone or the tyres missing. Would you mind keeping guard while Jack and I have a look around?'

'Suits me fine. If you think I'm going to come wading through cow pats in these shoes you can think again,' said Dani, and settled back in her seat, opening the window and lowering the sun visor. 'I could do with a nap after all the excitement of being a spy.'

Hannah opened the gate and walked over the cattle grid. Jack followed her closely. The air was dry with a healthy smell of livestock, while horses in a nearby field skittered around carefree, tails swishing and manes floating. Soft lowing and the occasional whinny on the breeze made the scene even more tranquil, in stark contrast to the churning Hannah felt inside.

They carried on down the road alongside a corroded fence. Jack wrinkled his nose.

'Phew, smell the eau de Cowlogne. Who is this guy we're looking for exactly?'

'He's a cleaner that works at the police station and he might have some information about what happened to your dad. It's a peculiar thing, the black staff is allowed access to the whole station, have keys to all the doors and yet everyone acts as if they're invisible as well as deaf. That's why people like them make such good informants. It's a lucky break for us.'

Jack grabbed the barbed wire fence and pulled it towards his body, then let it shoot back with a twang that reverberated the length of the field. The strain was showing itself in livid pimples that seemed to have erupted out of nowhere. Hannah had to stop herself from telling him not to pick. He had a wary look in his eyes too that troubled her and his moods seemed to be becoming even more erratic. At times he appeared to be handling events with almost adult maturity, and hope had certainly made him more sociable, but Hannah wondered how long the good mood would last before he suddenly he relapsed in a pique of childish impulsiveness.

Jack had been innocent and unspoiled when they first met, then he'd been propelled into an adult world in which he was ill-equipped to cope, experiencing things in the last weeks that no one, least of all a child, should ever have to see.

They walked down the dirt road for ten minutes until they saw a large thatched-roof house with a green lawn and sweeping brick driveway. This was the owner's home and the name T.Nel was inscribed on a fancy wrought iron gate constructed in the shape of two ostriches back to back.

'There,' said Hannah, pointing towards the left of the house. 'That's what we're looking for.'

Not far off was a group of buildings set to one side. They were square and flat-roofed; typical of servant's quarters the country over. The sun had baked the earth hard and a little grass verge divided one home from the next. A skinny chicken pecked hopefully in a forlorn vegetable patch and a pink doll with only one eye and missing a leg lay abandoned on the ground. The smell of paraffin hung in the still air.

The buildings appeared in good repair, although they were very basic, with only a door and two small windows for each room. A makeshift shower constructed out of a hosepipe and the nozzle of a watering can was rigged up

K.A.EDWARDS

on the side of one of the buildings. A torn and mouldy shower curtain erected to give some semblance of privacy hung lopsidedly on a piece of wire.

An elderly black woman approached. She wore a faded yellow dress with matching headscarf and was carrying a baby on her back secured in a bright red blanket.

'Hello…*dumêla*,' Hannah greeted her in Sotho, hoping that using the woman's own language would make her more co-operative. The old lady gave a toothless smile.

'*Ê, dumêla*,' she responded. The baby's liquid brown eyes stared at the white intruders.

'I'm looking for Silas. Is he here?' The old woman seemed puzzled.

'No, madam, Silas, he does not live here any more.'

'We were told he lived here with his mother. Are you his mother?' asked Hannah.

'If he doesn't live here? Where does he live?' interjected Jack.

'No, madam, I cannot tell you anything about Silas,' said the old woman, fear on her face.

'Cannot or won't?' said Jack, moving forward.

The woman recoiled as if he was about to strike her and the baby began to cry. Jack was taken aback and put his hands in his pockets self-consciously.

'Sorry, *mmê*, I won't hurt you, but it's very important we find Silas. Please tell us where he is. We'll pay you,' he said.

The woman shook her head rejecting the bribe and tightened the blanket. She walked away, glancing back over the screeching baby's head in case they followed. She went into one of the rooms and closed the door but stood at the window watching them. A curtain in one of

248

the other buildings twitched. The old lady wasn't the only one observing them. Hannah shivered as she felt the unseen eyes assessing them.

'You aren't just going to let her go, are you?' asked Jack.

'She doesn't know anything, and even if she does, she's too scared to tell us. There's something fishy going on here.' Hannah looked at her watch. 'Well, this has been a wild goose chase. I knew it was too good to be true Dani finding the information so easily. Come on, let's go before she starts worrying.'

They trailed back to the car across coffee earth.

Hannah and Jack hadn't been away more than half an hour but Dani was soundly asleep, sitting in the same position as when they'd left her. The windows were thick with condensation even though the door was open. Her left arm had slipped off her lap and dangled on the floor. Hannah put a hand on Dani's shoulder and shook her. Her friend's head lolled to one side.

'Dani, come on, Sleeping Beauty, wake up.'

Hannah's stomach folded in and her knees buckled. Jack made a soft sound behind her. Hands trembling, she slid the soft woollen jersey off Dani's shoulder. A deep ruby stain spread down her neck and onto her pink silk shirt, blood bubbling out of the wound in her head and it was then that Hannah noticed the spray of red across the windscreen interspersed with gelatinous globules of grey matter. Dani wasn't asleep. She was dead.

Icy calm descended. Hannah covered her friend tenderly and rearranged her hands on her lap. Then she stood, picked up her handbag, and turned towards Jack who was vomiting nearby, grabbed him by the arm and walked away.

At the corner of the road she turned back for one last look at Dani lying limply like a broken rag doll, her face soft and serene, a strand of hair caught between her lips. Hannah fancied she saw a slight smile on her lips as if she had died in the middle of an enjoyable dream. A dove flew overhead cooing.

'Ag, my friend, my lovely friend. I'm sorry, I'm sorry. Good-bye, Dani. Forgive me.' Her chest constricted and tears pricked her eyes.

It was imperative that she maintained a grip on her emotions and screaming hysterics were not on. She walked down the road on legs that belonged to someone else. Jack clutched her hand, a small moaning noise escaping with each lumbering step.

CHAPTER

Thirty-five

Hannah walked without thinking, her limbs heavy and her chest thudding. Jack was white and clammy, beige lips clamped together. Hannah's hands shook so violently that she nearly wrenched Jack's arm out of its socket. She twisted her ankle, pain shooting up her leg.

'Shit, shit, shit,'

Jack pried her fingers loose and put a supportive arm round her, in charge again. He had a way of going into a different gear whenever the need arose and Hannah was very grateful for it at that moment, knowing that if she had been on her own she would probably have curled up on the side of the road and waited for the killer to find her and finish her off too.

'I think I bit my heart in half,' said Jack.

Hannah gave a weak smile. She knew exactly what he meant; her heart was in her mouth too. They walked down the road, came to a bus stop and after some deliberation decided to wait for the next bus to take them back into town.

'It's a long walk and no one's going to attack us in full sight. Will they?' said Jack, far too calmly. 'I don't know about you, but my legs won't carry me very much further.'

They sat on the hard wooden bench. Hannah rested her head against the cool steel board advertising Fanta Grape. The air was still and silent. No sound but the beating of a pulse in her forehead and the surging current trying to explode out of the veins that held it captive.

'Bastard,' said Hannah angrily, 'I had a bad feeling about that information coming from Frik, but I still went ahead. All Dani ever wanted was to be helpful, and now she's dead.'

Her hand was tacky and a cloying sweet smell rose, making her abdomen tauten. Jack slipped his hand into hers, curling his inflamed fingers round her blood-sticky ones and they sat there in the fading sunlight. Hannah was trembling with grief and anger, recognising finally that she and Jack were truly alone now. Except for the killer that had followed them half way across the country and then killed her friend simply because she was trying to help or –

Jack spoke her thoughts. 'I wonder if they killed Dani by mistake. I mean, I wonder if they thought they were killing you. Your hair's blonde now and you look alike, sort of, you're prettier, but they wouldn't know it was her and not you if they were in a rush. You know?'

Hannah's mind raced. She felt as if she was trapped on an out of control roundabout, spinning, spinning. A group of giggling teenage girls arrived at the bus stop, confident that they were the only ones that mattered, that had the right to be there. They threw their school bags down and lolled on the bench next to them, leering at Jack while a cursory glance dismissed Hannah in an instant. Jack blushed, removed his hand from Hannah's and moved away.

Hannah stared at the graffiti-covered bus stop. Mary loved Peter. She had to think. What should she do next? Where could they go? What would happen to Dani when she was found? Rage surged through her, buzzing in her head, molten lava cascading through her nervous system.

Frik was behind her friend's death, of this she was certain. He had laid a careful trap and she had obligingly stepped into it, only someone had blown it and killed Dani instead of her and she would not rest until she found out who was behind it all. A calculating intelligence had directed everything that had happened so far, and she had more than an inkling of who it was.

After what seemed an eternity a bus arrived in a cloud of carbon monoxide fumes. Hannah and Jack climbed aboard, scanning the other passengers in case they were recognised, and rode in a stupor into town. The bus jerkily stopped and started through tree-lined suburban avenues, the grasping branches of the tunnel of Jacaranda trees scouring and tearing at the bus's roof with human-like screeching sounds that scraped at her sanity until she wanted to scream. The vehicle trundled on unconcerned about the lives of its passengers, disgorging or acquiring more at every stop. Hannah tried to focus.

They could not go back to Dani's house and her own flat was still full of builders. She noticed with a jolt that they were driving down the streets she had explored on her bicycle as a child. She knew each one intimately, where it led and how long it was. She could picture every house and sidewalk and pet dog that had chased her and could vividly recall the faces of the children that had lived and played there. She knew which houses the Afrikaner enemy inhabited. In her childhood it seemed as if they had infiltrated themselves insidiously into every part of her English world. She could still see the bushes that had given the best cover for hiding from these enemies so stones and insults could be thrown back and forth between the gangs of children, separated and made adversaries by their cultures and the language they spoke. Back then they were more concerned with still fighting the Anglo-Boer War, than they were with racial tensions between black and white.

Hannah found herself swamped by memories, but a simple solution occurred to her.

'Jack, my folks live near here and they have a shed at the bottom of the garden that no one ever uses. We can hide there for now, until I think of what to do next.'

Finally, when the forty-five minute journey they had undertaken since the discovery of Dani's body began to feel like it would never end, the bus stopped opposite Hannah's old primary school. She stood up and jumped out, struck by a momentary nostalgia as she noted the energetic pupils chasing a soccer ball round a field, a teacher nearby with hands on hips remonstrating with a scruffy little boy. Hannah smiled, remembering the happy days spent there.

'Come on, it's not far.'

They trudged up the hill and stopped outside her parents' house. Jack gasped. 'Sheesh, Hannah, you never told me you were rich.'

'My parents are rich and my mother likes everyone to know it.'

A large Cape Dutch style house with white walls and green shuttered windows below the attractive gables rested imposingly in a skilfully landscaped garden, the scent of flowers filling the air. A sprinkler swept a graceful arc of water across immaculate emerald lawns, the soft rhythmic clicking creating a subtle percussion accompaniment for the melody of the birds in the trees.

Relieved to see no cars parked outside the huge double garage, they slunk up the bricked driveway and round the side of the house towards the back garden where an enormous sapphire swimming pool pungent with chlorine glistened in the sunshine. Three white filigree metal sun-loungers with plump colourful cushions reposed neatly beneath a vast thatched umbrella. A bricked braai area with a bar counter made from a railway sleeper had a set of matching stools neatly arranged along its length.

Hannah led Jack past the rows of grapevines and plum trees, round the well-tended vegetable patch and towards a small wooden shed, almost hidden amongst the shrubbery at the far end of the garden. She pushed the door open, jumping in fright when it creaked.

'This was my secret place. I used to come and read in here when I was a kid. It was a good place to hide from my brother's bullying too. If we're lucky, some of my stuff should still be here,' she said.

She grinned when she saw a raggedy pink blanket and a large pillow with a pink 'Love Is…' pillowcase stuffed into a corner. She picked up a bundle of crocheted blanket and a copy of Little Women fell out, the pages well thumbed and the cover worn with use. She dusted off a rickety rocking chair and sat down. Jack dragged some sacks together to make a seat for himself. They stared at each other, unsure what to do next.

'Is there anything to eat?' asked Jack.

CHAPTER
Thirty-six

Jack confronted Hannah later that night. 'Here we are hiding out like criminals, again. I'm beginning to think you don't know what you're doing. We're sleeping in a shed and it's flipping freezing in case you hadn't noticed! And it smells. You don't seem to be very good at making the right decision, do you? You said we'd be safe with Dani and now she's dead. And what about Dudley? He's alone at Dani's house, locked up like some common criminal. He never sleeps outside and –'

'Get a grip. He's a dog. He'll be fine. Once Dani's body is found, the police will be all over her house. They'll find Dudley and take care of him.' She put her head in her hands and a tear trickled down her cheek when a vision of Dani lying dead in her car burst into her mind.

Jack stared out of the grimy window and pulled a spider web off the corner of the cracked glass. 'It's not like you even know what to do, is it? I thought you were supposed to be some hotshot reporter. Why can't you figure out how to get us out of this mess? Why don't you do something instead of just sitting there crying like a baby? And I'm starving, haven't you got any food?'

He watched a small grey spider scuttle across the windowsill, followed it for a moment then crushed it with one ruthless stab of the finger. He wiped its squashed remains on his jeans then banged his hand against the wall and sank to the floor, his head on his knees. Hannah mopped her face and stood up.

'You want food, do you? Well, there's a vegetable patch outside, why don't you go and dig up some carrots or something and there's plenty of fruit on the trees. There's a tap with a hosepipe attached round the back of this hut so at least we won't die of thirst. I'll creep into the house later when my folks go off to their usual Saturday night Rotary braai and see what I can find in the cupboards. When it's dark we can have a quick dip in the pool to get rid of the dirt but we'll have to make sure we aren't seen,' she said.

They slept fitfully that night, with Hannah waking at every sound in their dirty bolthole or outside in the streets. Between dozes, she had realised something: she would have to tell the boy about the files Marie had given her.

'Jack, you know the killers we saw aren't from the police?'

'Yes, I'm not an idiot. If they aren't from the police, or at least connected to the police, who are they?' he asked.

'I shouldn't be telling you any of this, Jack, and you have to promise you won't tell anyone?'

'Please, who would I tell? You're practically holding me prisoner here and I haven't spoken to a real person since before…'

'I have…had a contact high up in the Defence Force, and she gave me a document she had stolen from her boss. Someone must have found out that she'd given it to me because she was killed later that same day.'

'Killed? By who?'

'Well, officially they say she committed suicide, but I don't believe them, not having read the document.' She stretched her shoulder and wiped a grubby hand on her jeans.

Jack stared at his feet, slumped against a wheelbarrow. He picked up a carrot and nibbled the end.

'What are you waiting for? Tell me what you know.'

'I still don't know everything, there are gaps, stuff I'm not sure about. It's all happened too fast and -'

'You're too thick to work it all out?'

Hannah felt her hand itching, but restrained herself admirably, she thought.

'I've written everything down in chronological order to try and make sense of it based on what I know from Marie's document and from what I've discovered since.'

Hannah handed him the girly writing pad she'd found in a metal tin concealed in her secret hiding place in the shed.

Jack was ashen and his voice trembled slightly as he read the notes she had made and tried to absorb what she had concluded.

'Death squads? You think a death squad killed my dad?'

'Like I said, I'm not sure of everything,' How could she tell him she knew his father was somehow involved, if not an active member, of a death squad?

'We need to think about what to do next,' said Hannah. 'We can't carry on hiding out here. Sooner or later the gardener will notice that his prized carrots have been dug up and my mother will stop blaming the missing food on the maid and get suspicious. Anyway, I don't think she has enough groceries in her cupboards to feed you for much longer. Any ideas?'

'Yes, actually. The garden boy, Themba, maybe he knows something.'

'He might. And he's not a gardener, he's a reporter, I thought I told you that.' said Hannah, who had been thinking along the same lines herself. She was still edgy and irritated by his behaviour and couldn't resist having another dig at him, hoping to put him in his place. 'Jack, it's a bit insulting to call a grown man a garden 'boy'.' He glared at her. 'I know, I do it myself when I forget, but I just thought I'd make you aware that even though it's a commonly used way to refer to a black man in this country, it's not particularly polite, nor is calling your maid the 'girl', especially as your servants are older than your parents. It's a demeaning and belittling custom.' She couldn't have sounded more pompous if she'd tried and it had the desired effect.

Jack went red and gritted his teeth. With an effort, he said, 'Go and call him. I'll wait here.'

Hannah slipped out and after making sure no one was home, crept into her parents' ostentatiously furnished house and made a couple of calls, one to Themba asking him to meet her at the park. Next she raided the cupboards before running back to their hideout.

The shed was damp and musty, filled with gardening tools and fishy-smelling fertilizer. A few opened tins of baked beans and spaghetti in tomato sauce lay discarded on the ground, a mouldy loaf of bread and two empty boxes of Longlife milk: pitiful indicators of life as a fugitive. A fly buzzed urgently against the window desperate to escape into the clean air outside.

Hannah and Jack spent the evening going over Hannah's notes endlessly, looking for anything important they might have missed. Jack became more and more bad tempered as the evening progressed and she was relieved when he finally fell asleep, emotionally and physically exhausted.

Hannah woke early the next morning. She glanced at Jack sleeping in the corner. The face resting on a pile of soiled rags was the colour of old dishtowels, little lines that had not been there before wrinkled the corners of his eyes and a pathetic droop hung at the edges of the soft mouth. He stirred drowsily and groaned, the sleepy eyes filling with tears. She considered waking him, but decided against it and scribbled a note telling him where she was going and to stay put until she returned. She propped it up on the workbench where he would be sure to see it.

The floor was grainy under her feet, crackling as she crept past the sleeping boy, opened the door and slid like a wraith across the lawn and into the street.

CHAPTER

Thirty-seven

Themba was pacing impatiently when Hannah finally arrived at the park. She'd never realised before how difficult it was getting around without a car. Buses seemed to run according to whim, never sticking to the timetable and sometimes not turning up at all. Forced to walk, Hannah now had a large blister on her heel. By the time she pushed open the gate to the park she was sweaty and bad tempered.

'Walking, Hannah? I did not realise you white people knew how to do that,' said Themba, a lopsided grin taking the sting out of his words.

'Only when we must,' said Hannah, kicking off her shoes and stretching her burning toes. They sat down on the whites-only bench after checking to make sure they were alone.

'What have you found out? Are you okay, you look like you're about to explode?' she asked Themba, who was fidgeting uncharacteristically.

'I have lots to tell you, let me get through it all before you start asking questions, okay?'

'Okay.'

'First of all, about that list of names you sent me. It wasn't too difficult to find out that all of them, without exception, were trained as part of Special Forces. They're all experts in weapons amongst other things and most are trained snipers. None of them serve in the forces any longer. All the killings we're investigating may be part of a covert op known as Operation Barnacle and it's a lot harder to investigate. But, after extensive enquiries and a couple of threats, I've managed to track down someone that's involved, a dying man, who is willing to talk.'

'Great. When?' asked Hannah. 'My brain feels like it's un-spooling. I don't know how much more of this I can take.'

Themba contemplated her for a moment then said, 'I have a car parked down the road, we can go now if you want to. I think it's best we get on to it as soon as possible. I don't think he has much time left.'

Hannah didn't need further urging. 'Let's get cracking.'

Hannah stared out of the car window. The road they were travelling on meandered westwards through the foothills below the Voortrekker Monument standing astride its authoritarian perch. She had the sensation that it was manifesting its censure of their mission through the dark thunderclouds gathered behind the stout building and the occasional flash of lightning slashing the sky.

The suburb of Valhalla, on the western side of Pretoria, was calm and ordinary, painted white houses interspersed between new, more modern clinker brick homes squatting in large gardens. It was a middle-class suburb occupied by mainly military personnel, being close to Voortrekkerhoogte Air Force Gymnasium and Zwartkops, a dreary military area.

They drove past Waterkloof Air Force Base before turning into Valhalla, travelling down the quiet streets and past the English primary school, where little girls in royal blue tunics and crisp white shirts played hopscotch and scampered up and down the jungle gym, and a wild pack of small boys in khaki shorts and shirts raced after a soccer ball.

They found the innocuous red brick house they were looking for easily enough. The garden was unkempt and as they drove up a scruffy giner-haired mongrel ran to the fence yapping. It was delighted when they opened the gate and walked down the overgrown path, jumping up and licking Hannah's hands.

A cheerful black nurse opened the door and ushered them inside. The house was dimly lit and smelt strongly of disinfectant, cooked cabbage and death. The nurse gave Themba a curious look and they exchanged a rapid conversation in Sotho. Satisfied that they didn't intend any harm to her patient she led them into a darkened room. While it was now a serene bedroom with a view out of a large window, it must once have been the lounge. An old-fashioned glass display case brimming with china knickknacks and animals made out of seashells stood in a corner next to an upright piano with sheet music scattered across the keys.

A skeletal man lay in the bed barely distinguishable from the rumpled bedclothes. He had a drip in his arm and the table next to his bed was full of bottles of pills, a half-eaten apple and a jug of sickly-looking juice. A pile of blood and sputum soaked tissues lay on the floor. Hannah averted her eyes and tried to focus on the body in the bed.

The nurse swiftly cleared away the evidence of the man's illness muttering soothing words while she plumped the pillows and propped the man up efficiently before bustling out of the room carrying a full bedpan. Hannah almost gagged and took a deep breath.

'Mr Snyman? My name's Hannah Smith and I want to ask you about Operation Barnacle.'

The man's rheumy eyes opened wide and he gave a hacking cough.

'Why does a pretty young thing like you want to know about that? Why should I tell you about the evil I committed? You can't stop it now. No. The things I did will be buried with me when this tumour finally eats the rest of me.'

Hannah grasped his hand. The parchment-thin skin was almost transparent and she could feel the fragile bones beneath. She saw her reflection mirrored in his eyes, and somehow with what seemed immense strength of will, he turned them away from their view of what awaited him in the next life, to focus on her face.

'Mr Snyman, Danie, I need to know everything you can tell me about Operation Barnacle because it's not over. It's getting worse and you're the only one that can help. Please, tell me.'

The dying man closed his eyes briefly before staring intently at her, his gaze sweeping across her, lingering on her lips. Hannah sat motionless, waiting. Whatever he saw reflected in her face gave him courage and he started to speak.

'I did it all for money. Blood money.' He coughed again, his bones seeming to knock together as he gasped for breath and Hannah was afraid he would die before telling her what she needed to know. Themba proffered a glass of juice and Snyman drank thankfully. Revived, he continued to talk.

'It's a good thing I'm dying because if they ever found out I've talked I'd be dead in an instant. The things we did, the crimes I've committed…' His eyes glazed over as he stared into space, remembering. Themba touched his shoulder and he was back.

'We did evil things and we weren't accountable to anyone. I was only interested in the money and for a few thousand rand I killed many, too many men and women and even children. And now what good is the money? It sits rotting in the bank and I will soon be rotting in the ground. My penance and my punishment.'

'Tell us how it all works,' prompted Hannah. 'How did you get involved?'

'I was recruited soon after I left the army and started working for a large engineering company. They said I had skills that could be useful in preventing industrial espionage and they were right. They trained me well, the government, gave me the abilities they needed to make me an efficient killer. It helped that I'm amoral, sad but true, and they exploited that quality in me. What was I supposed to do once I left? Killing was the only thing I knew. When I was offered the chance to do what I loved, how could I refuse?

'I can shoot a man between the eyes from eight hundred metres and I never asked questions, never needed to know who or why. I'm the perfect employee.

My business was to make sure I didn't miss and I seldom did. Occasionally all I had to do was drop something in a drink at a party or braai, an overdose of muscle relaxants or a poison, it didn't matter to me. It was easy.

'It wasn't long before I realised that the people I was killing all had something in common. They weren't businessmen or industrial spies like I was told they were, they were mainly black and they were all working against the government, communists and terrorists and whites that were too liberal. That was our task, the clandestine elimination of enemies of the state. But you can't ask too many questions – not if you value your life – and I never cared who I killed, as long as I was paid.

'From time to time we were flown to a neighbouring country for an operation. That's where the terrorists are, you know. And we would kill them and get rid of the bodies. A couple of times our mission was to take a pile of body bags and dispose of them. They were terrorists that died while being interrogated or during an illegal military action and we were the clean-up crew.

'Sometimes we buried the bodies, sometimes we burned them, and sometimes we put them in the unit's aeroplane, flew out to sea and dumped them in the ocean. Usually they were already dead, but sometimes they weren't. If they were still alive we injected them with a sedative before throwing them out, but I don't know if they were all dead by the time they hit the water.

'Once one of the victims started to struggle and I had to strangle him with my belt, but I don't often kill with my hands, I don't like to touch flesh. I prefer a weapon or a drug. They'll tell you that South Africa doesn't have a chemical weapons programme, but it's a lie. Where do you think we got the Tuberine and Scoline to kill them or the Ketelaar to put them to sleep first? We even laced chocolates with anthrax, poisoned umbrellas tips and had screwdrivers fitted with poison-filled cylinders. Clothing was often infused with lethal chemicals. The whole idea was that an attack would look like natural causes.

'All those enemies of the state, gone just like that. I thought I was doing my country a service.' He rolled his head to the side and spoke directly to Themba, blue fire in his eyes.

'You lot aren't very different though, are you? You also kill in the name of freedom. You plant bombs and you *toyi-toyi* down the streets waving your cultural weapons, as if dancing can make up for rampaging mobs looting and smashing and beating innocent bystanders. Your children complain they have no education but they demolish their schools and burn their books and they assume this will make things change, but all it does is destroy the small chance they have for a better future.

'You believe that because you are oppressed your killings are justified. You place tyres filled with petrol round the necks of traitors and you set them alight and as they burn to death screaming you dance and shout and treat it like a celebration. You think blowing up buildings and massacring one another will force the government to change its policies. They watch the bodies burning and the villages being destroyed in tribal vendettas and all it does is reinforce their opinion that you're a bunch of savages that could never rule a country. How different are you from me, really? You and me, we're the same person in a different colour skin.'

Hannah and Themba sat motionless as the man spoke, lost in horrific memories, trying to make sense of his life now that it was at an end. Perhaps he felt talking about it would purge his soul.

'We work for private companies with no connection whatsoever to the government or South African Defence Force,' Snyman continued. 'We're all part of a top-secret unit that has its own money to get the weapons it needs and also to gather intelligence information. We're a paramilitary organisation, a group of civilians trained and organized in a military fashion. We learned from the best, the KGB, CIA, Mossad, the finest covert operatives in the world and the most efficient and effective killers.

'Most of us have no idea who else is in any cell. Some of us are part of the outer circle, men and women who aren't conscious of their connection with the SADF. Then there are those that are part of an inner circle made up of full-time members employed openly by the South African Defence Force.'

'Marie's boss, the general, must be one of them,' murmured Hannah.

'The unconscious members think they're working for a business corporation, the police or one of the other security force units. In the beginning I thought I was an assassin for the wealthy, but they were all enemies of the state and I was the government's dupe.

'There's a whole bunch of hit men out there that have no idea they're employed by the SADF. They do it for the money and are common businessmen and civilian companies and even ordinary people that don't know who they're working for. There are so many people willing to be killers. You'd be surprised if I told you about some of them, people you'd never suspect. I've heard rumours that there are other units too, even more secretive than ours.

'I thought, there are always people that need to die, for business or ideological reasons, it doesn't matter why or who because surely they deserve it and I had to earn my living. But women and children, no. Now I have another killer inside me and at last I am accountable, to God. May He have mercy and forgive me, because I cannot forgive myself.' He began to weep, each sob struggling to express itself through a chest crowded with cancer.

'He'll forgive you,' Themba reassured him. They sat in silence broken only by tortured breathing until the man fell asleep, his breath rattling in his chest, his yellowed bony hands clasping the sheet. Hannah and Themba gave their contact details to the nurse and crept soberly out of the room. They sat reflecting in the car. Snyman's story confirmed and clarified much of what Hannah already knew, but it didn't make it any easier to digest.

A motorbike revved and it shot past them and she jerked upright. 'What about Dani? I can't believe it, I forgot about Dani. What did you find out?'

Themba turned towards her with an inscrutable expression on his face. She braced herself, dreading what he was about to tell her.

'A passing motorist discovered Dani's body yesterday and the area has been cordoned off as an investigation gets under way,' said Themba. 'They are looking for you, it is probably a good idea if you stay in hiding for now.'

Hannah agreed, afraid of what would happen if the police took her in for questioning. She had a gnawing pain inside her that she couldn't ignore but was unable to surrender to either. She didn't have time now to grieve for her friend, to regain her equilibrium. She would have to leave that until later.

'Why don't you go back to Jack at -?'

'My mother's house, well, actually the shed at the bottom of the garden. But, there's something else I should do first,' said Hannah, feeling the last ounce of energy leaking out of her bones.

'Now what? I don't think I can take much more of this,' said Themba, for the first time beginning to look strained.

'I contacted my office this morning and they gave me a message from some guy that was in the army with Dani's husband, Richard. His name is Paul Fourie and I have to meet him at Church Square in about an hour, but I suppose I can put it off for a couple of days,' she said.

'Do not do that. You never know, he could be helpful, especially if he is in the army. We could use a bit of friendly muscle on our side,' said Themba. 'I will go and stay with Jack for now.'

'You'll have to climb over the back fence instead of going in through the front. We don't want my mother setting the dogs on you. Themba, keep a close eye on him. I have a horrible feeling his father is still alive and if he is, he'll do anything to get his son back.'

'Well, that would certainly explain why no one found his body,' said Themba with a frown, 'It makes sense now, all of it. I knew we could not trust him,'

'I don't know how I could have been wrong about him. He seemed genuine.'

'It is not your fault. He shared just enough with you to keep you on side and calm your suspicions. Now, you better get off to that meeting,' said Themba, his eyes filled with compassion.

All Hannah wanted to do was go home and sleep for a week and she was worried about Jack. She vacillated for a minute, but finally decided to meet Fourie as planned and get back as soon as possible. Jack would be safe with Themba.

CHAPTER
Thirty-eight

Hannah sat on the steps below the statue of Paul Kruger, the leader and president of the old South African Republic and regarded as the father of Afrikanerdom, waiting for Paul Fourie. Church Square, the historic centre of the city was busy, the air thick with car fumes and the scent of commerce. She could see the turreted Palace of Justice, scene of the Rivonia Trial, arguably the most famous political trial in South Africa's history. It was during this trial that Nelson Mandela and others were charged with treason and subsequently incarcerated. Now the city cared nothing about the history that had been created there over the years. It went about the business that mattered in the present, caring little about what was past or what was to come.

Hannah blushed inwardly as she remembered the offhand way in which she had treated the receptionist who answered her call to the office earlier that day. The middle-aged dowdy woman fired suspicious questions at her, demanding to know where she was and adamant that she present herself to the office at once, but Hannah had cut her off and asked about any messages. There'd only been the one from Paul Fourie.

A large blond man dressed in well-worn combat boots, jeans and a bottle-green jacket approached her. He had a freckled sun-tanned face, a friendly smile and very short hair, not that different from the average white South African male. As he advanced, his Ego deodorant bit at her senses and for a moment Hannah had a feeling of déjà vu. He reminded her of someone that she couldn't quite bring to memory. He proffered an enormous calloused hand.

'Hi, Hannah, how are you? Thanks for seeing me. I hope you don't mind me calling your office like that but I wanted to see you when I heard about Dani.'

'Hello, Paul. Thanks. It was a terrible shock.'

'Ja, it was. Richard and I were together at Tempe for Basics and then for about six months on the Border. We helped each other out, before they blew him up. It was hell up there and I liked him a lot. I couldn't believe it when he stepped on that landmine, he was always so careful, but that was Richard, just had to run back to save a fallen comrade and what good did it do? They both died. He was a good oke so I was sorry to hear about Dani. I've always liked her.'

'Me too.'

'Bloody kaffirs. Probably killed her for a few lousy rand. Wonder what she was doing out there on her own though?'

Fourie watched her in anticipation but Hannah said nothing, waiting for the right moment to ask him if he'd heard anything about Operation Barnacle during his time in the army. She impatiently made small talk for a while and though the man seemed pleasant enough, she was surprised that he and Richard had been friendly. Richard had tended to avoid the '*braai*, beer and *boerewors* boys' as he called them. He preferred the intellectual type and it was obvious Paul Fourie would be far more at home wallowing in the mud of a rugby field than in the philosophical meanderings of Dani's late husband and her cousin.

They sat on hard wooden chairs in a seedy coffee shop not far from Church Square. The walls were decorated in deep purple brocade and the atmosphere was thick with cigarette smoke and clandestine afternoon affairs. The coffee was weak and lukewarm, the melktert on her plate lumpy and unappetising with the cinnamon sticking to her palate and making her cough. The longer they talked, the more nervous Hannah became.

'Hannah, as a journalist, how do you like the way things are going now, hey? I mean, with all those bleeding-heart liberals threatening to surrender the country.'

Hannah remained tight-lipped since he obviously didn't share her opinions and she wasn't inclined towards getting into a political debate with him. She didn't care what he thought and since she would probably never see him again, it wasn't necessary that he knew what she thought.

'You're in the PF? What rank are you now?'

'Ja, that's me, a career soldier in the Permanent Force. I was promoted recently, I'm a Major now.' He oozed conceit and Hannah obediently put on an admiring expression.

Secure in the knowledge that she was swooning with admiration, Fourie continued his diatribe.

'Someone has to stop this country from being sold up the river. Next thing we know, they'll free the terrorists like that Mandela bastard and him and his armed wing will kill us all. Like they don't know that apartheid is the only way to handle the racial question in this country.'

'You think forced segregation and oppression are necessary?'

Hannah's skin began to prickle and the back of her neck was soon wet. This meeting wasn't going according to plan and with a sudden upsurge of bile she realised that Fourie reminded her of the ex-fiance that had tried once too often to beat her into submission.

'Ja, man, it's for their own good. We, as Christians, have to protect ourselves from the kaffirs and communists. That's what Richard died for, isn't it? I mean we all know that even the Lord doesn't consider the blacks part of the human race. They are condemned to being drawers of water and hewers of wood in the Bible.'

'I think that's down to interpretation,' said Hannah.

'No, man, if you think about it logically, their hair is rough like an animal's and their flat features are also more like an animal than a human so they certainly aren't part of the same species as me. It's nothing personal, but they have to understand that the whites built the country - made it what it is today – and that we are not simply going to hand it over to the blacks or worse, the reds.' He gave a little grunt. 'We all know the Russians and the Chinese have their sights set on us. They've already taken over half our neighbouring states – that's why we have to stay strong to defend our borders and keep on building our war machine. Let them come, that's what I say. Our weapons are more advanced, and there isn't a soldier in the world that compares to our guys.'

Hannah heard the passion in his voice and knew she had to get away from him as soon as possible. She couldn't possibly ask him about death squads run by the South African Defence Force now. He was probably in it up to his eyeballs.

She was starting to feel very weary, her shoulder was aching and the hammer behind her left eye had begun to pound in earnest. She decided to put herself out of her misery.

'I must be getting back now, Paul. It was very kind of you to call me.' She wanted to get back to Jack and hopefully never see Fourie again, but no such luck. He grabbed her arm preventing a speedy escape.

'Wait, one more cup of coffee. You can't let me come all the way here full of sympathy and then push off without at least telling me what you know about how Dani died. Okay, I'm morbid, but Richard was my friend and I did carry what was left of his body back to base.'

'Okay.' Hannah sighed. 'I don't know much about Dani's murder and I thought when you contacted my office that you could help in some way since you were Richard's friend and that perhaps you had heard something.'

Fourie gave her a strange look, his pupils dilating slightly.

'The police could probably be more help than I could, and anyway, wasn't she killed in a robbery?'

'Yes, I know,' she said, feigning female helplessness. 'I'm very upset about Dani and I didn't know where else to go. I don't know why I thought you could help. I guess any port in a storm.' She pretended to cry, covering her face with a trembling hand.

Fourie was ill at ease and muttered, 'I need fresh coffee. Where the hell is that kaffir waiter? I suppose I'll have to fetch it myself.' He pushed back his chair and strode off to give someone a piece of his mind.

Hannah thought she had conned him quite well. He returned carrying two cups of coffee but seemed edgy and distracted, looking around and plucking at the neck of his khaki T-shirt. Hannah took no notice, sipping the coffee as fast as she could, eager to get away. Fourie was restless and shifted around in his chair, whinging about how uncomfortable it was until she wanted to slap him. She took another sip of her coffee and grimaced, realising that it tasted bitter.

'What is this?' she asked, frowning at the self-satisfied expression on his face. She never did get to finish that second cup.

Hannah opened her eyes to a banging head and blackness. She sat up but wished she hadn't when a wave of nausea rolled across her. Her tongue was dry. She swallowed, lay back and waited for the undulating queasiness to pass. It dissipated after a while and she sat up again putting a hand to her head, inside of which was a loud brass band, and tried to make sense of her environment.

Hannah realised she was in the back of a *bakkie* travelling fast and she could see the dim flash, flash, flash of evenly spaced streetlights through the small window. She clambered onto her knees and tried to look out, but could see nothing much except sporadic lights indicating that they were passing through a well built-up area.

Without any distinguishing landmarks that she recognised they could have been anywhere, and she had no idea how long she had been unconscious. She tried to see the time on her watch but it was too dark.

She hammered on the partition separating her from the driver and was met with deafening silence except for the gentle sound of the radio playing Bles Bridges and two people talking in the cab of the van.

'Hey,' she yelled. 'Let me out!' She banged on the partition with her fists but the driver and his companion took no notice.

Looking out of the window proved futile. When the lights disappeared completely she was engulfed in darkness. Soon she could no longer hear passing cars, in fact there appeared to be hardly any traffic at all. Hannah sat down on the metallic floor and shifted around trying to find a comfortable position, but little ridges dug into her bottom no matter how she tried. She felt around blindly and her grasping fingers rested on what she discovered to be a pile of newspapers. She made a cushion for herself and sat on it, hoping the carbon monoxide fumes filling the back of the *bakkie* wouldn't kill her.

Hannah could have kicked herself for being so gullible. Paul Fourie – she'd never heard Richard mention him before he died, and had only met him briefly at the funeral. She hadn't even bothered to find out if they actually had known each other on the Border. Fine investigative journalist she was, stepping obligingly into the net.

They drove on and on through the night and Hannah tried to listen for anything that would indicate where they were, but gave up eventually. The road surface changed from time to time until finally it felt as if they were travelling along a dirt road.

The van bumped and jolted for approximately two hours and then the road evened out. Every now and then a light glittered and she lurched to the window to try and see out, but it was too dark. She arranged her newspapers into a makeshift bed and lay down. Might as well try to get some sleep as she would need her strength if she was going to succeed in escaping at the first possible opportunity.

Surprisingly, she slept soundly - probably the after-effects of whatever drug it was Paul Fourie had slipped into her coffee.

Hannah woke with a start in the early hours of the morning when the van went over a bump in the road and looked around disorientated. She shivered, rubbing her arms and wishing she had her coat and handbag. She wondered if they were still at the restaurant or if Fourie had them. She could feel the cold seeping through the floor and an icy draught coming through the cracks in the van sides. She knocked on the partition.

'Hello, I'm dying of cold in here!' The small black-painted window separating her from the cab opened and a thick, extremely large jersey was tossed through. Then it closed again and she heard the catch click firmly shut. Gratefully she pulled on the oily-smelling jersey, shuddering to think where it had been, and even though it was scratchy against her skin at least it was warm. This was no time to worry about her tender sensibilities.

Grey light started filtering in through the window. Hannah stretched as best she could and pressed her face against the glass but couldn't see much except that they were travelling through the countryside. She spotted grain silos next to dry khaki mealie fields and dusty veld streaking by, and assumed they were now in the Orange Free State but for all she knew they could have been driving round in circles all night. Her mouth was dry, her teeth fuzzy, her shoulder seized up stiffly.

The *bakkie* slowed down. Hannah scrambled on to her knees realising they were passing through a town. She saw a white church with a tall spire and desperately searched for someone walking by. As soon as she saw anyone, she would scream blue murder but it was too early. Not a soul was in sight.

They drove out of the town and into the countryside once more. She kept watch, trying to memorise the landmarks in case she managed to break out. An incandescent blue shimmered in the distance that she thought was the sea or a dam. They turned on to a bumpy road and she had to steady herself on the van sides to prevent from falling over. The *bakkie* stopped and Paul Fourie flung open the back doors and peered in at her.

'*Uit*,' he said in Afrikaans, motioning aggressively. Hannah climbed out gratefully and stretched, shaking her feet to get rid of the pins and needles. They were on a farm. She could see sheds and rusty pieces of farm machinery and two huge black Rottweilers barking furiously in a large enclosure. There was an empty chicken coop nearby and a large rusted water tank next to a steel windmill.

Fourie roughly pushed her towards a ramshackle stone building. She tripped on the rocky ground and nearly fell. He pushed her again, charm and smiles gone.

'Move. In there.'

Hannah staggered through the wooden doorway but didn't have time to look around as she was hustled unceremoniously up a dim narrow stairway and shoved into a room. The door slammed and she heard it being locked.

She was in what seemed to be a large cupboard. A narrow bed took up three-quarters of the room and the dirty beige mattress that sagged sadly on the flaccid springs was bare. A grubby pillow and a thick grey blanket with frayed edges were neatly folded on the end of it. The only large glassless window was well and truly boarded up with the planks nailed securely down and her spirits plummeted even further. She wouldn't be escaping out of there. Hannah squinted through a long thin crack between the strips of wood and saw a patch of blue sky and the top of a blue-gum tree.

She sat down and surveyed her bare prison. In one corner was a jug of water and a chipped enamel cup. It smelt as if something had died nearby, and she wrinkled her nose, clamping down on her imagination, visions of dead and decaying bodies would not comfort her now. The floor was worn beige stone, a piece of threadbare olive-green carpet remnant tossed in the middle of the room. A white bucket stood in the corner, and she realised with dismay that she was to use this as a toilet.

Hannah lay down wearily, pulled the blanket across her shivering body and started piecing her abduction together with the other things she knew. She knew Paul Fourie worked for Tom and was sure it wouldn't be long before he himself came up to see her. But she was wrong again, something that seemed to be becoming a habit.

CHAPTER

Thirty-nine

On the third morning Hannah was lying staring at the ceiling when the door opened. Paul Fourie and another man came in and stood next to the bed. The second man was tall and bulky, with tightly belted khaki trousers, which strained to close under a flabby belly. His face was red and she could see the broken veins running across his cheeks; his dung-coloured eyes stared at her, unblinking.

Hannah sat up, her fingers tightly grasping the hem of her shirt. Their stillness frightened her more than if they had threatened her, so she boldly stood up to ask what they were going to do with her.

Hannah didn't even see the blow coming. She flew backwards across the bed and cried out, raging pain in her face. She shut her eyes and waited for the spasms to subside.

'Where is it? Who did you tell?' She heard the question through a haze and turned her head, wishing the room would stop seesawing. Fourie was twisting an ornate gold ring on his finger. He grabbed her arm and yanked her upright. She collapsed against him as he tightened his grip on the tender flesh of her upper arm. His eyes were expressionless, the pupils dilated and she wondered if he took drugs.

'Where is it?'

'What? I don't - ' The blow to her chin caught her off guard once more, her knees buckled and she slumped to the ground. As she tried to sit up, she saw his foot moving forward and instinctively contorted her body. His shoes had hard toes and caught her below the ribs. Shafts of agony shot across her stomach, tears sprang into her eyes and she gasped for breath. Hannah lay still as the pain washed over her and then tried to sit up again. A large foot descended on her fingers.

Fourie stood looking down at her and ground the heel of his shoe into her hand. She realised with a sickening sense of unreality that he was enjoying himself. His skin was greasy, covered in a thin coating of sweat. He towered over her and his mouth curved upwards. She licked her lips, tasting the saltiness of her blood.

'You'll tell me. I can keep it up much longer than you can resist.'

The next few minutes blurred into a purple mist as the two men took turns beating her about the head and punching her in the ribs and kidneys. How was it that men seemed to know the exact spot to hit to cause the greatest pain?

Hannah had been beaten before, but nothing compared to this. Her body was ablaze. She clenched her jaw to stop from crying out, realising that the louder she cried out, the more they enjoyed it.

Then they stopped. Fourie motioned to the other man and they left, leaving Hannah lying on the rock-hard floor wondering how the hell she had ended up like this. So this was what it felt like to be on the wrong side of the authorities in South Africa.

Hannah dragged herself on to the bed and lay in a shattered heap. Her eye had swollen closed and throbbed in a primitive rhythm. She felt her ribs and was relieved to find that, despite breathing being torture, nothing seemed broken. She wiped a handful of blood from under her nose where the warm smell was making her feel ill, and probed the stinging cut on her cheek. Her fingers were distended and painful and she could make out an imprint from the sole of a shoe on the back of her hand.

She curled up covered in the hard blanket, its wool rubbing abrasively against her skin, lay as still as she could, taking only shallow breaths and finally fell into a pain-filled sleep.

When she awoke, she waited in a state of constant fear that they would come back. Every footfall and noise had her twitching and cowering on the bed in case it was the two men returning to take up where they had left off, but they didn't come back and the day dragged by in peace. So did the next and the next.

Hannah lost track of time, the days blended into one another and she became more and more disconsolate at her predicament.

They kept Hannah shut up in the tiny room for two and a half weeks and in that time barely a word exchanged between her and her captors. In the mornings the door was opened and a tray of food, usually watery porridge and dry bread, was pushed in. The same happened for lunch and supper. The menu was boring but adequate and if she never saw another baked bean, it would be too soon. It was no use complaining so she ate everything - from the porridge to the withered apples that occasionally appeared. Once in a while, if she behaved, she was served a cup of strong, too sweet, lukewarm coffee.

Once a day Paul or the other man with cropped brown hair and muddy eyes allowed Hannah out of the room and took her to a bathroom at the end of the passage. She was given fifteen minutes to bath in the icy water and complete any other necessary ablutions. They had made one concession to her requests, which was to provide a toothbrush, a used one with bent and worn bristles, but she was grateful for small mercies. Dirty teeth would have been more than she could bear. She had soon discovered that this brief sortie was the only time she was allowed to use the bathroom, so she was careful not to drink too much after she had had her daily outing, not at all keen on using the rusty bucket they had so considerately placed in her room.

Hannah surveyed her face in the cracked mirror and winced at her reflection. Her eye was still half shut, one corner sagging, and she wondered if it would ever be normal again. The ring on Fourie's hand had cut deeply into her cheek and she knew it would leave a scar. She opened her mouth, revealing a chipped front tooth, and realised that she resembled a worldly-wise hooker, especially since her hair had begun to grow back, brown roots showing between the brassy blonde streaks. Her bruises were changing from purple to yellow, which added to the beauty of her complexion.

The days dragged by and Hannah marked each with a scratch on the wall - something she had seen done in the movies. It was very effective. Her two guards did not speak to her at all and she had the impression they were waiting for something.

Once the memory of the beating she'd received started to fade, she recovered some of her spirit and began asking questions. When the door was opened one morning, she spoke to Fourie.

'Why am I being held prisoner? You can't keep me here forever. People will be looking for me.'

A blank look met her query. She tried again.

'Well, if I'm going to be here indefinitely, how about a book or magazine to read? Come on, Paul, show some humanity.'

Without a word, Fourie belted her across the mouth, splitting her lip and loosening a front tooth. She didn't ask again.

Hannah wondered how people could survive in solitary confinement for years and years. She felt as if she was going crazy and as she thought back on all that had happened, the despondency inside her began to ferment.

For a long time she drifted in and out of troubled feverish sleep, telling herself over and over how useless she was. Finally her natural resilience reasserted itself and she decided to pull herself together as it was evident she was here to stay. And to her relief, they had decided for some reason or other, not to try to beat any more information out of her.

Hannah began to learn that patience was indeed a virtue, and it did not come naturally to her. She agonised over what had happened to Jack and Themba when she failed to return to the shed and wondered what her parents were thinking at her lack of communication once more. She knew exactly what her brother would think.

CHAPTER

Forty

Days merged one into the next. To keep herself occupied, Hannah sang the scores of every musical she had ever seen, from *The Sound of Music* to *My Fair Lady* and *West Side Story*, and recited poetry out loud. She made up stories with happy endings and did endless mathematical calculations. Twice a day she exercised as briskly as her painful body would allow, stretching and jogging on the spot. Anything she could think of. She spent hours every day trying to loosen the planks over the window and anticipated her brief sorties to the bathroom with manic pleasure.

Whenever she was out in the passage she tried to see the rest of the building. It wasn't a house as such and she reached the conclusion that she was in a granary or grain storage facility. She'd noticed a room next to hers but the door was closed. Once it was open and she saw that it was a storeroom with a number of cardboard boxes piled up high against the walls. She couldn't see what was at the bottom of the stairs. If she tried too hard to peer down she was jabbed hard in the back and once, hit in the face. She gave that up.

At night she listened to the two men talking downstairs. She could only make out a word here and there but none of the fragments of conversation made any sense. She discovered that the other man was called Gerrie and they talked about their chief as '*die baas*'. Hannah knew exactly who they were.

The boss would soon be here and she longed for that day to arrive, even though the wait was postponing her inevitable execution. She had realised by the fifth day that Jack was not going to come galloping in to rescue her this time and resigned herself to her fate. She became encased in depression and lay immobile on the narrow bed. Hannah spent much time during those two and a half weeks thinking about Jack and Dani.

She considered her relationship with Themba and how lucky she'd been to have him alongside while she struggled to make sense of what was happening in the country. She wondered if he was safe and if he had been able to return home to the township.

In a sudden paroxysm of anger at her foolishness in allowing herself to be caught, she stood up and kicked the bed, venting her frustration on its sturdy metal frame. It skidded across the floor, hit the wall and toppled over. She went to set it straight and the seeds of an idea began to germinate.

Hannah turned the bed upside down. It was an old-fashioned model with springs that were stretched and slack from years of use criss-crossing the base, so it was an easy task to pull one of them loose. She tugged at it until it was unwound, smiling in satisfaction at the piece of wire she now held in her bruised fingers.

She went over to the window and was about to insert it between the planks to make a lever when she heard the key in the door. She jumped back to the bed, stuck the wire under the blanket then lay down feigning boredom.

When Hannah returned from her excursion to the bathroom, she hauled out the spring and went back to the window. If she could insert it between two of the planks and hook one of them, she might be able to lever it away from the window. It was a futile exercise. The spring wasn't strong enough, bending every time she applied any pressure. She gave up in frustration and left it dangling between the two planks and sat down. She glared at it and had another idea, one that might conceivably work. Why she hadn't thought of this before she didn't know, but decided to blame the beatings for her lack of ingenuity.

Hannah was filled with exhilaration as she plotted and schemed. She made her plans. It all depended on timing. And luck. She spent the rest of the day in frenzied activity, preparing.

She ripped the canvas mattress covering and made strips from the hard material. These she plaited together into a rope - once again a trick learned from the movies – and spent most of the night working on the window. She used her piece of spring to prise the nails out of their wooden home. All those seedy crime novels her mother so despised might save her life.

Her fingers were aching and raw from the wire and splinters of wood, her fingernails chipped and tore as she gouged away at the sturdy steel nails, flecks of blood and small pieces of skin trapped in the wood evidence of how hard she was working.

Finally one of them sprang loose. Encouraged, she set to work removing the remaining four. She sank back sweating, and picked up the little stack of nails and dropped them into a hole on the floor. She ripped back the plank and peered out of the window. The two massive black dogs growled up at her, showing their fangs. She shuddered at the thought of what would happen if those teeth got hold of her soft flesh.

Hannah could see freedom, smell it like an aphrodisiac and it sent her blood quickening round her body. She tore off a piece of her shirt and threw it out the window, quite impressed with this little theatrical touch, hid the canvas rope under the mattress, propped the planks back in place so no one would notice her handiwork, sat on the edge of the bed, and waited.

When Gerrie took her out, she pretended to stumble as they reached the stairs. She dropped her toothbrush, and as she bent down to pick it up, he bumped into her backside and swore. Catching him off balance, she rugby tackled him low and hard and he crashed down the stairs, arms and legs flailing.

Hannah scurried to her room slamming the door behind her, and with trembling hands removed the planks. She tied one end of the rope to the bed frame, dangled the rest out the window, opened the door and ducked stealthily into the spare bedroom next door. She crept in behind the stack of cardboard boxes and waited. She wasn't stupid enough to go anywhere near the dogs, but they wouldn't know that. As she had hoped, they fell for it.

Gerrie bellowed to Paul, 'She can't have gone far! Find her! Let the dogs loose!'

Hannah waited until the sound of their voices and the barking of the dogs faded into the distance, crawled out of her hiding place and went downstairs.

She moved through the deserted building, pushed the front door open and, seeing no one around, raced off in what she hoped was the opposite direction. She couldn't risk running across the open veld but had nowhere else to go. She ran towards a low wall, vaulted over and lay trembling behind it.

She caught her breath, and then, bent double, began to inch along away from the house. The farmer was very conscientious and his wall was well kept, running the entire length of his property. Her back was aching as she peered over the top, but she nearly cheered when she saw that she had reached the road. Now, if only a car would come by she could hitch a lift. No such luck.

Hannah waited, willing a car or truck to appear, but saw no traffic at all. On the other side was an expanse of mealie fields. She darted across the road, plunged over a barbed wire fence, and pondered which direction to take.

The fencing ran parallel with the road and from what she could see stretched on for a considerable distance. She went left, deciding this was as good a direction as any, and started a backbreaking crawl through the rows of corn. She was sweat-soaked, breathing in short, jagged gasps. Red-hot pains shot along her lower back and blood from her knees trickled down her legs. Urgency drove her on until she reached the end of the field and breaking cover, she stepped out into the open.

The ground was becoming rocky, with tufts of scrubby veld forcing their way up through the copper earth. She could see the outline of grey-green mountains in the distance. Her calves felt like lead, and she wasn't sure she could carry on so she found a vantage point behind a large boulder and sat down to rest. She had a clear view of the road and watched for any sign of Paul or Gerrie.

After catching her breath, she stood up knowing she had to keep moving as far away from the house as possible. Ignoring the pains stabbing her body and her frozen feet, having long since lost her shoes, she continued.

Time ceased to exist for her as she went on and on through the approaching night. Eventually she could no longer see where she was going and as she stepped forward, her feet shot out from under her and she pitched forward into shadowy wetness. She had slipped on a mossy rock and fallen into a shallow, sluggishly flowing river. She was face down, hands and knees stinging from the fall onto the stony bottom. She came up spluttering and dragged herself to the edge, soaking wet.

Her teeth started chattering and she was furious with herself for not being more careful. Now she would probably die of pneumonia before she reached safety. She dragged her shivering body forward and blinked. A watery light swam in front of her eyes. She started walking towards its warmth but it suddenly went out.

Hannah opened her eyes. She was warm, wonderfully warm. In the distance she could hear someone moaning and struggled up through the fog in her head. She realised it was her own voice and tried to tell herself to be quiet so that she wouldn't wake Dani who was sleeping in the car, but didn't have the strength.

She drifted off again only to waken in fright with something thick and woolly round her neck. She tried to fight it off but it only wrapped itself tighter. She screamed for help but no one came. Then she remembered the boy. He would save her but she couldn't remember his name. Dudley was barking outside her window. She thrashed around trying to escape and yelled for Tom to come and help her. He opened the door and came into the room but when he leaned over the bed, he had a hole in his head. He was wearing khaki trousers and his stomach was too big for them. He towered over her and she moaned again. He put a cool soothing hand on her forehead and mopped her face with something soft and damp. She started crying. Her neck was wet and she couldn't find her cousin but his friend started chasing her with big dogs. She was so scared, so scared, so scared...

Hannah woke to a quiet white world. She was lying in a bed covered in a thick grey blanket. It was bunched up and wrapped around the top half of her body. She disentangled herself and sat up, looking round in disbelief. Her world tilted as she realised that she had been here before. Some heroine. She had escaped straight back into the clutches of Paul and Gerrie. She was tired and felt so despondent that all she could do was sink back and close her eyes.

The door opened and Paul came into the room with a triumphant curling of his mouth.

'Thought you'd know by now you can't get away from us. You better pull yourself together because the boss wants to see you.'

As he closed the door he taunted her, 'Won't be long until you get what you deserve.'

Finally. The boss.

CHAPTER

Forty-one

Hannah sat on the edge of the bed, waiting. She rubbed the goose bumps on her arms and wished they would get on with it instead of keeping her in suspense. She gripped the blanket and tried to arrange her face into a calm expression when she heard voices and footsteps coming up the stairs. The door was unlocked and pushed open and she could see three figures outlined in the doorway.

Fourie wiped the sweat off his brow. 'It's about time you were punished for sticking your nose where it doesn't belong,' he said. 'You're right to look nervous, just seeing your stupid face makes it all worthwhile. I'm going to get great pleasure watching you die.'

She felt more relieved than afraid. Finally, everything would be revealed.

Hannah stood up, expecting to see the stocky figure of Tom, but instead Laurel drifted into the room smirking, and with an expression in her exquisitely made-up eyes that made the reporter feel as if a serpent was squeezing her lungs. Fourie and Gerrie, both quivering with triumph, took up positions on either side of their leader.

The room swayed and Hannah's mouth went dry. Laurel? That wasn't right. It was Tom. Wasn't it? What one earth...?

'Hello, Hannah, surprised to see me? Not so clever after all, are you? I was sure you'd figured it out. But you didn't, did you?' She laughed, her creamy throat vibrating, her vacant eyes more alive than she'd ever seen them before. Hannah was incapable of speaking because her tongue was stuck to her palate. She felt a trickle of sweat running down her back and clasped her shaking hands firmly together, trying to appear confident, as if she'd known all along, as if she wasn't rocked to the core by this revelation. The truth was she was now more afraid of Laurel than she'd ever been of anyone in her life. She had seen the fruits of this woman's labour and did not relish becoming another notch on her belt.

Her head was foggy, thoughts leaping about erratically as she tried to make sense of it all. 'Maartens', the name on the list, the holder of the secret bank account, was Laurel, not Tom. And it all made sense now; the military background, the dotty behaviour, the odd disappearances, the strange strength Hannah had sensed, even the netball skills, it all fitted. Tom had said she was an excellent shooter, but neither of them realised she was exactly that, a deadly sniper who could hit a target with barely a thought. The gun Themba had found belonged to her, not Tom. Her stomach heaved. The woman was a psychopath, more cunning and intelligent than they'd ever imagined and Hannah was now wholly in her grip.

Laurel leaned closer, minty-breathed and sweetly scented.

'Now, if you'll tell us who else knows about the document that traitor Marie gave you, we can bring this matter to an end. It isn't necessary for you to suffer any more, but I have to make sure my activities don't get made public. I'm sure you understand.'

Hannah stared at Jack's mother, standing there in a diaphanous lilac dress smelling of violets, a saccharine smile etched on her not-so-vacant face, and nearly vomited up her last meal.

'No one. I never told anyone.'

Laurel moved slightly. Fourie's arm shot out and a hand like the flat side of a cricket bat struck Hannah's cheek. She opened her mouth but no sound came out.

'Not even Tom? Surely you told Tom? You and my husband were such very good friends and I think Tom started becoming suspicious of his loving and oh so dotty wife long before you arrived on the scene asking questions, though he never said anything. His eyes were different when he looked at me. At first I thought it was because he was having a crisis of conscience about you.' A far-off look floated into her eyes and she spoke, almost to herself. 'I think it was the butterfly trip that did it. I should never have left that man's body in the Magaliesberg like I did. I was too careless, in such a hurry to get back and find out what he was up to with you. I think he worked it out shortly after that. He was a better detective than you'll ever be, Hannah.'

For a moment Hannah struggled to process what Laurel was saying, and she remembered the vague sense of something immense she had been unable to grasp after seeing the body in the Magaliesberg. The butterflies. She had seen them swarming but had dismissed their connection to Laurel. Her limbs felt heavy and she sat down on the bed, wondering how much more Laurel knew.

'How is Jack, by the way? I hope you hid him somewhere safe after Tom died. I'd never have thought you were callous. Who'd have thought that you'd abandon a man in his hour of need, so to speak.' She castigated Hannah with a shake of the head. 'When I think what you put my Jack through, making him leave his dead father and run off with you. You'll have to be punished.'

'We followed a car all the way from Pretoria because Jack recognised one of the men from the attack on your house, and we watched a man being executed in the plantation. Only, we didn't know it was you. It was you, wasn't it?' said Hannah, desperate to regain control and justify her actions and decisions.

Laurel went very still and her face tightened. Hannah could see thread-like wrinkles on her mouth beneath the mauve lipstick, a regular Revlon cover girl. She ran a pink tongue over perfect pearly teeth and contemplated Hannah with her head inclined slightly.

'I see. You know, I had a feeling we were being watched. I'm very good at sensing when things are wrong and my men did search for you up there, especially after you were stupid enough to go to the police. What on earth were you thinking? Surely you know the police aren't to be trusted? You should never have let my boy see something like that. Poor Jack. He thinks I'm such a scatterbrain, constantly forgetting him and getting lost. Well, I had to have some excuse, didn't I? I had business to attend to and I couldn't very well take him with me, could I?'

'And by business you mean?'

Laurel tut-tutted and shook her head. 'Don't pretend to be stupid because we both know you aren't, you know what business I mean. It's quite lucrative actually, but rather sad at times. All those lovely men and women and a poor child now or then, that was especially depressing. And Tom.'

Her eyes filled with tears. One spilled over and she wiped it away with a pink-tipped finger, playing the grieving widow to perfection.

Then her voice hardened. 'But that's over now. It never helps to linger too long on the gory details.' She stopped again and scrutinized her professionally manicured fingernails, clicking her tongue on noticing a small chip.

'Tell me where my son is, Hannah.'

Hannah shook her head. Laurel sighed and signalled to her henchman, who set about methodically and systematically beating out the last ounce of resistance.

Through broken teeth and a split lip Hannah panted, 'I don't know where he is. He could be anywhere. He was at my mother's but wouldn't have stayed hidden there for long when I didn't come back. I'm sure he'll have found somewhere else by now.'

They gave her one last kick in the ribs for good luck and left her alone. She knew they would find Jack eventually, but she had done her best to put them off for a while at least. She clung to the hope that someone as skilled at vanishing as Themba was would secrete him somewhere safe.

Hannah lay unmoving. It hurt to breathe. It hurt to think. Even her eyelids hurt. She tried to sit up and cursed herself for thinking she was brave enough to do so. Brown saliva clotted in her mouth as she picked a piece of broken tooth off her tongue with an aching finger. She saw a multi-coloured mist in front of her that changed colour like a kaleidoscope every time she closed her eyes. She blinked a few more times to see the psychedelic patterns and colours then drifted into semi-consciousness covered in an undulating cloak of pain.

Once again the days crept along, hope fading in degrees with each sunset. She surrendered to the pain of her body and her memories and lay lethargically, trying not to think of her fate or that of her friends.

Gerrie threw a cup of cold water over Hannah. She sat up, spluttering. Laurel was standing next to the bed with a smirk on her face.

'Oh good, you're awake. You've been asleep for days.' She smiled, trying to look sympathetic.

Hannah wiped her face and waited.

'Well, we found Jack. He's not as bright as you'd have thought and was hiding at that annoying friend of his, Joseph, I think his name is. His stupid mother calls me 'floral Laurel' behind my back and thinks she's funny. I might just send my men round there to have a word with her. That would teach the fat, vacuous bitch a lesson.' Her face was positively glowing.

'It's almost a month since you went off for your meeting with Paul Fourie and apart from your handbag being found in a coffee shop near Church Square, you seem to have dropped off the earth. So with no parents and no - whatever it is you are to him - my son had to find somewhere else to stay. Oh, he spun Joseph's parents some line about me and Tom being away visiting a sick relative and has been living there quite safely. Until now.'

Laurel was pensive and every time she faced her, Hannah caught a whiff of flowery perfume. The soft rose had turned out to be a Venus flytrap and she, the fly, was well and truly caught.

The door opened and Fourie entered. He whispered something to Laurel who went very still and then stood up and walked behind Hannah, who tensed and waited for a blow. Instead, Laurel put her hand on Hannah's back and started massaging, strong fingers kneading the taut muscles in a circular rhythm. Hannah pulled away, her skin crawling. Laurel pursed her lips in displeasure.

'Everything has changed. I have to be decisive and sacrifices must be made if I'm going to carry out the most important mission of my life. There's no time for sentimentality and I can't focus if I have baggage.' A chill settled in the air as she spoke in a blank, measured tone. 'Jack is dead, Hannah. He had an accident on the way home from school this morning. Killed instantly. Tragic, a young life gone in a flash.'

Laurel's voice disappeared in a discordant vortex of muffled sound and spots began jumping in front of Hannah's eyes. Ice-cold pinpricks tripped across her skin and she could hear a distant ringing in her ears. She tried to stand up but lead weights were dragging on her arms and feet and she couldn't move. A sad feeling of inevitability crept over her and Jack's forlorn face floated in front of her, a spectral accusing vision. Until that very moment she had not truly accepted she was going to die.

'Why, Laurel? I don't understand it at all. You have everything. You had a wonderful husband and Jack, how could you sacrifice them like that? Is it political? Do you hate those with different views from yours so much that you feel the need to kill them off?'

'Oh don't be so melodramatic, Hannah. Politics have nothing to do with it whatsoever; although I can honestly say that I don't have much time for the blacks and their constant complaining. They're parasites, every last one of them. It's business. You have a job and I have a job because we have to make a living. It's all about money and there's such a lot of it about, if you know where to look. Why else get involved? Oh, it was a thrill the first few times and I do love it when a plan comes together and how else could I use my special skills?' She giggled. 'There's always a sense of achievement at a task well done, even you must agree. But, it's only work, exceedingly well paid and if it helps rid the country of undesirable elements at the same time, that's an added bonus.

My Tom, dear man that he was, would never have understood why I have to do it. I'm afraid he rather neglected me, Hannah. He was too busy, although I pretended I didn't mind, and Jack didn't have time for his dear old mum either. He liked you though, didn't he? No, no, don't deny it, I could see his adolescent heart beating faster every time you came into the room. And it's obvious you felt the same. Now don't be coy, you got such a lovely flush on your cheeks when he spoke to you.

Stirred up some primal urge in you, did he? I'm not sure how healthy that is.' Her reptilian eyes narrowed, glinting.

'You, Miss Nosy Reporter, have spoiled my plans. I have a big job coming up, a bigger, more lucrative job than any I've had before. I've spent years preparing for this and you nearly ruined it for me. Very naughty.' Her voice changed register.

'Now, my dear, who else knows about the document? I can't have my business threatened and anyone who knows about me will need to be dealt with quickly and quietly.'

Paul was twisting the heavy ring on his finger, ready to use it on her again so she gave in. Laurel would find out anyway and she was too weak to take another beating.

'Only Tom knows – knew. But, I thought it was him, Laurel. I saw the name Maartens on the list Marie gave me and I thought it was him. I never suspected…how could I?' Her head dropped and she waited for the contemptuous chuckling to stop.

'How hilarious, and there I was thinking you were such a good reporter. But my Tom was a clever man and I'm sure he figured it out before he died. I'm certain he suspected something before though. I wanted to kill him myself, I am his wife, but like every good leader I know when to delegate and my men are willing to do anything I ask. It's such a pity because I would have liked to say goodbye and I could have ensured his death was quick and painless. He deserved that at least.'

Laurel inclined her head like a tiny sparrow, bemused.

'He was such a good detective Tom, but he never once realised that someone always died when I was away or lost. I even did some business while he was watching Jack playing rugby a few months ago. He thought I was working in the tuckshop but I was off putting a bullet in the back of a man's head and he didn't suspect a thing. Isn't that funny? I had to stop from giggling when he dashed off to investigate and was utterly clueless about who could have done it.'

Hannah didn't think it was funny at all. The woman seemed totally unaffected by Tom's death. She spoke of him as if he was a stranger, not the man she had married and whose child she had borne. Even worse, she had murdered her own son and yet she showed a complete lack of sadness or remorse.

'How did you get involved, Laurel? I mean, they don't advertise, do they? Killers wanted. No conscience necessary.'

'Yes, very witty. No, they don't advertise, but when Tom came back from the Border I met a friend of his and we got talking and you know how it happens.'

'No, actually I don't. Tell me how it happens. Tell me how Jack's mother came to be hired as an assassin for the South African Defence Force.'

'No, I don't think so. Just knowing you got it wrong is enough for me, and what good would such knowledge do you now? I can't believe I felt threatened by you, or that I was worried you'd worked it out and would bring me down.' She started laughing again, a guttural sound that made Hannah wince. Finally, she wiped her eyes and studied Hannah's flushed face for a moment. 'If I were you, Hester,' she snorted, 'I'd start saying my prayers, make peace with my Maker, because it won't be long until you see Him face to face.' She walked towards the door, turned and smiled sweetly, 'I'm not going to say it was lovely knowing you, because we both know that would be a lie, but it's been interesting. Now, get some rest and my boys will be up to deal with you soon.'

CHAPTER

Forty-two

Hannah lay on her bed shaken by Laurel's revelations. Her body was infused with pain, her mind with guilt. Five souls had perished because of her and it wouldn't be long before she joined them. She could hear the men and Laurel talking outside her door and a number of times heard her own name mentioned. They were deciding what to do with her.

Now that she knew with certainty that they were going to kill her, Hannah began making peace with herself and wished she'd had time to reconcile with her family. They would never know what had happened to her and would live the remainder of their lives wondering if they could have done anything to save her.

She lay back and waited calmly, expecting Fourie and Gerrie to collect her and take her off to be executed. She had seen how it was done and had no intention of begging for her life. Being dumped in an unmarked grave in some remote area of veld was dehumanising enough, but to go to her death pleading and hysterical would be even more undignified. The thought that they would burn her body afterwards was too horrifying to contemplate and she allowed herself a few tears as she weighed up her life and remembered all the buried dreams that would never be fulfilled.

She sat up when she heard loud pounding on the door downstairs and conversation outside. A visitor, no matter who it was, was unusual and unexpected. She dragged herself to the window and peered out. It had been boarded up again, this time from the outside, but a gap between the planks gave her a good view of the freedom outside, and being able to see it but not get out made her want to scream.

Hannah could hear a man's voice and craned her neck to see a burly figure in a dirty white vest with sweat-stained armpits and oily jeans standing outside. He was gesticulating wildly and his head bobbed up and down as he spoke. She heard Laurel's raised voice and the dogs barking angrily and ten minutes later saw the man running away, looking over his shoulder in anger or fear, she couldn't tell which. But it didn't matter who the man was or why he had come. Nothing mattered any longer except the fact that she would soon be gone. She stared out at freedom one last time, breathed in the fresh air that was blowing through the gap and then, about to turn away, she caught a glimpse of something behind a clump of trees.

Hannah blinked and stared harder fearing she was hallucinating, but there was no mistake. It was Jack, alive, and he had someone with him, someone sturdy and compact. Someone she thought was dead. Someone Laurel said was dead. It was Tom. A tall shadow moved behind him and Themba peered over his shoulder.

She ripped off a corner of her shirt, stuck her hand out of the small opening and flapped the scrap of dirty white fabric hopefully. It had the desired effect, catching their attention. Jack started jumping up and down, pointing. Even from that distance, she could see the flash of Themba's teeth when he grinned and gripped Tom's shoulder.

Jack's father grabbed him by the arm when he made a move towards the house and must have said something to forestall an impetuous dash towards Hannah. Tom gestured to her to wait and the three men slid back under the shelter of the trees.

Hannah sat on the chair gazing out the window in a state of heightened emotion afraid they would leave without her or that they would be spotted or that Fourie would arrive and drag her off. Impatiently she willed darkness to fall.

She heard the dogs barking again and Fourie yelling at them to be quiet. She felt as if she was going to explode as time dragged by, but finally, the sun began to set, the sky a riot of burnt amber colours and then in a distinctively African way, as if a switch had been flicked, it was night. Her eyes strained against the blackness as she watched three shadows approaching the building.

She heard Tom whisper, 'Jack, get on Themba's shoulders. See if you can reach those planks across the window. Here, take my penknife to help you.'

With her eye glued to the gap in the wood, Hannah watched Jack climb on to Themba's shoulders. To her relief he was able to reach the window. He opened the penknife and began to pry out the nails holding the planks in place. A board came loose with a loud crack and clattered against the wall as it fell to the ground. Jack almost lost his balance and they all held their breath. The dogs began barking and Hannah wanted to scream in frustration but a voice bellowed at them to shut up and when everything was quiet again, Jack began levering the planks off the windows one by one.

Hannah pushed as best she could from her side and finally the last one came loose and he handed it down to Tom. She watched as the window opened up and Jack's face looked in at her. He beckoned and indicated that she be quiet. Then he dropped down and stood next to his father, waiting for her to fall into their arms.

But Hannah couldn't move. Her muscles had gone into spasm and vicelike cramps gripped her legs. Sweat mingled with dried blood as she tried to stand up, but all to no avail as she collapsed panting against the wall. She shut her eyes, trying to steady her breathing and gather the strength to escape.

Finally she pushed herself upright and tried to grasp the windowsill but again her rebellious body had a mind of its own. Jack's face appeared at the window.

'Psst! Hurry up, Hannah!'

They could hear the men and Laurel downstairs and expected to hear a shout of triumphant discovery at any moment.

Hannah gathered her strength once more and climbed on to the chair, then stood wobbling precariously as she realised she didn't have the strength to lift herself up and through the window.

She could hear Paul and Gerrie's deep voices and the dogs' intermittent barking outside and knew it would not be long before they arrived with her evening meal. She had to get out.

Jack appeared again and hissed, offering his hand, which Hannah grabbed. He pulled and she jumped and somehow between the two of them, they managed to drag her up on to the windowsill. Jack dropped back to the ground and waited while Hannah wriggled out of the window. She swung her legs out until she was dangling by her fingertips, took a deep breath and let go.

Tom caught her deftly, noted her face and her bare feet, swung her neatly over his shoulder in a fireman's lift and carried her towards the cover of the nearby trees. They stopped, panting, and turned back towards the still-silent house. Tom deposited her on the ground, relief evident on his face.

Speechless, all she could do was hug him and Themba and embarrass Jack by kissing him on the cheek and then clinging on to his hand as if he was the only thing left on earth that could prevent her from taking off and floating away into the vast universe forever.

But emotional reunions would have to wait for now. Tom grabbed her hand and the three of them ran towards the parked car where Hannah was not surprised to see Dudley panting on the back seat. The guard dogs began to bark in earnest and the front door of the house flew open sending a stream of light into the yard.

CHAPTER

Forty-three

Tom drove at speed watching for anyone pursuing them. He had not turned the lights on, fearing they would be followed, and the car slid and skidded on a dark road, illuminated only by the full moon.

Hannah could hardly speak. She had resigned herself to unavoidable death and to be rescued so unpredictably was an anticlimax. Jack, sitting on the backseat, leaned forward and put his head between the two front seats.

'What happened to you? I don't understand why you were kidnapped,' he said, studying her battered face.

'Not now, Jack,' said Tom, to Hannah's relief, as she was in no state to start answering any questions.

'I thought you were both dead,' said Hannah, still not fully convinced she wasn't in the midst of a terrible nightmare.

'I very nearly was,' said Tom and swiftly filled her in on what had happened in the last month. But as he told her about finding Jack and Themba and how they had tracked her down by investigating Paul Fourie and following one of his colleagues, it became clear that he had no idea his wife was involved. It was also evident that Laurel was a master at psychological games and had successfully manipulated Hannah. She knew Tom and Jack were alive, probably knew exactly where they were, and yet she still allowed Hannah to be beaten.

In the eternity since she had last seen him, Jack had become someone else, most markedly his physical appearance. His skin was grey, unsightly pimples marring his once clear complexion, yet she noticed an unfamiliar clean decisiveness about all his movements. The coltish clumsiness was gone in both actions and speech. He had a thin hairy line above his upper lip and his voice seemed deeper too. His mood seemed more stable and the surliness she had become accustomed to had given way to a subdued slightly distant air. The peculiar colour of his hair and eyebrows made him even more of an enigma, the mixture of blond and brown over-long hair giving him the flavour of a teen singer from a bad boy band.

Tom did not look well, his skin was grey and pasty and she could see a puckered, bald patch on the side of his head where the bullet had struck him. How was she going to tell them about Laurel? She couldn't face it now, but she'd have to tell them eventually and she did not cherish the thought.

They sped through the night, desperate to get as far from the farm as possible. No one spoke, all caught up in their own thoughts. On reaching a junction with the main road a couple of hours later, Tom turned south, to Hannah's surprise.

'Pretoria's the other way,' she said, indicating the green and white signpost.

'I know, but there's somewhere else we need to go first,'

Themba, sitting next to Jack in the back seat, leaned forward. 'Snyman died two weeks ago, but he left a note for us,'

'Oh?'

'He wanted to die with a clean conscience, I think. He mentions a secret storage facility where Barnacle records are kept and we decided to go there to find out more,' he said, 'If you are up for it.'

'Hell, yes,' said Hannah.

As the misty pastel shades of the dawn appeared in the sky, they drove through the flat land of the Orange Free State past fields of cheerful sunflowers and row upon row of corn, before reaching the Orange River and crossing the grey steel girder bridge into the Cape Province. They continued steeply up the road on the banks of the river and after a sharp turn, entered the town of Aliwal North, well known for its hot mineral springs. Tom continued onwards through the town and Hannah fell into fitful sleep.

They travelled on and on and finally through a still slumbering town and into an overgrown caravan park. The grass was wet with dew, opalescent mist rising from a nearby stagnant pond. Tom parked under a tree and turned off the engine.

Themba opened his door. 'Tom and I are going to take a look around. According to Snyman's directions, we are close to the storage facility but we need to scout around a bit first. We must wait until it is dark before breaking in, so this is a good time for you to have a rest,' he said.

Hannah groaned and rubbed her ribs.

'We're safe here for a while,' said Tom, touching her cheek. 'Try to get some sleep. We'll talk later. Keep watch please, Jack.' He and Themba hurried away.

Hannah closed her eyes again and fell into a dreamless sleep. When she woke the blue sky had already softened to grey and the sun hung low on the horizon. The men returned and Tom was eager to get going. She stretched and winced, trying to suppress a moan as her body protested at the sudden movement. Every nerve was ablaze, she was covered in bruises and abrasions, her front tooth was chipped and wiggled when she touched it and one eye was swollen shut. She had a cut on her cheek and a laceration on her forehead that could have done with some stitches, and found walking painful, her ribs and kidneys aching every time she took a breath. It was a miracle none of her wounds had become infected.

'You need a doctor,' said Themba, 'But we cannot risk it. Your injuries are bound to raise suspicions and if we are being followed, that kind of thing will not be easily forgotten. We bought some things at a chemist. Hope they help.'

She swallowed a couple of painkillers thankful for the supply he had brought her. Themba cleaned and patched her up as best he could and gave her a stale sandwich to eat. The wounds on her body would soon heal. Those on her mind were an altogether different matter, but now wasn't the right time to detangle the mess of emotions that were flooding through her. To her shame, she found herself overwhelmed with sensations and wept every time she looked at Tom or Jack. She covered her chagrin by joking that they should ignore her while she had a bit of a breakdown, hoping they wouldn't realise how close to the truth that was. All the time the knowledge she was keeping from them made her feel even worse and she could no longer delay confronting them with the truth about Laurel.

'Tom, Themba, can we have a word in private?'

'Can it wait? We need to get going,' said Tom.

She nodded. What harm could a few more hours do?

Tom pulled off the road and rolled the car forward into a patch of woodland. The drive there had been silent, each one caught up in private thoughts. Since Tom and Themba had scouted the area earlier that day, it didn't take longer than twenty minutes for them to reach their destination and they now sat silent, waiting to ensure they had not been followed. Tom made certain the vehicle was well hidden and pointed down a red dirt track, 'This is it,' he said, 'Jack, you better stay here. You too Hannah.'

'Fat chance,' she said, 'I'm not completely useless.'

Before they could argue she was limping towards a building that was hidden about a hundred metres further along. She peered through the thickening darkness. The stillness was broken only by the occasional lyric call of a *Piet-my-Vrou* and the sound of the trees murmuring as a light breeze blew. She stepped cautiously through the copper-dust and approached the six-foot high barbed wire fence encircling a building that could just be discerned in the gloom.

The gate was padlocked, so she clambered painfully over, every movement an effort. Themba and Tom followed her and they moved towards the facility that had been erected at the foot of a hill. It was grey and squat, held together by corroded metal girders and surrounded by a circle of thorn trees. As they neared the building, Hannah saw camouflage webbing and tarpaulins draped over the roof and realised that part of the structure was below ground. If they hadn't been searching for it they would have missed it completely.

Silence told them that the area was deserted and the disrepair of the facility and its surrounding grounds indicated that it had been neglected for some time, but perhaps that was the idea. It would certainly raise no suspicions from the casual observer. A row of petrol drums partially blocked the front door and a rusted car skeleton lay abandoned nearby. They approached with care.

'We had a good look around earlier and have disabled the alarm. We saw a few workers, but they have all gone home now and the watchman will not be giving us any trouble. Unfortunately I could not find his keys so we will have to use a window. There is one round the side,' said Themba, leading the way. Hannah did not dare ask what had happened to the watchman.

Tom peered inside and removed what was left of the pane of glass. He gave Hannah a leg up and she wriggled through, biting her lip to stop from crying out in pain. She landed in a heap on a dusty floor. Themba and Tom followed and examined the room. It was more like a large cupboard and was filled with cleaning supplies, some brooms, a mop and bucket, three broken wooden shelves and a rickety desk. The air was damp and the walls were discoloured and stained with musty green mildew.

Tom opened the door and peered out into a dark hallway, which had a number of doors and a warren of passages leading off it. They made their way through the building, inspecting each room in turn. Most were empty offices with a coating of rusty-dirt, but so far there was no sign of any filing system.

'There are steps here leading to a basement,' said Themba. He went down a flight of stone steps and flipped a switch. A neon light flickered, throwing a harsh blue light across a row of refrigerated glass cabinets containing what looked like vials of chemicals. Tom examined them and removed one filled with an oily liquid and wrapped it in his handkerchief.

'I'll get the guys in our lab to analyse this. But I wouldn't be surprised if it's some kind of chemical or biological weapon.'

After examining the laboratory, they continued their hunt for evidence of Operation Barnacle.

Another room revealed a cupboard filled with racks of guns and some boxes of ammunition. Tom examined them, selected two and tucked them into his belt.

'Know how to handle one of these?' he asked Themba.

Themba nodded and selected a revolver for himself. Hannah saw a sturdy knife tucked into a leather holder on the shelf below the guns. She removed it and slid it into the back pocket of her jeans. You never knew when something like this might come in handy. She wandered out into the hallway and continued exploring. At the end of a long dark passage that branched off from the main one, she spotted a door hidden behind a steel cupboard.

'Over here,' she whispered.

Tom and Themba pushed the cupboard out of the way, but the door was locked, so Tom put his shoulder to it and after a few heaves, the lock splintered and the door sprang open. They waited for a moment in case the noise had alerted anyone, but the only sound was their breathing and the cooing of a dove outside.

'Jackpot,' muttered Hannah.

Rows of filing cabinets were stacked around the room and to their delight the drawers were bulging with files.

'Take a cabinet each,' said Themba.

Hannah pulled open a drawer and rifled through the contents. At first she saw nothing interesting but when she pulled open the first drawer of the next cabinet, she found a file labelled 'Barnacle'. She took it out and scanned the first page. It was a list of names and dates of operations that the unit had undertaken. Hands trembling, she opened the next folder and started reading. It was labelled *'Operasie Liefie'* and the first name she saw was 'Maartens'. She sank to the floor, engrossed in the full and detailed history of Laurel's involvement from her time in the army until her recruitment to the death squad that was laid out in black type.

'Quick, Hannah, someone's here. We have to get out!' whispered Tom.

She'd been so absorbed in what she was reading that she hadn't heard the vehicle pulling up outside, or the voices. She tucked the files into the waistband of her jeans and followed Tom back to the utility cupboard, meeting Themba on the way.

'We'll have to hide in here and pray they don't come in. They'll hear us if we try to get out the window and there may be others outside,' said Tom.

They moved into a dark corner and crouched behind the desk. Hannah was barely able to breathe and sank to the floor in agony terrified they would be found. Tom put his arm round her and signalled her to keep quiet.

Footsteps sounded in the passage outside and men's voices rang out. The next voice they heard was Laurel's. She began barking orders at the men and they crashed around going from room to room, kicking in doors and turning over furniture. Hannah winced and looked up at Tom, hoping against hope that he hadn't recognised his wife's not so dulcet tones. His face was frozen and his eyes flared for a moment.

'Is that ...?'

Hannah gripped his hand to prevent him leaping to his feet, her eyes imploring him to stay quiet. He restrained himself with visible effort and the vein in his temple beat faster and faster. Themba frowned and raised an eyebrow. Hannah shook her head, guilt written across her face. Tom released her abruptly and moved away, turning his back on her, and it felt like a limb had been amputated. He would never forgive her.

Laurel was standing directly outside their hiding place and they could hear her clearly.

'We must destroy everything to make sure no one ever finds out the truth. Typical fucking government bureaucracy, leaving files and a paper trail clear enough for any fool to find. Here, pour this over everything and then set the building alight. We'll burn this place to the ground along with my past,' she laughed.

Tom made a sound and Hannah wanted to put her arms round him and tell him it wasn't his fault, that he could never have known, but she was unable to move and his expression told her in no uncertain terms what he thought of her now.

They listened to the men rushing about, heard splashing and smelt petrol. A trickle of liquid flowed under the door. They waited. Then, a roar, shouts and running footsteps shattered the peace. The building was alight. Vehicles started up outside, revving as they sped away. Themba moved swiftly, grabbing Hannah by the arm, yanking her up and towards the window.

'We have to get out of here,' he coughed. The cupboard was filling with acrid smoke and they could hear the crackle of flames outside. Themba shoved Hannah out and the two men tumbled after her. They lay on the ground, eyes streaming and lungs desperate for clean air.

'We must move further away. Those petrol cans and the chemicals in the basement are going to explode,'

Themba stumbled to his feet and helped Hannah up. Pain made it hard for her to move, so he put an arm round her and dragged her away from the building.

An explosion rent the air, the blast knocking them to the ground as the building disintegrated in an eruption of fire and smoke. Burning fragments rained down, scorching their arms and backs, as they lay prostrate, cowering in the dirt.

'Tom…' Hannah sat up and to her relief he was lying nearby. He stood, dusted himself off and without a word turned towards the car. She and Themba trailed behind and she was relieved to see Jack and his dog standing on the side of the road looking anxiously at the billowing column of black smoke.

Without a word Tom climbed into the driver's seat and waited for the others to follow. Before they even had time to put on their seat belts, he reversed and drove away from the blazing building. They travelled in silence for the next two hours and Hannah grew more jumpy with every passing minute. The car careered down the road, going much too fast and she clung to the dashboard, afraid they would lose control and flip over. Finally she couldn't take the tension any longer.

'Tom, please let me explain.'

He ignored her, drumming his fingers on the steering wheel.

'Dad? What's wrong?' asked Jack.

Themba cleared his throat, 'Shall we discuss it in a civilised manner?'

Tom screeched to a halt on the side of the road and turned off the engine.

'Hannah, do you have something to tell me?' He turned to face her, his eyes narrowed.

CHAPTER

Forty-four

Hannah cleared her throat.

'Do you think Jack should hear this?'

'He needs to know,' said Tom.

'Know what?' asked Jack.

'Tom, you have to understand. All along, I thought it was you.'

'Thought what was me?'

'The killings. I thought you were the killer or at least involved in some way. I saw you talking to Bosman the morning he was killed and I recognised his body in the car park, but you pretended you didn't know who he was. We heard a telephone call with someone telling you to make sure I didn't find out anything important and then Themba found that sniper rifle in your house and your name was on a list Marie gave me. I didn't suspect for a minute that it was another Maartens. I thought you'd organised the attack on me and faked your own death. I was sure it was you that kidnapped me and I was convinced you were going to kill me too because I'd found out too much, but I was wrong. It wasn't you.' She paused, hoping to see some sympathy in his face, but it was blank.

'I was in such shock I wasn't thinking straight and when you came to rescue me, how could I tell you? We've barely had time to talk and I tried to tell you earlier, but you were in such a hurry to get to the storage place. I never imagined for a moment that she'd turn up there. I was going to tell you.'

'If you say so.'

'I'm sorry.'

'What's she talking about, dad?' asked Jack.

'How did you overhear the telephone call?' said Tom after a moment.

'I bugged your house,' said Themba, 'It was my idea entirely, as was working in your garden. Hannah did not think it was a good idea. I also searched your home while you were out and found the gun. Obviously, I thought it belonged to you. It never crossed my mind that it was your wife's property. Hannah was not the only one that did not trust you.'

'I see. You actually thought I was part of a death squad, after everything we've been through together? After all we've shared?'

'I'm sorry. I don't know what else I can say. I was convinced you were dirty and that it was you pulling Paul and Gerrie's strings. When I found out it was Laurel –'

'What?' said Jack.

'Hush, Jack,' said Tom, 'Tell me what you know and don't leave out anything,'

'She didn't talk to me much and when she did it was all lies. She said you and Jack were dead and I knew I was going to die, wanted to die. All I know for sure is that

Laurel orchestrated the whole thing and is part of a covert unit that assassinates enemies of the state, not Barnacle like we thought, Themba, but an offshoot called *Operasie Liefie*.' She remembered the files and pulled them out of her waistband, 'I found these in a cabinet back at the storage building. I didn't have time to show them to you. Here.'

Tom opened the first folder. He read it from cover to cover without a word. When he was done he turned to face Jack.

'Basically, everything your mother ever told us about her life was a lie.' he said. 'Her whole life was a pack of lies.'

Hannah was concerned. He seemed too cold, too matter of fact. 'Tom, that's enough,' But Tom continued speaking as if she didn't exist.

'I met her at a *braai* and married her almost without thinking. Then you were born and she couldn't cope very well. I let her go off to George because I thought the structure would help and it was something she wanted very much. I just couldn't deny her the chance to make more of herself.

'She must have loved being in the army, especially the camaraderie. She once told me that her whole life she'd wanted to be part of 'the gang', and now she was. But she didn't tell me the truth about her time there. She told me her version of events, which were nothing but lies. But reading this, well, it seems she found her true calling after all.

'She had weapons training, on the old R1, the nine mil star pistol and on the Uzi submachine gun. She could field strip an R1 and put it back together again in about twelve seconds, blindfolded,' He jabbed the page with his finger, 'It's highlighted here, in her file. I can just imagine how much she must have loved the sniper rifles. Even to a novice like me there was something about the sensation of the barrel's cold curved steel and the precision of the telescopic sight that's above any other emotion in the world. It's power at the touch of a finger. It's the ability to save or take a life. It's the chance to make a difference and for the first time in her miserable existence, she was in complete control. God, she must have wanted it to last forever.

'Finally she was good at something that mattered. She was top of the class during Basics and could put a bullet in a man's head from over a thousand metres, better than the men. That's why they earmarked her for greater things.'

Jack did not move, barely breathed, and Themba's face was filled with such empathy Hannah felt ashamed. All she could think was that Laurel had betrayed Tom who'd done nothing but love her, despite her peculiarities. Her face must have reflected her thoughts because his lip curled and his voice cut through the silence.

'Why do you have that expression on your face?' he said, 'Aren't you proud of yourself? Exposing my wife for what she is? No, don't try to stop me, it gets better.'

Hannah wanted to scream at him, defend herself, but her throat had seized up.

'This bit is interesting, 'decisions have to be made about Maartens', it says. They couldn't risk letting her go when her time was up, not knowing how good she was, so they singled her out and decided to train her with the men instead, just to see what would happen. I imagine a few eyebrows were raised about that, and I suppose they were just waiting for her to fail.

'The fact she even made it through Basics is quite impressive. The running and swimming and leadership survival involves being chased up and down the mountains for three days without ropes or torches and only *takkies*, not hiking boots. And there I was thinking she's such a fragile little thing. Her medical notes say her toes became infected and that her toenails fell out,' he grunted, 'She told me she had an infection and fell down a ravine because she was delirious and had to be casevac'd off the mountain by helicopter. Another lie. But none of that can possibly have compared to what she must have gone through when they put her in with the recces.

'You have to be exceptional to survive the training, parachuting, water-orientation, diving and mountaineering, and she was. She learned about survival, evasion, resistance and escape techniques. They taught her how to camouflage herself and there's a highlighted section here that says she was so good she could hide a metre away from the target and not be spotted. It's obviously the skills she learned then that have kept her going for so long. I don't know how I didn't see it.

'You have no idea how gruelling it is. The psychological testing is brutal and they don't choose wimps. I suppose they thought she would crack because she's a woman, but oh no, not my wife. Most men would run off crying, but not her. She's tougher than anyone ever imagined.'

He stared out the window for a moment and the air around them was thick and tight, clinging to their skin as they waited for him to resume his tale. Hannah's hands were sweating and in spite of herself she was eager for Tom to continue. It was a story like none she had ever heard before and she experienced a momentary pang at the realization that writing about it would seal her place as a serious journalist, maybe even win her some awards.

Tom continued, breaking the silence, and without exception his audience was spellbound.

'I can hardly believe I'm reading this, but it seems she was trained as a sniper for Special Forces, the first and only woman to ever have that privilege. They kept her a secret and never acknowledged her officially. That must have driven her crazy. Doesn't like being ignored, my Laurel. She was their little experiment, but her life was finally complete. Dressing in fatigues and camouflaging herself must have seemed like she was living in her own private fantasy. I can just imagine it, her disintegrating, morphing into someone else, invisible and untouchable. She became the perfect hunter. There's nothing that gets the adrenaline flowing like creeping through the veld towards the prey and when you line him up in your sights and squeeze the trigger to make the kill it's better than sex. That's what I found on the Border, anyway. I understand now why I was never enough for her.

'But this is a man's world, Hannah, you must be aware of that in your line of work. She's not part of Barnacle. That's one of the other mistakes you made, but of course you thought it was me, didn't you, so you aren't quite as bright as you think, are you? They couldn't handle a woman being better than them so they kept her isolated for special missions, afraid of what she'd do to the morale of the men if she outshone them, I suppose. They wouldn't let her go to the Border or get involved in the action or go off to fight with the men. It must have driven her crazy. She passed all their tests and they couldn't look beyond her breasts.

'She was probably hoping they'd release her to do what she was best at, challenging the men – and believe me, you don't want to mess with the guys in the reconnaissance commando. They're tough and cruel and they wouldn't have responded well to having Laurel thrust into their tight clique for research purposes.' He stopped and looked at his son, but Jack was immobile with his face buried in his hands.

'Surely you aren't going to tell him the rest?' said Hannah, who still felt sickened by what she'd read in the file.

'Oh, what difference can it make? If you'd told us about her earlier…if we'd known…'

'It is not Hannah's fault, Tom,' said Themba,

'Go on, dad,' Jack kicked the back of his father's chair.

'One day they were in the bush and a few of them cornered her and tried to force her to give up and go home. They said she was bringing the unit into disrepute and that if it ever got out that she'd passed tests that so many men had failed, their credibility would be shot. But she wouldn't back down so they tried to break her. They took her into the veld and gang raped her through the night and left her for dead,' said Tom. Then he chuckled, almost as if he admired her, thought Hannah.

'They forgot how good she was. They'd trained her themselves and she escaped and went after them. She stalked them in the dark and when she found them she lined them up in her sights and pulled the trigger. You have to give her credit. She hunted them like vermin and took them down man by man and left their bodies for the birds and wild animals.

'Obviously they couldn't let what had occurred get out, they couldn't reveal what happened to her or what she'd done. After a massive cover up the powers above suggested she leave and nothing more would be said. They fabricated a medical discharge and said that one day they'd need her to do them a favour and I presume she felt obliged to co-operate because they'd let her go and kept those terrible events a secret. Despite everything, they knew her worth.'

'If she were a man she would have become a mercenary, I think, ' said Themba, 'She could have been useful to any government that wanted her, but as a woman she had to settle for married life because that is what is considered suitable and right.'

Even he sounded like he pitied her. Did neither of these men get it? The woman was evil. Hannah's face was hot and she had to make a concerted effort not to explode in a stream of vehemence and sarcasm.

'She slipped into her new role as suburban housewife and mother and fooled everyone,' she said, earning a glare from Tom.

'A year or so later she met a man at a braai who recruited her as a courier,' said Tom, 'She started off as a delivery girl but it looks like it didn't take long for them to move her up in the ranks. That was probably the plan all along. They knew all about her and that she'd never be content as a messenger but a housewife assassin? It is a novel idea, don't you agree?'

'It is certainly something no one had thought of before,' said Themba, 'Quite brilliant, when you think about it. They knew all about her special skills and she had already proved they could trust her. They must have fine-tuned her into a model killing-machine and it is blatantly obvious that she had quite an aptitude for it. Who would suspect her? She doesn't exactly look dangerous.'

Hannah interrupted. The situation was getting out of her control. Laurel was the enemy and they were talking about her as if she was the hero of the piece.

'All she had to do was tweak her character a bit, act spaced out, get lost a few times and her cover was in place. Anyone can act caring and loving, even if they feel dead inside. She spent most of her life pretending to be someone she wasn't and she certainly fooled you, Tom.'

She didn't know why she said it, just wanted to hurt him in some way, get a reaction that showed he felt the same disgust as she did, but he only blinked and stared at her with glassy eyes. She tried again, 'You have to admit it was ideal, simple suburban housewife: an assassin for the government. Floral Laurel, it was a faultless cover and audaciously arrogant considering who you are.'

'Yes, very clever. You thought I was a killer, now you clearly think I'm an idiot as well and perhaps you're right,' said Tom.

Hannah ignored him. 'They devised a clever scheme and created another unit, a splinter group even more anonymous that only a few know about. It operates the same way as Barnacle, using the same methods,' she said, 'But the difference is it's all about her. They even nicknamed it 'Operation *Liefie*', as if calling her 'little darling' would annoy her. It keeps her out of their way and preserves their fragile perception of their manhood.

'They gave her a squad of rejects to work with, men that were in disgrace for some reason. Fourie was out of control and had an inappropriate relationship with his commanding officer's wife, and Gerrie, as I can tell you from personal experience, is too fat and stupid to be of any use in a dangerous situation, but he does what he's told. They're a perfect team.'

Hannah didn't know why, but she was becoming angrier and angrier, furious with herself and with Tom, who was taking it all far too serenely. She wanted him to rant and rave and denounce his wife, but he didn't and it felt like a personal insult.

Tom's feline eyes were gold in the late afternoon light and his face was pale, anger etching harsh lines across his forehead. 'And basically that's it. She isn't the same mum you know, Jack,' said Tom, 'Not the woman who worked in your tuckshop and took you shopping for school shoes. The mother you know who played taxi every afternoon and fetched and carried you from rugby and swimming and made you tidy your room and clean the pool on Saturdays is gone. I think she disappeared a long time ago, only no one noticed, I certainly didn't.'

'Look at these dates,' And just in case Jack intended standing up for his mother, even though he hadn't spoken a word, Hannah snatched the file from Tom and passed it to Jack, who studied the list of operations his mother had been involved in.

'Every time she was late or forget to fetch you it was because she was off somewhere shooting someone in the head or blowing up a hut somewhere. That's why she was always late. That's why she was never where she was supposed to be. That's why she'll kill us if we get in her way.' Jack sat silent, holding the file, and began drumming his fingers on the seat.

Hannah was hell-bent on impressing upon Jack the savagery of his mother. The boy didn't say a word so she carried on,.

'The week of your school play when she missed the opening night, a man disappeared near Rustenberg and they found his body floating in Hartebeespoort Dam. Then that time you went to Swaziland for a holiday and she got lost while she was hiking, the house of an exiled activist was bombed. It was only a few kilometres from your hotel. When she took you and your friends to the planetarium and wandered off for a few hours, she went and killed a black man that worked at Wits University. Heaven only knows what crime he had committed, but months later Dani and I found his body rolling around in the surf in Natal. That's what started off this whole nightmare,' said Hannah.

'And a few weeks ago when you were scoring the winning try and your mom was supposed to be working in the tuckshop, a man was shot in a parking lot near your school, remember, when you first met Hannah?' said Tom, his voice so weary Hannah wanted to weep.

'And the week Hannah's flat was petrol bombed your mom left us to go to Beryl, only she didn't go there. She and her unit went and abducted a man from his village and killed him in a plantation. Shall I go on?'

Jack shook his head and went still, his chin dropping to his chest. Hannah could see delicate wrinkles at the corners of his mouth and eyes. He was too young to have worry lines like that. He raised his head.

'That was her? In the plantation?' The light in his eyes faded with every word. Hannah nodded, 'I'm so sorry.'

'Something went wrong with her a long time ago, but she hid it from us, made us believe she was someone else. Made me believe she loved me. I should have realised she wasn't right years back,' said Tom.

Jack stared at the road ahead, his face ashen. A luminous moon sat suspended in the sky and the scattered stars stretched towards infinity. A moth headed for the car, its dusky wings beating, carrying it towards the burning headlights that would fry its soft furry body the moment it landed. The night air was soft and syrupy, caressing their skin.

'Tell me what happened to you, Hannah,' said Tom.

She told him everything that had been done to her while in captivity, and watched the light in his eyes go out too.

'What are we going to do now?' asked Themba.

Hannah studied the documents again and on the last page found something that made her stomach churn.

'Look at this, there's another operation planned for this weekend, and here, oh my God, look at this name…Roli…it can't be…can it?' She gave the file to Themba, an unbidden emotion washing over her unexpectedly, making her ashamed.

The internal struggle Hannah now felt was almost physical, and she realised that the years of indoctrination had sunk so deep into her veins that she was actually more afraid of coming face to face with the man Laurel was planning to kill, than she was of the killer herself.

She'd been brought up to believe this Roli was a vicious terrorist out to violently purge the country of all whites should he get the opportunity. Now, battered and bruised though she was, the features of the evil she knew were far less frightening than those she had been told about. She was forced to face the unpalatable fact that part of her hoped Laurel would succeed.

And yet, the voice of reason still spoke loudly. The killing of another dissident wouldn't simply be an unfortunate death in detention, especially if it resulted from a sniper's bullet. It could not be written off as a suicide or an accident in the shower or a fatal escape attempt as too many such deaths were. It would be seen for what it was - the desperate ploy of an apartheid government to keep the status quo as long as possible.

Laurel was the perfect assassin for the job, part of an elite and secretive unit with no known connection to the regime. If she failed and was captured, they would refute any association with her. If she succeeded, she would simply melt back into the shadows until the next time she was needed and could leave the ensuing chaos to take its own course.

Themba read the file and handed it to Tom, 'We have to prevent this happening, but we are going to need help and I know just the man,' he said.

'You're right. We have to stop her, even if we die trying,' said Hannah and no one said a word, because that was a very distinct possibility.

CHAPTER
Forty-five

Hannah had only been in a township once before and then under heavy police escort. Her palms were sweaty and her breathing was laboured, having to constantly remind herself to continue forcing the air into her lungs. There was a fetid smell from piles of rubbish lying next to the road, the air was grey with pollution and smoke that stung her eyes and made her cough. She wrinkled her nose.

Jack, beside her, was grim-faced. They drove down dusty roads past dilapidated houses and shacks and people that screamed at her conscience. The sky, fighting to hold on to the last vestige of light and keep out the darkness that would soon smother them all, was a peculiar dusky orange colour.

Hannah kept low in her seat, fearing that a white face would not be welcome in Soweto. Jack followed her lead and they both sunk down, their bodies alight, the atmosphere around them charged.

Tom was driving unhurriedly and she knew it was more dangerous for him than for her. The police, for obvious reasons, were viewed with suspicion and hostility in the township. It was only the presence of Themba next to Tom that gave them some credible reason for being there.

'Tell me again why we're here?' said Jack.

'We can't cope with this next stage alone and I'm still not sure who I can trust,' said Tom, 'Le Roux is too busy to help and gave me permission to do what I could alone, for now. He's doing some detecting of his own.'

'Laurel's next target is someone so important we need help to get near him. That's where Themba comes in,' said Tom.

'My friend Solomon will help us. I have known him for a while and he is the one man I can trust to help but he is hard to get hold of and that is why we had to come out here. At least with him I know what the agenda is. He has contacts and I am certain we can rely on him,' said Themba.

'Why?' asked Jack.

'I know him from way back and he is committed to peace. He does not think that violence is the answer to our problems like so many do. He is one of the few who believes that education should come before revolution and not the other way round. He says, what is the point of a revolution if the people are so uneducated they do not know how to handle it afterwards? Democracy and all it encompasses can only be truly understood by the educated. I think he is right,' replied Themba.

Hannah concurred but was afraid that too few of them thought alike to have any real effect. 'This country is on course for a revolution and whether or not the full implications of such a revolution are fully understood by the masses advocating it is neither here nor there. They're going to win their freedom no matter what the cost,' she said.

Jack touched Hannah's arm, pointing at a burnt tyre on the side of the road.

'Is it safe for us to be here?'

She could see the vision in his eyes of that tyre being placed, burning, round his neck, and remembered the first time she had seen photographs of what had become know as 'necklacing'. A police informant had been captured by a mob, a car tyre filled with petrol and then placed over his head, pinioning his arms to his side. The tyre had been set alight and the mob had surrounded him, chanting and singing and watching him burn alive. It was a horrific type of death that was becoming more and more popular as a means of punishment in the townships, and there were few whites that didn't fear retribution at the hands of a toyi-toying mob with a tyre and a lighter. Some, particularly the militants of *Umkhonto we Sizwe*, advocated necklacing as a means to achieve reform.

'No. It's not safe. But don't worry. Your dad will look after us.' His dad shot an unfriendly look at her in the rear view mirror.

Tom had wanted to leave them behind, more because he was still angry with her, than out of any concern. Her wounds hadn't fully healed and she was still weak but she and Jack had worn him down, neither one keen to miss out on the action. Besides, what kind of story could she write if she wasn't in on it all, blow by blow, Hannah had argued? Themba understood her need for a story, but expressed his concern about her frailty.

Secretly she was worried that she would let them down if she couldn't cope physically, but was unwavering in her decision to see through what she had begun. Tom consented reluctantly, and Hannah harboured the hope that he was impressed with her fortitude.

It was twilight now and there was a wary stillness on the streets. Weary workers returning home walked by, watching the passing car curiously, but Hannah noticed few hostile faces at the sight of a white skin so deep within the soul of Soweto. She wondered what expressions those faces would hold if they knew who they were. Themba pointed and the car stopped on the side of the road, such as it was, and Tom switched off the engine.

'He has a house down here.' Themba jerked his head in the direction of a small winding track through the veld. Hannah's spirits plummeted. She didn't fancy bundu-bashing in the middle of a township with not a speck of light to help them.

'Come on, we can't take the car any further.' Jack and Hannah were welded to the back seat.

'Hey, where's that spirit of adventure I've come to know and love?'

'I lost it about five kilometres back,' answered Jack in a trembling voice.

'Maybe we should stay here, with the car, in case someone steals it,' Hannah suggested, not fooling anyone.

'It's not safe here.' Tom's tone was firm and she recognised the stubborn detective again. She could see the pulse beating in his temple.

'And it is out there in the middle of the veld in the pitch dark?'

'Yes, and I thought you wanted to be in on all the action. Come on, we're wasting time.'

Somehow she managed to get her legs to obey and she and Jack, close together, followed Tom and Themba into a new, mysterious world.

The ground was uneven and Hannah wrenched her ankle stepping in a hole. Jack was unsympathetic and yanked her up and on, the grass scratching their legs and blackjacks attaching themselves to their clothes.

Assorted tin shacks hemmed them in, the smell of paraffin and rotting food all-pervading. Hannah stood in a dirty puddle of water, and her shoe squished soggily, her slimy toes battling to keep a grip on the wet canvas of her *takkies*. A mangy cat hissed and spat and a raggedy one-eyed dog barked furiously, their smell an offence. A scrawny chicken squawked and scuttled across their path, its beady eyes regarding them with suspicion. It seemed that neither beast nor fowl was happy with their presence there.

Tom stopped abruptly and Jack bumped into the back of him.

'What's...?' Hannah stopped the indignant question that leaped to her lips and moved behind Jack's left shoulder. She peered over his shoulder, into the eyes of five very large, very black men.

They encircled them in a silence more frightening than yells or cries. They held knobkieries and spears and one what seemed suspiciously like an AK47 assault rifle. Tom and Themba raised their hands in greeting.

'I'm looking for Solomon. Tell him Themba's here.'

One of the men, followed closely by Themba, slid off into the shadows. The moon cruised out from behind a cloud, bathing them in dim silver light. The night was motionless, chirping and scraping sounds of insects in the grass breaking the silence.

Hannah's senses were out of control, heightened to react to the slightest noise or movement, while her arms and legs felt curiously detached from her body. She could feel Jack shaking. His hand, grasping hers, was wet with sweat, and she could see a thin line of dampness glistening on the back of his neck.

Tom, on the other hand, seemed completely at ease, looking around with interest, never moving too fast or too suddenly. Time seemed to slow down as they waited for each sluggish second to pass until the man returned. When he finally did, he signalled for them to follow him, then led them further and further into a labyrinth of tin and wood and despair.

Hannah could hear the sound of rhythmic music from crackly radios and sporadic laughter sailing overhead on a path of smoke. She saw dirty snotty-nosed children playing with rusted and dented bicycle tyre rims and a mother breastfeeding her baby outside a shack. Grave-eyed women sat on upturned crates, their solemn suspicious eyes watching them pass.

There was vibrancy and a nerve-jangling awareness amidst these ruins of humanity that she had never experienced before. A shrivelled old man coughed and spat on the ground at Jack's feet. There was life amongst the dirt and the dust; life that she had never known existed. Flesh and blood lived and survived a diamond-hard existence here.

The ebb and flow of life from the city back to the townships had only been a vaguely alluded to event that had no place in her world, except to spew up a never-ending supply of labour for the whites who chose not to acknowledge what she was seeing tonight.

People that lived here, as comfortable in the squalor as she was in her prim neatly painted and carpeted flat. Her face felt hot and there was a pain above her diaphragm that had nothing to do with fear. In the instant of time between getting out of the car, to this microcosm of intensity, Hannah felt a pang of pity and guilt so intense she knew she would never forget it.

The little procession finally stopped outside a neatly constructed corrugated iron shanty. Hannah was interested to see a television aerial, secured with an old wire coat hanger.

They were ushered inside where Themba was waiting and in the gloom she saw an old man sitting on a mattress. He rose gracefully, greeting Tom with a solemn handshake. Jack he acknowledged with yellowed eyes. Hannah, he ignored.

Like an oracle of old he spoke.

'My friend tells me you need my assistance.' What teeth he had left in his shrivelled mouth were black with decay. Jack and Hannah looking on. They sat together on the mattress, and Tom explained why they were there.

Hannah surveyed the neat home with interest. The dirt floor was well swept and covered in sheets of newspaper. A few pictures of Kaiser Chiefs soccer team were sticky-taped to the wall along with a picture of a serene Jesus with a rosy-cheeked child on his knee, that came straight from an illustrated children's Bible. As a child she'd had that same picture on the pink walls of her immaculate cocoon in her mother's house. There was a battered stove in one corner with a blackened pot balanced on top. The smell of paraffin mixed with a strangely sweet aroma filled the small room, making their eyes water.

A pile of old clothes next to the stove coughed and she realised it was another antiquated person, asleep under a blue and green tartan blanket, oblivious to their intrusion. An upside-down box served as a table, two dented tin mugs and a small chipped and cracked china plate resting on the unstable surface. A small TV was propped precariously against the corrugated iron wall.

Solomon was silent for a while, his ancient lips puckered, his eyes still young and all seeing.

'If this is true, I'll send my sons and my nephew to help you. They are strong and brave and as you can trust their father so you can trust them. We'll do this for you and we'll do it for our people. We'll do it now because I fear that there is no time to waste.'

He placed a gnarled hand on Tom's shoulder and spoke with the understanding of a man who had suffered and survived.

'You will go on after this, Tom. You and your son. You must be strong and you must never look back.'

The audience with the sage was finished. A feeling of unreality swept over Hannah. She was awake in a dream, images and visions sweeping over her, sounds roaming through her consciousness and touching her soul. The sleeping behemoth of humanitarian awareness had awoken and she knew she would never be the same again. Surely none of them could ever be the same again.

CHAPTER

Forty-six

Her calling hadn't always been that clear. At first, the world was a mixed up and confusing time, but Laurel, who desired to be strong and good and do whatever she was told, paid attention and allowed the roots to deepen until finally, there came a moment when she understood fully that this country was the perfect place for her to satisfy the burning desire to take life that she tried so hard to ignore.

She had to bide her time and hone her skills in a legitimate way. She had to behave, not answer back or think out loud, never express a contrary opinion or draw attention to herself, never let on how she truly felt. And it was perfect, because that was what the system demanded anyway. But finally, she'd been released to fulfil her destiny, to do that for which she had been created. And she wasn't going to let Hannah Smith get in her way.

Laurel had learned at a young age about Christian love and charity, about the natural order of things, that the blacks were subservient and inferior, that men could not be trusted and that death was an inevitable part of life.

Hannah had turned her back on it all, embracing her colonial roots and the sentimental humanism that made her believe everyone was equal. It was a travesty.

She smoothed her hair and clenched her fists, determined to make the reporter pay. There would be no escaping again. Her moment had finally arrived, and gathering all her inner strength she set off to fulfil one last mission. She knew that she had to make every instant count from now on. Hannah would waste no time in telling Tom and the police about her activities, and even though she'd destroyed the storage facility there would be other documents detailing her activities. She knew she should get out now, take her false passport and leave, but she was no coward and would not go running off with her tail between her legs. Hannah Smith was not going to prevent her sealing her place in history.

***

A few anxious days passed as they waited for information from Solomon's network of informers, but finally the news they'd been waiting for arrived. Laurel had been spotted in the Cape and even without the files they'd found, it didn't take a genius to figure out who her next target was.

Solomon sent his sons Jacob and Isaiah and his nephew Saul to help them on the next stage of their mission, tall proud men with dazzling smiles. They met up with Tom, Hannah, Jack and Themba on a deserted airstrip in the middle of nowhere under a funereal sky that promised more rain, faces stinging in the sharp wind.

Hannah shivered. The air was full of unseen electrical charges that threatened to ignite and blow them all up. Her tongue was stuck to the roof of her mouth making speech almost impossible. Jack was bouncing up and down trying to get warm, little puffs of dust jumping up every time he landed. Out of the quietness Hannah heard the gentle purring of an aeroplane. It flew in straight and low, touching down with barely a sound. Bumping gently it taxied towards them and a door flew open.

'Come on.'

They followed Tom across the dry ground and climbed into the coffin-like interior. Surely it was not possible that this feeble craft could fly them safely to their destination?

Tom surveyed the grim faces, 'All set back there?'

Hannah stared straight ahead and pretended she was at home in her own bed with a good book and her cat purring gently on her lap. Jack pressed his face against the tiny widow. His mood had become mercurial over the last few days and his emotional barometer suddenly plummeted once more. He spoke, almost to himself.

'How come I never knew?'

Hannah saw conflicting emotions traversing his face.

'How could you?' she said.

His leg began to jiggle. Hannah listened to the pulsating engine and tried to stifle the terror that gripped her. She had always been sure of herself, her identity well defined. She knew who she was and what she wanted out of life and considered herself a confident and self-assured woman. Now she was a bundle of insecurity struggling to hang on to the parts of her she still recognised. Her life had spun so wildly out of control it felt as if portions of her intrinsic being had spun off into the ether never to be seen again. She had begun to question every thought and action and trusted none of her decisions. Even the instincts that had proved so trustworthy in the past had betrayed her.

She had snatched Jack from the safe harbour of his life, uncaring about the devastating effect her actions would have upon him and his family. She had pushed and pushed, determined to solve the murders and even as she began to uncover the truth had been too stubborn and arrogant to share her information with Tom, the one man who could possibly have averted the escalation of subsequent events. If she had been disciplined enough to rein herself in they wouldn't be here now. They wouldn't be at the mercy of a ruthless killer and Jack would still have two parents.

The plane landed with a judder two hours later and the passengers spilled out onto the makeshift runway. The next phase of the operation was about to begin.

The wind raged, drops of rain stinging their skin. The sea was sinister and intimidating; with the impossibly unsafe boat that Tom had procured for them bobbing up and down, about to tip over at any moment.

'Okay, this is it. You ready?'

Tom's words blew by her in a gust of wind and fled out to sea. Hannah tucked her hands deeper beneath her armpits. Jack, his face soaked and his clothes sodden like the rest of them, rubbed his hands together and inclined his head briefly. He licked salty chapped lips, then jumped on to the rocking gangplank and ran up and on to the deck of the tiny fishing trawler. He put out a hand and helped Hannah aboard. She wrinkled her nose at the fishy smell and averted her eyes from the dead flat gaze of the pile of limp glistening fish imprisoned in a net.

The fisherman at the helm grinned, revealing toothless beige gums and set the creaking and complaining boat seawards, heading into the darkness. Hannah swallowed, grateful that she had been unable to eat before they set out, but after ten minutes she realised to her surprise that the tossing boat had far less effect on her than the plane. She liked the rolling feeling below her feet and gripping the railing she stared out over the forbidding sea, the boat's white wake the only relief against the bottomless water.

Themba stood with the boat's captain, keen eyes scouring the seas ahead. Saul, Isaiah and Jacob huddled together behind a crate trying to get accustomed to the pitching motion. Jack paced up and down while Tom stood in the prow staring into the inky world before him. Every now and then he lifted his head and seemed to be straining his ears for the sound of anything following, but there was only the splashing of the water and the hum of the engine.

A feeling of unreality and the heavy, almost physical weight of what they had to do descended on Hannah's shoulders. What if they failed? What if Laurel arrived there before them?

Out of the grim waves a rocky coastline confronted them, ready to snatch and send them to a soggy death. Their captain was a local fisherman who had navigated these waters before and he managed to avoid the rocks that wanted to rip out the underbelly of their boat. The unexpected sleek shape of a diving seal caused ripples in the water nearby, making them all jump. The rain stopped and as they moved away from the mainland and through the starless night towards a ragged blister erupting out of the ocean, Themba joined Hannah and put his arm around her shoulders.

'It is going to be okay,' he said.

She tried to believe him.

Hannah wasn't sure how they managed to land on the rocky shore. She climbed off the relatively safe trawler on to the slick rubbery surface of the small dinghy that Tom had acquired to transport them through choppy water to a craggy beach. They crouched among the rocks on Robben Island and on seeing Tomk's bleak face, Hannah for the first time began to appreciate how difficult it was for him.

The fishing trawler would wait for them to return. If they did not, it would leave.

CHAPTER

Forty-seven

Hannah approached Tom. He was silent and hostile and for a moment she was afraid of him. His wife was a paid assassin about to try and exterminate the world's most famous political prisoner and they were all that stood between her and a country tipping over into chaos.

Tom turned his back on her and faced the black men, his frame rigid with tension. 'Jacob, will you have a look around?' he said. He motioned and Jacob stepped closer, but despite his whisper, Hannah heard every word . 'If you find her, shoot first, ask questions after, okay?'

Jacob nodded, swiftly spoke to the others, instructing them, and vanished into the night, his dark skin and clothing making him invisible. The others set off after him and Hannah then saw them splitting off in different directions, intent on finding Laurel before she had a chance to do any serious damage.

'You'll stay with Hannah, Jack,' said Tom.

'I don't want to hide somewhere with Hannah. I want to come with you,' said Jack.

'No.'

'Why? Stop treating me like a kid!'

'Stop behaving like one then,' said his father, and Jack took a step backwards.

Hannah could see from the tormented eyes and sagging mouth that he was not handling the situation as well as he imagined.

'I'm not going to argue with you. Go with Hannah!'

Out of the darkness came a sound that propelled them forward. Another small craft was approaching, and at this time of night on this barren island, there could only be one explanation. It was Laurel.

'Hannah, go. Now,' Hannah grabbed an unwilling Jack by the hand and the two of them rain, the rain lashing against their faces and trickling down their necks. She was afraid, for Jack, and for herself. She was under no illusion as to what would happen if Laurel spotted them.

Half an hour later Hannah and Jack were hidden in a blue gum plantation, hoping to see Tom or one of the others returning with the news that Laurel had been captured. The wind blew in sharp wet gusts, rustling the leaves on the trees, which moaned in protest like tortured souls.

Jack sat leaning against a tree trunk, a shape carved out of the darkness with the moonlight casting shadows on his gaunt cheeks. He watched Hannah without moving, making her uneasy. She couldn't tell what he was thinking but had a suspicion that he was planning something. She walked over to him and looked into the young eyes. He stared unblinkingly back, but his leg bounced up and down ceaselessly.

'It'll be okay,' she said, knowing it was a lie but incapable of saying anything else to reassure him. He turned away from her and stared out into the darkness.

'You aren't planning on being a hero or anything, are you, Jack?'

His head rotated. In the dark Hannah could barely make out his features and was unable to read his expression. He put his hand on his forehead. She resisted the impulse to wrap her arms round him, knowing he would rebuff her offer of comfort.

She had never witnessed anything as sad as the corruption of this child. His mind had been pure and uncluttered until the world unleashed its fury upon him and plundered his innocence.

Then she saw him stiffen and peer forward, his head tilted, ears straining. Above the cries of the birds and the sound of the waves and the wind whipping their hair, she could hear a faint rasping sound. Like shoes over rock.

'Hannah, there's something out there. I can see a light moving, like a torch or something. I think it's her.'

It was.

Hannah wrapped her arms around her body, a slithering sensation crossing her skin. Laurel was here, planning an assassination that would plunge the country into a chasm from which there would be no escape. They had to stop her. When Hannah turned back to Jack, he was gone.

As quietly as possible, she hurried through the thinning darkness in search of Jack. He would be heading for the nearby quarry, where they suspected Laurel would spring her deadly trap. Consternation at his disappearance had given way to anger as she realised that his impetuosity might very well cause the death of all of them. She had to find him before he ran into his mother. Catching her foot on a tree root, she crashed to the ground, banging her head on a rock. Standing up dizzily, blood on her cheeks, her surroundings reeled in front of her. She grabbed a branch to steady herself and then heard someone thrashing through the undergrowth up ahead. Taking a moment to re-orientate herself, she set off after Jack.

The screeching of gulls and the sibilant hissing of the surf as it pounded the rocks led her towards the infamous prison and the quarry where prisoners spent their days chipping away at rock. Grey shapes slid into focus as the sun ascended higher in the metal sky, brightening the scene but too muted to shine. She burst out into an open area unexpectedly and immediately took cover behind a hardy shrub. Raising her head cautiously, her muscles tightened as she spotted Laurel ahead, crouched on the ground. She was inching forward, sometimes leopard crawling, sometimes scuttling crab-like across the patchy earth.

Hannah felt the situation spinning out of control but was incapable of intervening now and stopping the inevitability of what was about to happen.

Laurel lay flat and unhurriedly slid forward until she had a clear view of where the prisoners would soon appear. She pulled a rifle out of a canvas bag and propped it on a rock, squinting through the telescopic gun sight. She made some adjustments and then aimed it down and pointed it where she expected her target's head to appear some time soon.

Then, eerily, Hannah saw her neck stiffen and her head turn. Somehow, like a hunted buck, she had sensed Hannah's presence.

Hannah moved back quickly out of sight and ducked behind a large rock, disturbing a dassie, which hopped away in fright. She cautiously raised herself up to get a better view and confronted Laurel's deadpan face. Laurel pointed a handgun at her and without pause shot her in the shoulder. Hannah fell forward with a grunt, landing in a crumpled heap on the ground.

Cursing her carelessness she tried to sit up, but found herself pinned to the earth. She kicked out and grunted in pain then felt a fist smashing into her face. She reached up and jabbed a finger in Laurel's eye and she cursed, rolling away.

Despite the rushing in her ears, Hannah could see Laurel's frenetic fingers scrabbling and clawing the ground. She spotted the gun half hidden beneath a loose stone and stretched out a hand too, but it evaded her grasp. She tried to slide forward but Laurel clamped an arm around her leg and pulled her backwards. She threw herself on top once more, the weight of her body on her arms preventing Hannah from struggling.

Laurel straightened up, no expression on her face, the lids of her eyes red and watery. A soft hand fastened around Hannah's neck and squeezed.

Hannah twisted her body, reached for the knife tucked in her waistband and slashed wildly, the blade slicing through her attacker's skin. Laurel let go and clutched her bloody arm, and Hannah managed to scramble away. She stretched out an arm towards the gun and her finger touched the barrel before a sickening blow to the side of her head stopped her. The knife fell to the ground as she fell forward and found herself in a stranglehold, being pulled violently upright by the collar.

The malignant eyes of the woman she'd tracked for so long, stared down at her. The creamy face was dusty, the makeup smudged and a long oozing cut ran across the forehead below a perfectly shaped fringe of hair. Hannah could see the shiny layer of oily sweat on Laurel's skin and above the rancid smell of her own perspiration, could make out the familiar tantalizing fragrance of flowers drifting on the wind. She caught a glimpse of flawless teeth as Laurel smiled quite sweetly and drew back her fist to finish off the job.

Then behind her Hannah heard a small sound, a gasping muffled cry and saw Jack watching, eyes wide, arms outstretched, stumbling towards his mother.

Laurel turned in one fluid movement and fixed her eyes on her son.

'Jack! I wondered if I'd see you here. Come to Mummy, darling.' She held out a hand to him but Jack stood frozen, staring.

Catching Laurel unawares, Hannah sprang at her and smashed her hand as hard as she could into her nose. There was an audible squelching sound as the bone broke and flesh connected sickeningly with flesh. Blood spurted, spraying over the front of her jacket and spattering her face. Jack made a sound like an animal caught in a trap.

Hannah spun round, picked up the gun and pointed it at Laurel, who was beginning to straighten up, breathing agitatedly. She levelled the gun and her finger tightened on the trigger.

'Hannah, no!'

Jack rushed forward towards Laurel, who grabbed him round the throat. He gasped, thrashing about and looking at Hannah for help.

'Stand still, sweetie, or you'll get hurt. You always were a silly boy. Never stop to think first. Stand still!' She punched him in the back, her fist thudding into his kidneys and he cried out, disbelieving.

'Mum, please, let me go, I can't breathe.'

Laurel's grip tightened and he struggled for air, his hands flailing as she exerted more pressure on his tender windpipe.

Jack's eyes began to glaze over. Hannah wanted to scream at him to stay focussed on her image in front of him but couldn't make a sound. He was quiet, with a sad look in his already blank eyes. He was dying and there was nothing she could do to save him.

CHAPTER

Forty-eight

'Laurel! Let him go, for God's sake, he's your son! He's your son.'

Tom appeared behind them at a run, hands outstretched, gaze riveted on Jack's blue-tinged face and his beseeching bulging eyes.

Laurel's head tipped to one side. 'No, he's Tom's son. He wasn't ever mine. Not really. I nearly aborted him once, but it was too late because I was so far along and he was growing and kicking and making me sick. And Tom had that soppy look on his face. I had to have him, but I didn't want him. They say you forget the pain of childbirth but I haven't. I thought my body was going to be ripped in two and I've never forgiven him for doing that to me.

'I'd have given him up for adoption if I could have, only Tom wanted him so badly. He fell in love with him the first time you saw his red bawling face. He fell in love with his son and out of love with me. He was so small but he ruined my figure and my life and he took away my freedom.'

'I never stopped loving you.' Tom's voice caught in his throat, but Laurel didn't even turn her head, speaking solely to Hannah, her eyes fixed on the reporter's face, unmoving.

Jack slumped forward. His mother tossed his limp body to the ground in disgust.

'I wanted to love him, but I didn't know how, and no matter how hard I tried to conjure up some maternal feelings, I couldn't. Everyone told me I'd love him in time but I didn't. I tried to lose him so many times when he was a baby because I simply couldn't cope and it seemed the easiest way out, but someone always found him and brought him back. Tom was so busy playing the hero he didn't even notice that I was drowning and losing my mind. It's not my fault though, you must believe me.'

Tom stood rooted, as if he was unable to move and get to Jack who was lying inert in a contorted heap. Laurel continued speaking in a calm monotone.

'My own mother never loved me, Hannah. She sold me to her uncle when I was only twelve, and he handed me on to his friends who stank of beer and cigarettes and thought it was so funny when I screamed and kicked and spat at them. I had an abortion in a filthy backstreet clinic when I was fourteen and swore I'd never have another child, but then Tom came along and I fell pregnant with Jack and he was so concerned and caring so I thought I'd do it for him and that I'd love the baby when he came, but I didn't. I tried to love him but it was no good, and he's not a bad boy, but it doesn't feel as if he belongs to me.'

'Laurel, you aren't well. Let me help you.'

'No. You can't help because I'm not ill, Hannah. This is who I am, this is the real me. I know you think I'm mad, but I'm not. I'm as sane as you are, I just think differently. Morally bankrupt, that's me. It's such a pity that everyone had to find out the truth. It's your fault, Hannah. If it wasn't for you we could all have carried on, Tom with his job and me with mine and enough money to keep me happy and no one would have been any the wiser. Jack could have carried on living in oblivion like everyone else in this cursed country and he wouldn't have known any different. But no, you had to come along and poke your nose in where it wasn't wanted. Panting after my husband like a bitch in heat. Don't you look so horrified, Tom's fallen for your big eyes and long legs like Jack has, don't you dare deny it. The minute I first met you I knew you'd be trouble, I knew Tom would get all hot under the collar so I tried to get rid of you, but you're like dog shit on the bottom of my shoe, you won't let go. That's why you have to die. I'm sure you understand that.'

Hannah saw Jack's eyelid flicker and threw herself at Laurel. Laurel grabbed her jacket and dragged her down, a large hand snatching for the gun that she had lowered while trying to keep his balance. Involuntarily her finger tightened on the trigger and a shot, muffled by Laurel's stomach, loosed off.

Jack's mother slumped forward, her eyes wide open in surprise. She swore once, and then lay still. Hannah stood up panting, looking at the figure supine across her feet. A pool of red began to spread out, seeping into the ground.

She wiped her face with her undamaged left hand. Leaning forward she pulled the blood-soaked shirt down over the percolating black hole in Laurel's stomach.

Hannah watched unmoving as Tom approached and stared at the body in front of him. Once Laurel had been a bride in white who had promised to love, honour and obey until death did them part. How had it come to this? How could Tom ever put the day she killed his wife and lost his son behind him?

He leaned closer and yanked the wedding ring off her finger. He gripped it tightly for an instant then flung it over the cliff in a swift savage movement.

Jack stirred and sat up groggily, coughing and holding his bruised neck.

'Dad? Where's…?' He saw his mother and crawled over to her. 'Is she dead? Mum? Mum? It's me, Jack!' He shook her and she opened her eyes.

'Jack?' Laurel tried to sit up. Jack, obviously thinking she wanted to hold him, put an arm round her back and pulled her into his lap, gently pushing her hair off her face.

'Mum, we'll get you to a hospital, you'll be fine.'

'Don't be ridiculous, Jack. I won't be fine, and neither will you.'

In a spurt of strength Laurel wrenched herself away and staggered to her feet. The gun that had fallen to the ground during the struggle now appeared in her hand. She pointed it steadily at Jack, gave a slight shrug and the sound of a shot ricocheted across the bay.

Hannah's heart contracted with fright. She waited in terror for Jack to fall, instead Laurel faltered, turned and tottered towards the edge of the cliff. With a look of surprise and a muted cry, she toppled over the edge and was gone, leaving only the sound of the waves and screeching seagulls.

Hannah heard a sound behind her. She swung round, ready to fight, but saw only Isaiah and Saul, two shadows with staring white eyes. Isaiah lowered his gun.

'I'm sorry, Tom, but your wife was an evil woman. We'll take care of her body for you and then we'll forget what we've seen. She will disappear like so many of those she killed have. We'll make sure she's never found.'

Themba and Jacob appeared behind them, curiously surveying the scene. Saul quickly apprised them of the situation and like a well-oiled military unit they sprang into action.

'We need to move fast,' said Themba. 'No one must ever know we were here.'

They disappeared down the cliff face as invisibly as they had arrived. Tom ran towards Jack and pulled him close.

Hannah watched Jack and Tom, wishing she could have spared them the disintegration of their lives, done something to prevent the implosion that almost destroyed them. No one could ever know what had happened that day. This was one story she could never write. They would return home to rebuild their lives, Themba and his friends would melt back into the cauldron of activism and resistance and they would all pray that if a New South Africa ever arrived, it would be everything they hoped for. Perhaps Tom would allow her to help him heal Jack, if the boy could ever forgive her for her role in the tragedy his life had become.

'Hannah?' whispered Jack.

'I'm here, Jack.' She hesitated but Tom beckoned her forward.

Hannah knelt with her arms around Jack and his father. Tom took her dirty hand in his red one. As they clung together, Hannah wept.

'I don't even know who Nelson Mandela is, or why we had to save him,' said Jack, before burying his head in his father's shoulder.

Author's Note

FW de Klerk became the leader of the National Party in February 1989 and in September of that year was elected State President. In his first speech as party leader he called for a nonracist South Africa and for negotiations about the country's future to resume. He lifted the ban on the ANC and released Nelson Mandela, who walked out of Victor-Verster Prison on 11 February 1990. He ended apartheid and paved the way for the drafting of a new constitution based on the principle of one person, one vote. Many considered De Klerk a traitor and predicted a civil war. This did not happen and the transition occurred peacefully.

In 1993 De Klerk and Mandela shared the Nobel Peace Prize. On 10 May 1994 Nelson Mandela became South Africa's first black democratically elected president and the 'Rainbow Nation' was born. De Klerk was his Deputy President until 1996. Despite the fears of so many, Mandela advocated peace and reconciliation as the way forward instead of revenge.

During the Truth and Reconciliation Commission hearings, the activities of the death squads based Vlakplaas and covert operations such as Barnacle and Project Coast, the chemical weapons programme, were made public and many families finally found out the truth about what had happened to their missing relatives.

The New South Africa, so eagerly anticipated, faces many challenges, unemployment, rising violent crime, rolling power cuts, and the 'brain drain' as thousands of skilled whites, unable to find work due to the policies of affirmative action leave the country. The greatest challenges of all are corruption within the government and the AIDS pandemic that is devastating the African continent.

Democracy has brought new freedom, but the masses remain uneducated and stuck in poverty. The gulf between the haves and the have-nots grows ever wider, with the middle class almost disappearing, as the rich, both black and white, grow richer and the poor, both black and white, get poorer.

Nelson Mandela spent 27 years in prison before being released in 1990 and died on 5 December 2013, aged 95, following a prolonged illness. His funeral was televised around the world.

ABOUT THE AUTHOR

Katy was born and raised in South Africa where she qualified as a teacher, teaching English and Music. She wrote five children's musicals that were published in SA and sold extensively throughout the country and Africa, but left teaching to become a full-time television scriptwriter in 1994, working on an award winning South African children's programme, Kideo. During a nationwide scriptwriting competition she was selected to be on the writing team of Generations, a multi-lingual soap. Katy also wrote advertising copy, radio jingles and adverts and then moved into writing industry specific textbooks and readers for illiterate and semi-literate adults. She emigrated to the UK in 2000 and became a naturalised citizen in 2005. She lives on a farm in the wilds of Gloucestershire.

MESSAGE FROM THE AUTHOR

If you enjoyed *When Killers Cry*, (or even if you didn't) please leave a review on Amazon, Goodreads, Barnes and Noble etcetera. Reviews are so important for us authors and I'd love to know what you thought.

You can also get in touch with me on:

🐦 @katykrump

📘 www.facebook.com/katykrump

www.glue-publishing.co.uk

BOOKS BY THE SAME AUTHOR

The Blue Dust Series:
Blue Dust: Forbidden
Blue Dust: Destiny
Blue Dust: Insurrection

Children's Fantasy:
Drippy Face

Lightning Source UK Ltd.
Milton Keynes UK
UKOW04f0014031015

259782UK00002B/8/P